Praise f

"With her debut romant̶ established herself as a c̶ ̶ ̶ ̶ ̶ ̶ ̶ ̶ ̶ ̶ ̶ ̶ and an instant favorite of mine! Mistaken identities, love at first sight, friends to more, and even a delicious tease toward marriage of convenience come together to create a rom-com treat for readers to devour. Simultaneously a sweet romance with the perfect amount of heat and a laugh-out-loud comedy with a surprising dose of depth, *Dear Henry, Love Edith* is a witty and heartfelt gift from first word to last."

BETHANY TURNER, author of *Plot Twist* and *The Do-Over*

"This delightful tale of mistaken identity is a must-read for romance lovers! Charming, witty, and with plenty of comedy, *Dear Henry, Love Edith* pairs well with tea, a cozy blanket, and a penchant for happily ever afters."

BETSY ST. AMANT, author of *Tacos for Two* and *The Key to Love*

"What a quick, sweet, and charming romance to brighten your day! A lovely debut by Kinzer that had me cheering for the unlikely, and yet so perfect, pair, Edith and Henry."

MELISSA FERGUSON, author of *Meet Me in the Margins* and *The Cul-de-Sac War*

"Rarely have I read a romance with such sparkling personality. Everything about Kinzer's vibrant voice and freshly told love story tugged at my heartstrings and widened my smile. Henry and Edith's quirky story as told with a dash of mistaken identity and peppered with epistolary flair is deepened by a cast of colorful supporting characters, zippy dialogue, and resonant themes of loss and hope. Fans of Katherine Reay and Pepper Basham will be enchanted."

RACHEL McMILLAN, author of *The Mozart Code* and the Three Quarter Time series

"I couldn't put it down! Becca Kinzer's debut novel kept me turning pages well into the night. *Dear Henry, Love Edith* is a delightful story, with lovable characters in a town packed with quirks and charm that will have you laughing out loud. I can't wait for what this author puts out next!"

TARI FARIS, author of the Restoring Heritage series

"In *Dear Henry, Love Edith*, Becca Kinzer marvelously toys with favorite romance tropes such as mistaken identity, love at first sight, fake relationship, and May–December romance to create a fun romp full of heart and humor. With pop culture references and values from bygone eras, readers of all generations are sure to fall in love with Henry's charm and Edith's passion for helping those near and far."

JANINE ROSCHE, author of *Aspen Crossroads* and the Madison River Romance series

Dear Henry, Love Edith

Dear Henry, Love Edith

BECCA KINZER

Tyndale House Publishers
Carol Stream, Illinois

Visit Tyndale online at tyndale.com.

Visit Becca Kinzer's website at beccakinzer.com.

Tyndale and Tyndale's quill logo are registered trademarks of Tyndale House Ministries.

Dear Henry, Love Edith

Designed by Libby Dykstra

Edited by Kathryn S. Olson

Published in association with the literary agency of Gardner Literary LLC, gardner-literary.com.

For information about special discounts for bulk purchases, please contact Tyndale House Publishers at csresponse@tyndale.com, or call 1-855-277-9400.

Library of Congress Cataloging-in-Publication Data

A catalog record for this book is available from the Library of Congress.

ISBN 978-1-4964-6608-2

Printed in the United States of America

29	28	27	26	25	24	23
7	6	5	4	3	2	1

For my husband. You told me to keep writing,
so I did. And I'll always be grateful.

CHAPTER ONE

Henry grimaced, not sure which irritated him more—the persistent ache in his knee or the relentless voice in his ear.

"Please, Uncle Henry. She has nowhere else to stay."

The voice. Definitely the voice. "Last time I checked, there were these things called hotels." Henry adjusted the phone against his ear as he raised the dishwasher door with his cane and shoved it shut.

"Uh-huh," Kat's droll voice responded. "And when was the last time you checked? 1945?"

"If you're referring to the fire that destroyed the Westshire Hotel, I think you mean 1937." Henry punched the quick-wash button.

"*Ugh!*" His niece's frustration competed in volume with the sound of spraying water. "I didn't call for a history lesson."

"Well, maybe next time you should. And maybe you should also read the newspaper every once in a while, because it mentioned the town fire in the 'This Day in History' section just yesterday."

"And what a riveting read that was, I'm sure. Point is our town doesn't have a hotel. Let the woman stay with you."

Henry shifted his weight, the floorboards beneath him creaking as much as his joints. "Why can't she commute?"

"From where?"

"I don't know. Peoria."

"She's flying into Moline."

"Okay then. Moline." Henry grabbed the frying pan coated in egg residue and plopped it into the sink. He'd get to it later. Along with the pile of dirty casserole dishes he needed to return to his office manager, Peg. The scent of garlic marinara still lingered in the air from last night. Not Peg's best dish, but Henry knew what they said about beggars and choosers.

Perhaps his niece needed the reminder. "Look, if this lady doesn't want to commute, there's always the bed-and-breakfast downtown. Built sometime *after* the fire. You ask me, she's got plenty of places to stay."

"Not for free."

"What is she, a charity case?"

This time Kat growled loud enough to completely drown out the dishwasher. Loud enough to make Henry's lips twitch as he hobbled into the living room, his cane thumping a slow beat across the wooden floor. With the way life had been going lately, he'd take whatever pleasure he could find. And pushing his niece's buttons was one particular pleasure he never tired of.

"She's doing volunteer work," Kat said. "She's donating her time to a good cause. She shouldn't have to pay for shelter—not when I promised her a place to stay rent free."

"Sounds like your problem, not mine."

"Oh, for crying out loud, would you stop acting like a crotchety old miser? How was I to know my kitchen would flood as soon as I left for the summer?"

"You know why I don't have to worry about stuff like that?"

"Because you never go away?"

"No." Henry eased onto his worn brown leather sofa and propped his right leg on the coffee table, stifling a moan as he massaged his knee. "Because I have crotchety old miser insurance. Keeps me protected from kitchen floods and impromptu displays of hospitality."

"If only it protected me from your mediocre displays of humor."

Henry cracked a smile, scanning the couch for the TV remote. "How long would she need to stay here?"

"Not long. My landlord's already on it. Edith can move into my house once it's livable. I promise, you won't even know she's there. She's the quietest, sweetest lady you'll ever meet."

"I thought you'd never met her."

"I haven't," Kat said. "But that's what Ruthie says."

"Who's Ruthie?" He aimed the remote at the TV.

"One of Sharon's cousins who lives in Pittsburgh."

"Who's Sharon?"

"You know Sharon," Kat scolded.

He smiled. He did know Sharon. In a town like Westshire,

Illinois, everybody knew everybody. Once he found the Cubs game on the flat-screen and noted the score, his smile turned into a groan.

"Oh, come on. It won't be that bad."

"Nothing could be that bad," he muttered, punching off the game.

"What?"

"Nothing. What's this lady's name again?"

"*Edith.* She's a nurse. Or used to be a nurse. I'm sure she's retired by now. Sharon said she's a widow. She probably spends all her time volunteering because it's the only way she can cope with the loss of her one true love." Kat sighed. "Isn't that so romantic?"

Henry rolled his eyes. His thirty-year-old niece sounded worse than a lovestruck teenager. She would probably find the Three Stooges romantic if she ever watched them. "How soon until your kitchen's fixed again?"

"Soon enough. But it's not as if you can climb stairs yet anyway. Someone may as well put all that remodeling you did to good use. Besides, you can't throw a little old widow out on the street. We both know Jesus frowns on that one. And really, between your morning therapy sessions and work hours, you probably won't even see her. How's your leg doing, by the way?"

Better than his pride. "It's still attached."

"When I think about how much worse it could have been—"

"Don't." *Please.* Last thing he needed was to rehash what a fool he made of himself the first week taking over his family's painting and construction company. Yeah, the injury could have happened to anybody. But he wasn't anybody. And as the man in charge now, he couldn't afford another misstep. Not in this town. Not after all the time it had taken to get back on his feet in the first place.

"Look, if this old lady needs a place to crash for a few nights, fine. Just so long as she stays upstairs and out of my way."

"Thank you!"

"But as soon as your house is ready—"

"She's gone. Promise."

Henry sighed into the phone. "After all this time, how do you still do it?"

"Do what?"

"Get me to cave to anything you ask."

Kat chuckled. "That's the power nieces have over their uncles—especially nieces who are only two years younger. Thanks again, *Uncle* Henry."

"Why am I already regretting this?"

———— ♥ ————

Edith read the email again.

> Hi Edith! Hope you landed safely. There's been a slight change of plans. One of my kitchen pipes decided to spring a leak on me. I know. Great, huh? So I'm afraid my house is more appropriate for FEMA than visitors. Don't worry though. My sweet uncle Henry lives close by and has graciously offered to host you for as long as needed. He hasn't been able to climb the stairs for some time now, so you'll have the entire second floor

to yourself. Make yourself at home. I'll let you know when my house is habitable again. Sorry for all the last-minute changes.

Kat

PS—My uncle really is a sweet man, but you know how bachelors get set in their ways. If he gives you any trouble, just tell him he'll have to answer to me. That ought to scare him! Ha!

Edith clicked her phone off and sank against the seat of her rental car. Why couldn't anything in her life ever go as planned?

She blew a layer of hair away from her eyes, wondering for the hundredth time if she'd made a mistake. Honey-colored strands fluttered back down, catching on her eyelashes. "I mean, really, Edith?" she muttered to herself. *"Bangs?"*

If she were going to go through a quarter-life crisis, couldn't she at least have been brave enough to get a tattoo?

Although planning to fly halfway around the world to a remote South African village by the end of summer surely accounted for something akin to bravery. Must be why the idea of sharing a house with a little old man didn't bother her. Because she was so darn courageous.

Starting her rental car, Edith flipped her visor down to block the late-afternoon fireball threatening to blind her. Then gasped. "What? Oh, you've gotta be kidding me."

She'd taken Benadryl as soon as she bit into the salad with blue cheese, but obviously it hadn't helped. Angry welts rose in ugly red blotches all over her neck, taunting her from the visor mirror. No wonder the man who'd signed out her rental car seemed afraid to touch the same paper she'd signed. Probably thought she had leprosy.

Well, that's what she got for not paying attention at the airport when she'd grabbed a quick bite to eat. Thankfully her allergy didn't amount to anything more than some annoying hives. But man, they usually weren't this bad. She scratched at a few, then forced her hands back on the steering wheel.

Edith met the gaze of the frowning reflection staring back at her from the visor mirror, the reflection that looked an awful lot like her mother when she went through her retro 1970s hairstyle phase. "Oh, what are you looking at?"

Edith flipped the visor back up, preferring to squint into the sun than be reminded of her mom. Thinking of her mom only led to thinking about her dad. Which led to thinking about regrets. And that sent her right back to thinking about her bangs.

Edith's stomach grumbled, taking her mind off everything but the fact she'd had only one bite of salad for lunch. She grabbed her phone. After typing the address Kat sent for her "sweet uncle Henry"—which Edith knew full well meant stubborn old mule—Edith breathed a sigh of relief. Less than an hour's drive. Good. Because a hamburger with all the trimmings was screaming her name. And according to the flight attendant, Westshire had one of the best mom-and-pop diners in all the Midwest.

If Edith was going to blow her diet, she might as well blow it big. Especially since she hadn't actually started her diet.

Before Edith made it out of the airport parking lot, her phone trilled a piano jingle. Her shoulders tensed. *No. Not already.* She didn't even have to look at the caller ID to know who was calling. *Just ignore it.* The piano continued its trill. *You don't owe him anything.* The phone finally stopped ringing.

Only to start up again a few seconds later.

That's it. She pulled to the side and threw the car into park. Better to get it over with now. She wasn't about to listen to that piano jingle the entire drive to Westshire.

"Hey, Steve," Edith said after a deep breath, relieved at the calm in her voice despite the trembling in her fingers.

A long stretch of silence followed. Then, "Are you insane?"

"No, I'm good. Thanks for asking. And you?"

"Knock it off, Edith. Why would you do this?"

"Do what?"

"Leave."

"I'm a grown woman, in case you've forgotten." She had the quarter-life crisis bangs to prove it.

Steve's deep breaths filled her ear. She could picture him as easily as if he were standing right in front of her. Jaw clenched, nostrils flaring, the Sherman scowl stamped on his face. It must be an inherited trait. She'd seen her husband wear the same look often enough.

"The least you could have done was tell me you were leaving."

She took a breath to respond, but he cut her off. "In person."

Edith scrunched her eyes shut. "I know. I'm sorry." So yeah. Maybe she'd taken the coward's way out by leaving him a letter when she knew he was out of town. But the last thing she'd wanted was a face-off with her late husband's brother. Especially since things between them had gotten so weird.

"When are you coming back?"

Edith looked to the ceiling of her car, blinking her bangs from her eyes as she prayed for the right words. "No." Well, it was a word at least.

"No what? No, you're not coming back?"

"I need to move on."

"From me?"

"From . . . everything." If Edith had any lingering doubts about her sudden decision to fly to Illinois until her passport arrived, this phone call laid them to rest. No way would she have survived an entire summer in Pittsburgh with Steve's suffocating behavior.

Overhearing Ruthie mention her cousin's crisis nursery house this past Sunday at church had to have been divine intervention. Sharon, the director, was over the moon when Edith contacted her about volunteering. And Edith was over the moon to place five hundred miles between her and Steve for the next several weeks.

"Look, Steve, it's been a rough go. You know that. I just need a fresh start. On my own. I explained it all in the letter. You should have—"

"I got your letter. I know what it said. But you're making a big mistake. South Africa? No. That's crazy. Come home. Let's talk about this."

"But that's just it. Pittsburgh isn't home for me." Not since Brian died. Maybe not even before then.

"Where are you right now?"

Oh, she hated this. Edith tugged on her shirt collar. Why did confrontation always have to make her so sweaty? "I know Brian told you to look out for me after he was gone. And I appreciate all that you've done. I do. But you don't need to take care of me. I'm good."

Or at least she would be once her passport arrived. Who knew passports could take so long to process? Clearly not Edith. If she'd known that, she would have started the application process back in kindergarten. Then maybe she would be boarding a flight to the Eastern Cape of South Africa right now instead of sweating in a rental car in Illinois simply to avoid conversations like this.

So much for being courageous.

"What if I want to take care of you?"

Okay. This phone call was going from awkward to downright painful. She turned the air conditioner up higher. "It's not what I want." And now she was itching. Everywhere. At this rate, the hives wouldn't disappear until mid-December. "Please, just let me go. It's time for both of us to move on." Before he could offer any further protest, Edith said, "Goodbye, Steve," and ended the call.

CHAPTER TWO

Henry winced as he adjusted his right leg beneath the diner's red- and white-checkered tablecloth. "Let's Twist Again" blared from the jukebox in the corner. "Sure, Chubby Checkers," Henry muttered under his breath. "Rub it in a little more, why don't you?"

According to his ortho surgeon, Henry's progress was right on track. Well, if this was what *on track* felt like, he pitied the poor soul who ever fell off track. Six weeks after the accident and Henry's right knee felt like it belonged in the body of an arthritic eighty-year-old on a cold, damp day.

Speaking of arthritic eighty-year-olds . . . Henry sighed, reading Kat's text message before sliding his phone back into his front shirt pocket. So the landlord discovered mold in Kat's basement, did he? Well, cue the theme song to *The Odd*

Couple. Looked like Henry and ol' Edith were going to be housemates for the long haul this summer.

Though Henry would never say so to Kat, the thought of having someone under his roof, even an elderly someone, didn't actually sound all that bad. Spending the past six weeks at home with little more than pain and the scent of Icy Hot serving as company, Henry hungered for a taste of something different. Something besides office work, physical therapy, and Peg's leftovers.

Besides, Kat was right. Well, mostly right. He hadn't remodeled; he'd *restored*. But either way, no point in letting all that space in his house sit unused and empty if there was someone who could benefit from it.

His eyes trailed the young family finishing up their meal at the booth next to him and heading out the door a minute later. A wistful smile hovered over Henry's lips, watching the dad tug playfully on his daughter's dark ponytail, then give his wife a gentle tweak on her neck before she leaned into the car to strap their toddler son into his car seat. The look she sent her husband a moment later communicated more than words ever could. So did the quick kiss she planted on his cheek.

Henry couldn't help the stab of envy that pierced him. What would it be like to have someone like her? Someone to share a look with. Someone to share a family with. Someone—

"Sorry I'm late."

—not like Angela. Henry swung his gaze from the window. "Oh. Hey." He rescued a napkin from sliding off the table due to the breeze kicked up by Angela's arrival.

"It was crazy today. You have no idea."

Angela never ceased to amaze him. Within five seconds, she had unloaded her oversize purse onto the table, raised a finger in the air to notify the first waitress who came into her peripheral vision—because Angela had yet to take her eyes off her phone—that she'd "like a chef salad with half ranch, half French, one egg, no croutons, dried cranberries if you have them, and just water please, but could you get a clean glass? This one looks dirty. Thank you."

Then as quickly as she sat down, she scooted out of her chair. "Sorry, babe. Gotta take this." And with her phone pressed against one ear and a finger pressed into the other, she made a hasty retreat out the door, a soft ding announcing her departure.

"Um, was she talking to me?" A freckle-faced girl with tufts of red hair arching her head like a frazzled rainbow stood next to his table. "It's my first job. I mean, my first day. I mean—" She swallowed and the pink blotches on her cheeks turned red. "All I heard was chef salad."

The bell dinged again, and the young waitress sent a nervous glance toward the door but exhaled when a different woman entered. Henry, however, felt his entire breath lodge inside his throat.

"Did she want an egg and no croutons? Or was it one crouton and no eggs?"

"Goldie Hawn," Henry murmured.

"Excuse me?" the waitress said.

Henry couldn't stop himself from staring at the young woman at the door. Ever since he watched the movie *Overboard* years ago as a kid, he'd always had a giant crush on

Goldie Hawn. And shoot if this woman wasn't the spitting image of her. Except for the eyes. Somehow this woman's dark eyes were even more beautiful than Goldie's blues. "Um . . . sure. That sounds fine."

"The egg or the croutons?"

"Oh. Ah—" He watched the Goldie Hawn look-alike make her way past him and about dropped his glass of water when she met his gaze. Up close, her big brown eyes were even more of a knockout.

"Sir?"

"Yes." He snapped his gaze back to the waitress. "Both. The usual. Whatever you normally put on it will be fine. And I'll take a burger." He handed back the menus, then chugged several gulps of water.

"So you'll never believe this," Angela said, dropping back into her seat with a flourish. "Marsha Derby fired her daughter's wedding photographer. Apparently due to some sort of hush-hush scandal. Nobody's talking. But now she wants us to take on the contract. Can you believe it? *Marsha Derby.* I'm telling you, honey, this has been the craziest day of my life."

She picked up her water glass, frowned into it, then set it back on the table. "I need to get together with Chad to start planning the shots. The wedding is less than two months away. It's going to be at their villa in California. *Their villa.* We do this right, we will never have to worry about clients again. Oh, my word. We have so much to do to get ready. I'll bet Chad is *freaking* right now."

Angela took a breath and searched the diner. "Where is that waitress? I hope she didn't screw up my order. I might have to get it to go. You understand, right? This is just such a huge break for us. Wow, okay. I'm sorry. Enough for two seconds about me, right? What's going on with you? How was your day? Is your knee back to normal yet?"

"It's—"

Her phone pinged and she let out a gasp. "I told you Chad would be going crazy." She showed the message to Henry. A GIF of Will Ferrell from the movie *Elf*.

"Funny," Henry said with a polite smile. "Look, if you need to go, I get it. Sounds like you have a lot to get ready for."

"No, no, no." Angela made a display of dropping her phone into her purse. "I'm all ears. Tell me what's going on with you. I feel like it's been forever since we've talked."

Probably because it had been. "Well, let's see," Henry said, rolling the saltshaker between his hands. "Not much. A lady's going to be staying at my house this summer, I guess."

Angela straightened. "A lady? Staying at your house? What exactly does that mean?"

Henry shrugged. "Just that. She was supposed to stay at Kat's place for the summer while Kat was away, but a pipe burst and now they found mold and—"

"Is she pretty?"

"I don't know. Haven't met her yet. She's a widow who used to be a nurse but now does volunteer work and likes to travel, apparently. She's here to help out with Sharon's crisis house for the summer. Anyway, Kat dumped her on me, and I couldn't really say no. She sounds . . . old." He shrugged again.

"What's her name?"

"Edith."

"Yep. Definitely old. I guess that's fine then. What about your knee? Are you done with therapy yet?"

"Almost. It's still sore and pretty stiff—"

"Great. Sounds like everything is falling into place for both of us then. Hey, honey—" Angela snapped her fingers at the waitress—"I'm going to need mine to go. Actually, you know what? Just keep it." Angela rose from her chair and dug her phone out of her purse. "I'm too excited to eat. Bye, pet." She brushed a kiss against Henry's temple and left, texting the entire way out the door.

Henry sagged back in his chair. Wow. Dating Angela was like dating a force of nature. At first, sort of fun and exciting. But lately . . . downright exhausting.

"Here's your burger, sir." The waitress set a plate in front of him. "Was your wife coming back for the chef salad or should I box it?"

"My wife?" Henry choked on his first bite and reached for his water glass. If he'd had any doubts about his relationship with Angela, hearing the word *wife* put the final nail in that coffin. He coughed and sputtered into his napkin, certain the entire hamburger had leapt off the plate and cannonballed straight into his lungs.

"Are you all right?"

Through watery eyes, he looked up expecting to see the adolescent waitress. Instead a concerned Goldie Hawn stood next to him, constricting his airway even further.

"Try putting your arms up," she said.

"Why?" he rasped between coughs, lifting his arms above his head.

"No idea. But moms make their kids do it all the time."

She smiled at him, and he was sure he'd be tempted to smile back if he could only stop dying.

"Oh no." A plate of salad flung through the air. Smacked the floor. "Somebody help him," the waitress yelled, waving her arms around. "He's making the universal sign for choking!"

"What? No, that's not it." The brown-eyed beauty clutched her own throat. "*This* is the universal sign for choking."

"Who's choking?" A bear of a man, who used to be a bear of a teenager when he played linebacker on Henry's high school football team, raced from the kitchen. When his eyes landed on Goldie, he barreled toward her as if she were the end zone. "Ma'am, don't panic. I know the Heimlich."

The woman's eyes widened in terror. She jumped back, thrusting a finger at Henry. "Not me. Him."

Before Henry could protest, two beefy arms wrapped around his torso and yanked him out of his chair. His sore knee banged against the table and an explosion of stars flooded his vision. When a scream sounded, Henry could only pray it hadn't erupted from his own lips.

"Did anything come out?" the chef demanded, hoisting Henry up and down. With each thump to the floor, searing white pain shot through his leg. *Lift, thump. Lift, thump.*

"Stop," Henry gasped. "Stop!" As soon as the chef let go, Henry's bad knee buckled and his body slammed to the floor. A lightning storm flashed in front of his eyes. The whimper that slipped past his throat, sounding more pathetic than the mew of a kitten, only added to the pain.

"Oh, my." The woman knelt to the ground. "I'm not sure

whether to call for an ambulance or the police. That was . . .
Oh, my. Are you okay?"

Was he okay? He wished he was dead. Henry gritted his
teeth and growled when she tried to assist him. "Get back."

"What can I do to help?" The Goldie Hawn look-alike
leaned farther over him.

"I said get back." With a great deal of effort, Henry managed to roll onto his side and use his good leg to climb back
onto his chair. Sweating with the exertion, and at the same
time wanting to scream at the setback this might have cost
him in his therapy sessions, Henry worked hard to control
his breathing.

"I called 911," the waitress shouted as she raced back from
the kitchen. "And I also grabbed this." She cocked her arm
back, then stabbed a syringe into Goldie's thigh.

"What was that?" The blonde beauty's voice rose two
octaves.

"An Epi shot. My little brother has a peanut allergy. I
know what anaphylactic shock looks like. And don't worry.
I've got another one in my purse if we need it."

Goldie scowled as she rubbed her thigh with one hand
and scratched her neck with the other. "I'm not going into
anaphylactic shock. It's just a few hives."

While she was distracted, Henry worked up the courage
to stand. He wouldn't be able to put much weight on his leg
without bawling like a baby. But he sure as shooting wasn't
getting carried out like a baby.

"That's more than a few hives," the waitress said.

"She's right," the chef said. "That's like a whole constellation of hives." He motioned with his thumb toward the kitchen. "Better grab the other shot."

"Don't you dare!" The woman picked up a spoon and peered at her image. "This is pretty much how I always look."

"That's too bad," the chef mumbled.

Henry dropped some cash on his table and limped away while the three of them argued about the state of her face. Welts or no welts, her face was gorgeous. And the last thing he wanted was that gorgeous face to see him crumple again.

Not that it should matter. It wasn't as if he knew this woman. She was probably only passing through. Why should it matter if she saw him fall flat on his face?

Maybe because she was the only person in this town who wasn't so used to seeing it.

♥

"If you're not going to let us take you to the hospital, will you at least sign this waiver?" A stocky EMT wearing a navy T-shirt with the word *Volunteer* on the back handed Edith a napkin covered in ketchup stains. "Oh, whoops." He switched the napkin with a piece of paper covered in ketchup stains.

"You know what?" He crumpled the paper and returned to eating the plate of french fries abandoned by the handsome man who had started to choke. "I'll track you down later. You sure you're okay?"

Edith couldn't believe someone had called for an ambulance. "I'm fine." Other than her pounding heart and jittery nerves. But what did she expect after getting stabbed with a dose of adrenaline? It certainly had nothing to do with the Paul Newman look-alike. Nope.

"Mack the Knife" sounded from the jukebox as the EMT headed outside. Edith eyed the waitress, prepared to fend off any further attacks. But this time the young woman came bearing a fountain glass piled high with a chocolate shake, whipped cream, and a cherry.

"The rest of your order should be ready soon. Still think you should go to the hospital," the waitress murmured on her way to the kitchen.

Please. If anybody had needed to go to the hospital, it was the guy choking, not her. And good night, he hadn't even been choking. Edith tried shaking the image of his face from her mind. Especially his expression when she'd first entered the diner. Something about the way he had looked at her, almost like he recognized her. But it was most likely just the hives that had caught his attention. That or the bangs.

No way had they met before today. She never would have forgotten a pair of blue eyes like that. Heat blossomed in her cheeks, remembering the way those eyes had followed her across the room. It had been a long time since she'd felt such an instant attraction.

Stop it. Edith dug her spoon into her shake. What was wrong with her? She was here to kill time until South Africa. Lie low. Avoid Steve. Not make moon eyes over some handsome stranger. A handsome stranger who not only had a girlfriend but was just humiliated in front of half a dozen burger-eating patrons and probably preferred to never see Edith or her hive-covered face again.

Especially since you had him raise his arms in the air like a toddler. Really, Edith, is that your idea of flirting?

"You okay?"

"Oh!" Edith flinched, dropping her spoon.

The waitress stood next to her booth, a hamburger basket in her hands and an uneasy expression on her face. "Your airway's closing up, isn't it?"

Edith retrieved her spoon and released an embarrassed laugh. "Was I thinking out loud?" She'd been known to do that on occasion.

"Not exactly." The waitress set the hamburger basket in front of Edith. "But your lips were moving and you were making all sorts of scrunchy faces."

Edith shrugged, the embarrassment radiating off her cheeks enough to char the hamburger. "Just gathering wool, as they say."

The waitress pulled a bottle of ketchup from her apron pocket and plopped it next to the basket. "Anything else I can get you?"

"No. Well, actually, Miss . . . ?"

"Gabby." The young waitress pointed to her name tag.

"Gabby. Cute. Say, Gabby, any chance you know the man who just left? The one who—"

"Almost died? Yeah. A little bit. I mean, not really. I don't know his name or anything. Me and my family just moved here a few months ago. This is only my first day working here. He lives in our neighborhood, but no, I don't know him." She buried her hands in her apron pockets with a shrug.

"That's fine. No worries. Just curious. Thanks." *See?*

Nobody even knows who he is. If that's not a sign to forget about him, then I don't know what is. Best just eat your burger and get on with your business. So what if he looks like Paul Newman? Tons of people probably look like Paul Newman. But you're not sitting here, thinking about them, are you?

Edith froze with a fry halfway to her mouth as she realized Gabby hadn't stepped away from her table.

"Gathering more wool again, ma'am?"

CHAPTER THREE

"Well, Henry, you sure did a number this time, didn't you?"

Sweat drizzled down Henry's forehead as he tried focusing on Frank Sinatra's voice crooning "You Make Me Feel So Young" from speakers perched above a row of empty treadmills soon to be filled with Westshire's Spicy Citizens Club, formerly known as Westshire's Seasoned Citizens Club, formerly known as Westshire's Seventy-plus Citizens Club, previously known as Westshire's Senior Citizens Club.

Whatever name they were going by these days, Henry guaranteed they felt younger than he did.

Henry grimaced at Lance, his physical therapist and drill sergeant and yeah, might as well say it, new best friend, considering the amount of time they'd spent together these past several weeks talking about every topic under the sun. Henry learned early on, when it came to rehabilitating his knee, it was either talk or cry. Today might be cry. "Is it as bad as I think it is?"

"Nah." Lance lifted Henry's leg into another stretch and nodded in greeting to a gray-haired gentleman wearing a blue T-shirt with *Westshire SCC* emblazoned across the front. The man returned Lance's greeting with a raised coffee mug, never breaking his stride to the treadmills.

"A few dozen more exercises today," Lance said, returning his focus to Henry, "a few extra sessions this week, at least one month of hard, grueling therapy tacked on at the end . . ."

"Is that all? Here I was afraid I may have set myself back."

Lance finished the stretch, then stood and snapped a resistance band at Henry. "You did set yourself back. In case you've forgotten, you're not in high school anymore. You're practically middle-aged."

"I'm three years older than you. Remind me again what the average life expectancy is these days?"

"Remind me again what possessed you to participate in a full tackle scrimmage football game?"

"It was the alumni match. Nobody else from my graduating class could make it. I had to . . . you know . . ." *Redeem myself* sounded pretty pathetic, no matter how true. "Represent."

"Well, how about next time you stick to representing the marching band, like me." Lance folded his arms across his chest and motioned his head toward the crew assembling around the treadmills. "'Cuz now you're going to be sporting a limp the rest of your life that represents your teammates' granddads."

Henry grunted. Lance might have a point. Not the marching band bit. He'd take walking with a limp over wearing a hat with a plume any day. He finished his last repetition of leg exercises on the floor mat before leaning up on one elbow. "Can I ask you something?"

"Sure, as long as it's not 'Am I done yet?'"

"What do you think of Goldie Hawn?"

"Goldie Hawn." Lance frowned, stretching the resistance band between his hands. "To tell the truth, she always sort of rubbed me the wrong way."

Henry lowered himself onto a recumbent bike and began to slowly pedal. "Really? I've always kind of had a thing for her myself."

"Huh." Lance scratched the back of his smooth shaved head. "Well, different strokes for different folks. I suppose if she hadn't ratted me out to my parents back when I tried switching book covers in grade school because I believed my brothers when they told me 'Wee Willie Winkie' was an adult story, I might think she was okay. Can't say I can ever imagine having a *thing* for her though."

Henry stopped pedaling. "What are you talking about?"

"Goldie Hawn. The librarian. What are you talking about?"

"That's *Gloria Haughn*, you dingbat. She's gotta be a hundred years old. I'm talking about Goldie Hawn. The actress. Didn't you ever see *Overboard*?"

"If I did, it would have been a long time ago. Isn't she kind of getting up there in years too?" Lance twirled his finger in a circular motion for Henry to resume pedaling. "Either way, it sounds to me like you've got a thing for old ladies."

Henry laughed, ignoring the ache in his knee as he pressed the pedals. "I saw a woman that looked just like her yesterday. The *young* her. And she was beautiful."

"Did this woman have anything to do with you reinjuring your knee?"

"No. Well, maybe. Yeah. She was there. And got to see me look like a complete idiot." Henry winced at both the memory and the increased pedaling speed. "Doesn't really matter. I'm sure I'll never see her again."

Lance stepped on the middle of the resistance band and raised the ends of it above his head. "Should you even be wanting to see her again? If memory serves me correctly, you have a girlfriend. A girlfriend who doesn't strike me as the type to be very understanding if she ever heard you talking about beautiful women, be they young or old."

"Angela and me . . . man . . . trying to keep our relationship moving has been like spinning wheels on this bike. We're not going anywhere. Next time I see her, I'm going to end it. Should have done it already, to tell the truth."

"Wow," Lance said, dropping the band and glancing at his watch. "This is turning into a pretty deep therapy session for us. I feel like we've covered a lot of ground, and we're only twenty minutes in. What other confessions do you have for me?"

"Twenty minutes? I thought it'd at least been an hour."

"Quit being such a bawl bag. You see any of those guys griping?" Lance hiked his thumb over his shoulder.

"Griping? They're not even moving. They're sitting around the treadmills, drinking coffee."

"But the point is they're not griping about it." Lance did the circle motion with his finger again.

Henry sighed, wiped a towel across his face, and pressed on. After several minutes of silence, needing something to distract him from his leg and the repetitive motion and the thousandth time hearing Frank Sinatra sing the same song, he said, "So . . . 'Wee Willie Winkie,' huh?"

Three hours later Henry stopped off at home to get cleaned up. After a quick shower—quick being relative—he limped into the kitchen. The welcoming scent of cinnamon and baked bread took over his senses. A note sat on the middle of the kitchen island.

Dear Henry,

I just wanted to leave you a quick note to say thank you. I'm sure having a houseguest wasn't part of your summer plans. Kat said you had physical therapy sessions in the morning, so I thought that might be a good time to use the kitchen without getting in the way. I didn't catch you before you jumped in the shower. I hope you don't mind I used up some of your older-looking bananas to make banana bread. Please enjoy! Consider it a small token of my appreciation. All right. I'll stop writing. My husband used to say even in letters I could talk a person's head off.

Sincerely,

Edith

PS—Since I don't know what hours I'll be coming and going, I'll continue using the back stairway so that I don't disturb your sleep. Thanks again.

Henry held the note in his hand as he scanned the kitchen. Dirty dishes he'd been neglecting in the sink were washed, dried, and stacked on the counter. The island had been wiped clean. Two loaves of banana bread sat on the stove.

Well, how about that. Place looked downright homey. Put him in mind of long-ago summer nights when he played dominoes and ate chocolate chip cookies in this very kitchen. His grandma Dee's kitchen. Her warm smile, coupled with the taste of gooey chocolate, always had a way of unraveling Henry's tongue. He told her things he would have felt silly telling anyone else. Like who the cutest girls in his class were. Or how his teacher was always telling him he had ants in his pants—and how one day he really did.

Sometimes he wondered what he would say about his life now if Grandma Dee were still sitting across from him.

Henry helped himself to a slice of banana bread. Then helped himself to two more slices as he washed it down with a glass of milk and reread the note. Maybe banana bread had the same power to loosen his lips as chocolate chip cookies, because for some reason Henry was feeling a bit chatty.

He grabbed a blue pen out of the oversize coffee mug he used as a pencil holder on the counter, then turned Edith's note over.

Dear Edith,

You are more than welcome in my home—especially now that I've sampled your baking. Help yourself to any ripe bananas from here on out. I haven't had anything this tasty since my grandma was alive. My mom, God rest her soul, never did inherit her mother's knack for baking. I, unfortunately, did inherit my mother's knack for baking. Or should I say, lack of knack? Probably I should just stop talking. Seems you're not the only one who gets chatty on paper.

A few more things. Don't worry about waking me up. I sleep like the dead. As for using the back stairs—please don't. A frayed rope ladder missing its rungs would be more dependable than that poor excuse of a stairway. Been meaning to get to it for years. I'd feel much better if you came in through the front door at night. I'll leave the porch light on. The last thing I want is for you to fall and have to join me in my physical therapy sessions, although you'd probably handle it with more grace than I do. I've always admired the stamina of women in your generation.

Henry

PS—Just out of curiosity, as a woman, what do you think of Goldie Hawn?

Henry set the note in the same spot he'd found Edith's, right where Grandma Dee used to leave a plate of her cookies. Since his parents had him later in life—a big surprise to both them and his twenty-one-year-old brother at the time—Henry didn't remember his other set of grandparents. Barely remembered Grandpa Joe. But Grandma Dee, he not only remembered, he adored. She was special. Something told him this Edith might be special too.

And now a glance at his watch told him he better get moving if he wanted to swing by the historical society and touch base about an upcoming project before he put in a few hours at the office. He grabbed his grandfather's cane, wincing at how stiff his knee felt from just that short time sitting. He'd hoped to not need the extra help by now, but after the assault his leg took at the diner, he feared he and this cane might turn into lifelong partners.

He squeezed the curved wooden handle. *No.* Before he could change his mind, he propped it against his chair and forced his feet to keep moving.

Behind the closed doors of his own home was one thing, but as the new boss of his family's company, he needed this town to see him standing on his own two feet without any assistance, be it a cane or his retired brother. He limped out the back door toward his truck.

And prayed he didn't fall flat on his face again.

CHAPTER FOUR

"I feel bad putting you to work right away." Sharon, the director of the crisis nursery center, twisted open a set of white window blinds. Golden sunlight flooded the beige walls.

"Tomorrow night isn't right away. Besides, the whole reason I'm here is to help." And avoid Steve. Okay, maybe the whole reason she was here was to avoid Steve. But that didn't make her desire to do something helpful as she avoided Steve less worthy, did it?

Edith stared down at the crib where a potted elephant ear plant and three succulents sat. Her eyes wandered over to the baby changing station. A fern and maybe an African violet? She wasn't sure.

"Um . . ." Edith cleared her throat. When she jumped at the opportunity to volunteer at this crisis nursery center, she'd assumed it was an *infant* crisis nursery center. So far the only thing she'd seen swaddled in a baby blanket was the potted snake plant downstairs in the living room. "Is this a typical day here? I mean, you do get babies. Not just . . ." Edith waved to the plants.

Sharon chuckled, running her finger over the crib rail. "Yes. I assure you the purpose of this home is to provide shelter to human babies in crisis. But somehow Gladys—you'll see her flying around town in her motorized wheelchair—got the impression this was a nursery center for plants in crisis. She kept dropping off all her houseplants. Pretty soon others started following suit and well, now . . ." Sharon inhaled a deep breath. "Let's just say every room of this house is very well oxygenated."

"Isn't that a good thing, though? I mean, to have a house full of plants rather than babies?"

"It is if we're not needed. But I've worked too many years in social services to know that can change on a dime, even in a small town like this. We might go an entire week without seeing a single baby, then be up to our ears in dirty diapers because four single working moms suddenly lost their child-care arrangements and need us to fill in for a few days. We've seen all sorts of scenarios. Which is why I need at least one person on-site twenty-four hours a day."

Sharon plucked a dead leaf from a plant on the dresser and dropped it into the trash. "Now you're certain you won't mind covering some of the night shifts? You'll need to stay awake. One of our volunteers slept through three drop-offs. We can't have that."

"Nights won't be a problem. I worked nights in the ER. Nights, days, wherever you need me, just let me know."

"Wonderful. The summer months are usually the toughest to schedule because of vacations. Of course, some of the college students are home on summer break, so they're able to help fill in some of the holes. I promise not to work you to death. This town may be small, but you'll be surprised at the number of activities we have going on throughout the summer. I do want you to be able to enjoy your time while you're here."

The wooden floorboards creaked beneath their steps as Sharon led Edith out of the upstairs bedroom to the stairway. "The gala is always a blast, especially if you like to dance. There's also the annual pancake breakfast out at the old airport, the Fourth of July carnival downtown—we usually help out with the medical tent—then the summer league baseball tournament . . ."

Edith followed Sharon down the stairs, half-listening. Black-and-white photos, mixed in with more recent photos, captured her attention on the wall. Pictures of Westshire, she assumed. The town square. A marquee advertising *Gone with the Wind*. A barbershop quartet. Ribbon-cutting ceremonies.

She recognized the crisis house in one of the photos near the bottom. A sea-green Victorian with white trim on the outside, original woodwork and crown molding on the inside, it reminded her of Henry's house. "This house is gorgeous."

"What?" Sharon grabbed the banister at the bottom of the stairs and twisted around, following Edith's gaze. "Oh, thank you. You should have seen it when I first bought it. It would have sent chills down your spine. My husband thought I was crazy when I told him I wanted to use it as a service to the community. He said the greater service would be bulldozing it to the ground. Thankfully once Walter got rid of the wallpaper and pulled back the carpet to reveal the original flooring, my husband started seeing the potential."

"Walter?"

"Yes. Wonderful man. Talented artist too. Maybe you've seen the mural he did on the side of the old boiler factory? No? Well, very talented. Just like his older son. Or I should say *was* talented. He's dead now. Walter, not the son. His son is very much alive. He just retired from running the company so he could move closer to his wife's parents because you know how it is. They're starting to get up there in years, could use the extra help. So now Walter's younger son has taken over, and I have no idea why I'm telling you all of this."

"I wasn't really sure either, but you were on such a roll." They shared a laugh, and Edith knew she and Sharon were going to get along just fine this summer.

Sharon lifted her palm. "Next time hold your hand up like a stop sign. It's what my kids do whenever I get carried away—or start telling a story they've already heard a dozen times."

Edith followed Sharon into the kitchen. A plant with long vines spilled over the top of the refrigerator and several smaller plants were spread across the countertops. "How many kids do you have?"

"Five. All grown and out of the house. Coffee?" Edith nodded and Sharon grabbed two mugs from a cabinet. "Only James, my youngest, still lives in Westshire. The rest have pretty much spread out to every corner of the country. Cream or sugar?"

"No thanks." Edith accepted the hot mug, inhaling the

fresh aroma of coffee. "Five kids. Wow. Bet your house never knew a moment of quiet."

Sharon's eyes widened in feigned terror as she leaned back against the counter. "I think that's why this crisis center is so important to me. I remember how hectic it was at times. Good, don't get me wrong. But very hectic. Very loud. Very stressful. Especially when James came along. We had not been planning for a number five. And we certainly hadn't been planning for my husband to lose his job the minute number five arrived. Believe me, I know what it feels like to be in the midst of a crisis. To feel like you don't have enough support. To feel like you just need somebody to take this screaming baby out of your hands for a few hours before you do something bad. Like get in the car and drive away, never to return. I was about there. Oh, honey, I was about there."

A clock on the wall with a different birdcall for every hour ticked off the next few seconds while Sharon blew on her coffee. "And that's why I'm here now. Why this house is here. To be a resource not only for Westshire but all the surrounding communities. And so long as we don't run out of funds, I hope someday to extend that reach even further."

Sharon took a sip of her coffee, then lifted her mug toward Edith. "But enough about me. What about you? My cousin Ruthie said you're planning a trip to South Africa at the end of summer. For how long? And what will you be doing?"

Cradling her mug in her hands, Edith gave a small laugh. "To be honest, I'm not entirely sure. My hope, if everything works out with my visa, is to stay for three years. As for what I'll be doing, all I know for now is I'll be volunteering for a nongovernmental organization called Ithemba. It helps support a rural hospital located in the Eastern Cape. I don't know how familiar you are with South Africa . . . ?"

Sharon shrugged and shook her head.

"Well, it's in an area known as the Wild Coast. Apparently a lot of adventure travelers like to go there because it's so remote."

"I imagine it's beautiful."

"Yes, but also very poor. They say the infrastructure is practically nonexistent because it's so rural. Sometimes people walk for hours just to get to the hospital."

"I see. So will you be volunteering as a nurse while you're there?"

"That was my original intention, but I guess there's a bunch of bureaucratic red tape to get through. Things like registering with the South African Nursing Council and taking written exams. I've been told it's a nightmare of a process that may take up until my dying day to accomplish. So I'm not sure yet what I'll be doing. Kaya Reddy, the operational manager for the organization, is supposed to contact me again later this summer. Considering I don't even have my passport, she probably wants to make sure I'm serious about coming before she spends too much time deciding what to do with me."

"Well, I'm sure she'll be grateful to have you. Just like we are here. And whatever you end up doing, my goodness, it sounds like it'll be quite the adventure."

"Exactly." Coffee sloshed over the rim onto her fingers. "Whoops. Maybe I shouldn't talk about South Africa with coffee in my hands. I tend to get a little animated whenever I think about this next chapter of my life."

"I can tell," Sharon said, her kind eyes softening with compassion as she handed Edith a napkin.

Edith wiped off her fingers, then started to sip her coffee when she realized what that soft look of compassion meant. It meant Sharon was thinking of broaching the last chapter of Edith's life. A topic Edith had no intentions of broaching. Ever.

How long has your husband been gone? How long were you married? Do you think you'll ever remarry? Tell me about him.

Edith popped out of her seat as an owl hooted from the clock. "Oh, my. Noon already." She dumped her coffee down the sink. "Thanks for the coffee, but I should probably get going and, you know, do something. Stuff. Things." She backpedaled out of the kitchen. "Thanks again for the coffee. I'll be here bright and early tomorrow night. Or dark and late, rather."

"Don't forget your phone," Sharon called to her as she was halfway out the door.

"Right." Edith spun and snatched it from the entryway table. Fourteen missed calls. For. The. Love. Good thing she'd kept it on silent.

Sharon followed her out the front door. "Oh, hey, I meant to ask, where are you staying when you're not here? I heard about Kat's house. Please don't tell me you're paying to stay at the bed-and-breakfast all summer."

"No, no." Edith jogged down the porch steps. "I'm staying with—" Edith's phone buzzed in her hand. She glanced at the screen. "Steve," she muttered.

"Steve? Surely not Steve Winters. I knew he was looking for a roommate, but my goodness, he's only nineteen."

Edith shook her head. "Not that Steve. My Steve. I mean, no. Not my Steve. Not any Steve. I'm not staying with Steve. I want nothing to do with Steve. Not Steve Winters. I'm talking about my Steve." She winced and held up her phone. "This Steve. Who is not my Steve. I don't know why I keep saying my Steve."

Edith blew her bangs away from her eyes. "What I'm trying to say is my man, my roommate, my—" Steve's incessant phone calling had her so flustered she couldn't even form sentences. "An elderly gentleman. Over there. That's who I'm staying with." Edith pointed in the general direction of Henry's house. "It was nice meeting you."

Edith took off down the sidewalk. Would it be selfish to pray that hundreds of babies were thrown into crisis situations this summer? Probably. But Edith was going to need something more than keeping houseplants alive to make time fly while she avoided Steve until she could escape into the next chapter of her life.

———— ♥ ————

Dear Henry,

I'm glad you liked the banana bread. We must have just missed each other this morning. I was anxious to get over to the infant crisis center and meet some of the, um, plants?

But onto serious matters.

Goldie Hawn . . . hmmm . . . Well, Henry, to be honest, as a woman, I can't say I ever gave her much thought. I think she's pretty.

And she certainly seems fun. But for some reason I've always veered more toward movies before her time. Especially movies starring Paul Newman. I love, love, love him! And you want to hear something crazy? I saw a man who put me in mind of him just the other night.

One word, Henry—HUBBA-HUBBA.

And on that note, I'll bid you good night. May your dreams be filled with visions of Goldie.

Edith

PS—I couldn't resist a quick pit stop to the grocery store today. I put some butter pecan ice cream in the freezer. Help yourself.

Henry set the note down on the kitchen island before sinking onto a stool and massaging his temples. The past few hours had left him with a dull steady headache. He'd spent the better part of the day finagling business negotiations with the local historical society on projects Henry thought were already locked. Or at least they were when his brother Nick ran the company. Now that Henry was in charge, it seemed the president of the historical society had all sorts of concerns.

Henry shoved back from the island. Maybe he was reading too much into it. Maybe the president was just being thorough.

His phone chimed on the counter. Shoot. Probably Angela again. He'd meant to call her back before he left the office. Henry's knee flared with pain as he maneuvered off the stool. He'd call her in a minute.

First, ice. He opened the freezer, intending to grab the bag of frozen peas dedicated solely to his knee, when his eyes landed on the carton of butter pecan ice cream.

Not his first choice when it came to ice cream. Probably not even top ten. But considering her age, he should be grateful Edith hadn't picked up orange sherbet. That had been his grandma's favorite.

He yanked the carton out, retrieved a spoon, then settled back on the stool, knee forgotten for the moment, and glanced at Edith's note. His lips tipped up in a small smile, rereading her words. Sometimes she sounded more like Kat than his grandma.

Despite her abysmal ice cream decision-making skills, Henry couldn't help enjoying Edith's presence. For some reason, it offered a small taste of his childhood again. Back before he messed everything up.

Henry scooped a small bite into his mouth, letting the creamy, nutty taste melt on his tongue as he angled his head to the side. Okay, so maybe not the worst. Maybe top ten potential.

Henry shoved another spoonful in his mouth and stared at his phone. He should really give Angela a call. His eyes closed as the headache that had receded to a whisper threatened to come back with a vengeance. It wasn't so much he didn't feel like talking; it was more about the type of conversation he didn't feel like having.

He dug his spoon into the carton. He'd call Angela later. First, he had a letter to write.

———— ♥ ————

Edith bit her lower lip as she turned the key in the front door. In the silence of the night, the gentle click sounded more like a gunshot. She clasped the door shut and removed her shoes to soften her footsteps, stifling a giggle as she realized she was behaving like a teenager who'd broken curfew.

As promised, Henry had left the front porch light on. She smiled, thinking of his worry over her climbing some rickety steps. If he only knew the living accommodations she was going to have once she made it to South Africa. *"I hope you don't mind lots of mud. Oh yes, and frogs, spiders, cockroaches, and the occasional snake."*

Resting against the door, Edith recalled Kaya's cheery warning, followed by her own quick response. *"Don't mind at all. Nope, not a bit."*

At least not the mud. She'd worry later about whether she minded frogs, spiders, cockroaches, or the occasional snake.

Edith palmed her stomach. She'd only seen pictures of the remote village online, but those images never ceased to set off butterflies. The same flutter she used to get when she trained for marathons and knew race day was growing closer and closer—a steady flow of nervous excitement mixed in with several drops of self-doubt. Although this time, the proportions felt reversed.

What if, after years of dreaming about living a grand adventure overseas, she didn't actually have what it took?

What if instead of staying for three years like she hoped, she ran home after three days because of a bunch of spiders?

Stop. Edith straightened from the door. Of course she had what it took. She was her great-great-aunt Edith's namesake, wasn't she? The same call to adventure that had buzzed through Edith Genevieve McClintock's blood decades ago now hummed through her own veins, didn't it? *Yes.*

With a new resolve in her step, Edith took to the stairs, pausing halfway to the second floor. Maybe the butterflies in her stomach would feel better if she fed them.

After visiting the crisis nursery house and dropping ice cream off at Henry's house, she'd wandered around town the remainder of the afternoon, checking out a few of the shops, then catching a double feature at the theater. But she never did eat supper. She ate a tub of popcorn at the movies—starting tomorrow she really was going to get back to eating healthier—but popcorn didn't count for supper. Everybody knew that. Especially the butterflies in her stomach.

And if she was going to start eating healthier tomorrow, she should probably take advantage of the butter pecan ice cream tonight.

Edith padded back down the stairs and to the kitchen. A night-light over the counter revealed another note on the kitchen island.

Aww. Sweet Henry. She grabbed the note and tucked it into the back pocket of her jean shorts, then opened the freezer door and pulled out the ice cream. "Or should I say, Sweet Tooth Henry?" she said, gaping into the mostly empty carton.

———— ♥ ————

Back upstairs in her room, ready for bed, Edith settled under the covers and unfolded Henry's note. She couldn't say why, but she looked forward to reading it as much as she would a favorite novel. What would he have to say—other than confessing a serious addiction to butter pecan ice cream?

> Dear Edith,
>
> So you love, love, love Paul Newman, huh? Good to know. More than a few of the older women at my church have commented that my baby blues put them in mind of the late great actor. Should our paths finally cross in this house of mine, I'll be prepared to catch you when you swoon.
>
> Speaking of hubba-hubba, I think I'm in love with this ice cream. Who knew butter pecan was this great? The next gallon is on me, Edith.

"Darn right it is, buster," Edith muttered with a smile.

> So I hear you're doing some traveling? Good for you. It's never too late to chase after a bit of adventure. Even if that guy's eyes are as pretty as mine or Paul Newman's (which hardly seems possible), don't let him stand between you and this opportunity. If that guy had half a brain, he'd beg to go with you!
>
> Kat mentioned you're a widow. I'm sorry for your loss. If you don't mind me asking, how long were you

and your husband married? How did you meet? Do you have children? My mother would tell me to mind my own business, and she would be right. So if I'm nosing into things I shouldn't, just tell me to buzz off. I'll understand. I might cry for a while, but I'll understand.

Henry

Edith folded Henry's note in half and sank further into her pillow. Though the walls were bare, the room had a cozy feel to it. A subtle scent lingered, making Edith wonder if all the upstairs had been recently painted and Henry hadn't gotten around to rehanging anything on the walls. Probably because he couldn't make it up the stairs anymore.

A cherry dresser with a curved mirror sat against the wall facing her bed. Next to the window a rocking chair with a quilt draped over the back rested next to an antique-looking steam trunk.

She stared at the ceiling for several minutes, lost in quiet thought. Only the occasional creaks of the house settling in for the night filled the silence. Her eyelids grew heavy. How come Henry never married? So far she hadn't been able to find any pictures around the house to show what he looked like, but she imagined he was quite the charmer back in his day.

A handsome young face kept bobbing to the surface of her mind. She tried pushing it down, only to have it pop right back up. What was it about that guy from the diner? Other than the handsome face and gorgeous blue eyes?

She really needed to stop thinking about him. And she would. Tomorrow. Once she finished dreaming about him tonight.

Van Halen's "Jump" blared on the stand next to the bed. Edith responded accordingly. "Yeesh," she squealed, clutching her chest. Time to switch her ringtone back to the piano trill before she had a heart attack. Patting her chest to soothe her heart, she scooted up and read the caller ID with a groan.

Well, really now. Who did she expect it would be? Paul Newman?

She'd sent a text to Steve earlier. Clearly he hadn't received the message to kindly back off. She really ought to block his number.

Edith closed her eyes as the phone continued blaring. She should answer. She should. That would be the adult thing to do. Though he wasn't really acting like an adult, was he, pestering her nonstop? Besides, what was left to say? Nothing. She had nothing left to say to this man.

Inhaling a deep breath, Edith turned her phone off and slid back beneath the covers.

The silence that had almost lulled her to sleep moments before threatened to suffocate her. Times like this, she wished she wasn't an only child. How nice it would be to have a sister to talk to. A brother. Someone.

She thought of a few friends she could call. But it was late. And she didn't want to turn on her phone. She could always go downstairs and wake up Henry, ha-ha. They'd shared a carton of ice cream, after all. Everyone knew late-night emotional conversations came next. Or maybe they hadn't reached that point in their sharing-a-house relationship status.

Edith rolled over, eyeing her notebook and pen on the floor next to the bed. But that didn't mean she still couldn't share some of her feelings with him. In fact, who safer than an elderly man she'd never met to share some of the hurts of her past with?

Edith yanked the notebook off the floor. He wanted to know about her marriage? Edith bit the cap of her pen off and began writing. "You're going to be sorry you asked, my friend."

When early morning dawned, Edith slipped down the stairs, placed several sheets of paper on the kitchen island, then scooted out the front door.

CHAPTER FIVE

Henry startled awake. What was that? He rubbed his eyes, taking a moment to orient himself. Even though he'd spent the past several weeks sleeping on the futon in the downstairs guest room–slash–office space, it always took him a few seconds to remember why he wasn't in his upstairs bedroom. Usually by the time he finished rubbing his eyes, his knee began aching, and he remembered all too well why he was stuck on the first floor.

Henry glanced at the digital clock on the corner of his computer desk. Then rubbed his eyes again. Had he forgotten to set his alarm last night? He reached for his phone. "No . . ."

He was going to be late for therapy if he didn't move fast. And considering Henry couldn't move fast, he was going to be late for therapy.

Henry rolled out of bed with a groan. At least whatever noise he'd heard had woken him up before he overslept any longer. Probably the newspaper. Chelsea, the delivery girl, had developed a mighty strong throwing arm this past year.

Henry hobbled into the kitchen. A gray overcast sky greeted him through the window. No wonder he'd overslept. His gaze drifted to the ceiling. Hopefully the noise hadn't woken Edith. He'd have to have a talk with Chelsea if it did.

Scratching his chest, Henry yawned and ambled to the front door to swipe the newspaper before it got rained on. He had just bent over to grab it when he caught sight of her. His her. Goldie Hawn *her*. Crossing the street at the corner.

It *was* her, wasn't it? Blonde hair trailed down her shoulders beneath a red headband. Oh yeah. It was her all right. He needed to go after her.

His bare feet froze at the edge of the porch, a voice screaming inside his head. *And do what?* Good question. Henry glanced down at himself. He was still wearing striped pajama pants and a worn gray T-shirt with a hole in the armpit. Hardly the attire a man wanted to wear when he was attempting to redeem himself from a bad first impression.

But he had to do something.

Henry spun back inside his house, ripping off his T-shirt. He hadn't seen any sign of her since the night at the diner. He'd even driven by the diner yesterday like a creepy stalker, trying to see through the windows in case she'd gone back there to eat again. All he'd accomplished was getting honked at twice for driving so slowly. He couldn't afford to lose this opportunity.

Henry yanked on a clean shirt, glanced at the time. *Shoot.*

Physical therapy started in ten minutes. What was he doing? He didn't have time to chase after Goldie Hawn. Who was he kidding? He didn't have time to chase after anybody.

If his multiple surgeries, extensive rehab, and ever-constant ache in his knee had taught him anything, it was that he wasn't exactly a young man anymore. The accident had forced him to slow down, look at his life, and face the truth.

And truth was, if he wanted to start that family he'd planned on starting over a decade ago, now was the time. With the girl he already had. As much as he admired his parents, he didn't want to follow in their footsteps, becoming a dad in his forties.

Crazy as Angela made him, at least she was real. Not some dream girl. He just needed to try a little harder to make it work. Forget Goldie. For all he knew, she could be some lunatic who'd escaped from a maximum security prison, out on the lam. Best to forget about her right now.

He picked up his phone and dialed the physical therapy department's number. "Can you let Lance know I'm not going to make it today? Something important came up."

Henry pocketed his phone. He'd forget about her tomorrow once he found out who she was today.

———— ♥ ————

Edith's only plan after a restless night with little sleep was to walk until she came across a place that looked like it sold a decent cup of coffee. A two-story yellow house with a sign in the front that read *Marvel for Sheriff!* next to a sign proclaiming *Coffee Forever!* seemed a good place to start.

A wooden door painted in purple sat propped open. Edith opened the screen door and stepped inside to the intoxicating aroma of warm caramel mixed with cinnamon, honey, and roasted coffee beans. She had chosen wisely.

A black cat curled up in a wicker basket on the counter greeted her through bored, slitted eyes. "Hi there, kitty," Edith returned his greeting.

A round, flush-faced woman holding a tray of cinnamon rolls burst through a set of saloon doors behind the counter. She spotted Edith. "Oh. Hi. You're new." She shoved the tray onto one of the shelves. "I'll have fresh baked scones out in two shakes of a tail." She pointed to herself. "Julie." Pointed to a chalkboard menu above her on the wall. "Our specials." She disappeared through the doors before they'd had a chance to stop swinging.

Edith sniffed appreciatively as she read the board. She'd made it to the chai tea options when the screen door behind her opened and slammed shut with a bang. Edith jumped. The cat yawned. The tiny wrinkle-faced woman who'd entered yelled.

"What's that cat doing on the counter? Julie! I told you last time I was calling the sanitation department and this time I'm going to do it!"

Julie reappeared, carrying a tray of scones. "Now, Opal, you know he doesn't bother anybody. He's practically dead. Just let him be."

"All the more reason to get rid of him. Nobody wants to be served a donut from where a dead cat's been lying. It's filthy, I tell you. Filthy! Now you give me one of those cinnamon rolls and if I see one speck of hair on it, I'm calling the sanitation department." The irate woman plunked cash onto the counter. When the black cat shifted his head to look at her, the old woman hissed.

Julie bagged up a cinnamon roll and handed it over the counter with a smile. "See you tomorrow, Opal. Take care, sweetie."

"Not sanitary, I tell you. Not sanitary!" Opal slammed the screen door shut behind her.

"Sorry about that." Julie wiped her hands on a flowered apron wrapped around her ample waist. "Some people just aren't cat people," she said with a shrug. "Are you new to town?"

Edith nodded. "I'm just here for the summer. My name's Edith. I'm volunteering—"

"At the crisis nursery." Julie's face lit up. "Sharon told me about you. Wait right here." She spun around, disappearing into the back for a minute, before returning with a yellowing waxy-leafed plant. "You mind taking this with you next time you go? I don't know if I'm overwatering it, underwatering it, or what." Julie handed it to her over the counter. "Thanks, honey. Really appreciate it. Now . . ." She wiped her hands on her apron. "Have you decided what you'd like?"

"Just coffee, please," Edith said, looking down at the plant in her arms. "Black."

"Why don't you set it by the door? You can grab it on your way out. Anything else besides a Chester coffee?"

Edith did as Julie suggested, setting the potted plant down, before stepping back to the counter. "I'm sorry. A Chester what?"

Julie winked and pointed toward the cat. "Chester. He's black."

"Right," said Edith. This town was so weird.

"Sure you don't want anything else? The cinnamon scones are always a hit."

"No," Edith said, though the cinnamon scones did smell rather tempting. *I really shouldn't though. Especially since I ate popcorn for supper last night. Although that wasn't really supper. More like I didn't have supper. I just had a snack. Missed supper completely. And I certainly didn't get any butter pecan ice cream. Probably need to make up for lost calories today.*

"You okay, honey?" Julie waved her palm back and forth in front of Edith's face.

"I'm thinking." Edith blew her bangs from her eyes. "You know what, on second thought—"

"She'll take the scone," a deep and slightly winded voice said from behind her, the screen door clasping shut a second later. "We both will."

Edith whipped her head around. *Him.* She reached for the counter, needing to steady herself. Especially when she looked into those blue eyes. Oh, dear. Paul Newman. Here. Mr. Hubba-Hubba. She opened her mouth. Nothing. Speechless. Or maybe she just couldn't breathe. Oxygen. She needed oxygen. And at least two scones.

"And go ahead and add another coffee for me, too," he said to Julie, though his eyes never left Edith's. How was it possible he was even more handsome than she remembered? Granted, the last thing she remembered was his face contorted in agony. But still. She should have stayed home this morning. With Henry. Where it was safe.

Say something. A strangled sound made it past her throat. She cleared it and ducked her face into her purse. "Here, let me, ah . . . uh . . . oh . . ." Edith didn't know what she was saying, other than vowel sounds, as she fumbled for money.

"I've got it. It's the least I can do for the way I acted the other night at the diner. You were only trying to help. I shouldn't have—"

"No," Edith said, shaking her head side to side, unable to meet his gaze again, especially since all she could find so far was a quarter and a piece of gum. "No. You were fine. I mean, you weren't fine. You were choking. Then obviously you were in pain. What I meant is that you had every right to be horrible—"

"Ouch."

"Not that you were horrible," Edith rushed on. "I'm saying this all wrong."

"No," he said with a self-deprecating laugh, "you're probably saying it all right."

Julie interrupted them with a polite cough. "Here's your coffee and scones, you two."

Paul *Hubba-Hubba* Newman paid while Edith took her coffee and scone. "Thank you." She shifted back and forth on her feet. What was she supposed to do now? Join him? He didn't ask her to join him. He only offered to buy. She hesitated as he doctored up his coffee with cream and sugar sitting on a turquoise baker's rack near the front door.

Edith glanced at Julie, who had her elbows propped on the counter, watching the two of them like they had the lead roles in the community play. Maybe Edith should go sit down.

Julie waggled her eyebrows at Edith while Mr. Hubba-Hubba's back was still turned.

Or maybe she should just leave.

Part of the reason Edith never planned to remarry barreled down on her like a freight train. The whole idea of starting over at square one with a man—having to *date* a man—terrified her. But this wasn't a date. She had no reason to freak out. No reason to sweat.

So why was she sweating?

Scattered tables—some wooden and round, others concrete and square—filled the room attached to the front bakery area. Edith crossed the creaky wooden floorboards. With a shaky breath, she chose a round table near the back. A round table for two. Why had she chosen a round table for two? Was it too late to choose another table? For say, eight or twenty?

The slow, uneven gait of Paul Newman's twin drew closer. She held her breath.

He limped past her table.

Edith exhaled, a mixture of relief and disappointment. He lowered himself into a chair at the next table, facing her, and gave her a small smile. Her lungs refilled with a mixture of anxiety and delight.

"This scone is so good." Edith realized she hadn't taken a bite yet and shoved a chunk into her mouth. "Thanks again," she mumbled around a mouthful.

"You're welcome." He held up his coffee in a sort of salute.

Edith swallowed and saluted back with her coffee. They both sipped in silence. Edith wished she had a newspaper or her phone or anything right now that would keep her eyes from drifting back to the man across from her. She wished even more he had something to keep his eyes from drifting toward her.

She scanned the walls. A few tin signs with quotes about coffee. A couple of framed newspaper articles, one headline saying something about a town fire. A mirror. Windows. She sighed. Nobody else had entered the coffee shop yet. It was still early in the morning. Edith racked her mind for something to say. Couldn't this place have some music, at least? A coffee grinder? What was Julie doing back there?

When he shifted in his chair and made the slightest frown, she leapt on it. "Do you need something to prop your leg on? It's your knee, right? It might feel better elevated. I can grab another chair for you."

He held a hand up to stop her. "I'm fine. Despite every impression I've given you, I promise I'm actually a healthy, able-bodied man."

"Oh, believe me, I noticed." Edith inhaled a sharp breath, realizing she'd spoken out loud. "The healthy part," she quickly added. "Not that your body isn't able. It looks extremely able. I just meant you look good. Your *health* looks good. Your cholesterol levels are probably really good." She blew on her coffee. "That's all I meant."

His gorgeous blue eyes stared at her as if she were a piece of abstract art he couldn't quite figure out, before a slow grin spread across his entire face. "Who are you?"

"Who am I?" Edith asked.

"Yeah," he said with a laugh. "Where did you come from?"

"Pittsburgh."

"Okay. So what brought you here? And don't say a plane."

Edith blew her bangs from her eyes. "That's kind of a long story."

He leaned forward, propping his elbows on the table with the coffee mug cradled between his hands. "I'm in no hurry."

What was it about this guy? The eyes, obviously. Edith tried reining in her silly infatuation. But goodness. *Those eyes.* She marveled that for the second time in less than twenty-four hours she was ready to pour out her life story to a complete stranger. Although Kat's uncle Henry was hardly a complete stranger. They'd shared the same tub of ice cream after all.

Edith blew her bangs off her forehead. "Well, if you really want to know—"

"Babe!"

Edith flinched at the outburst. She turned toward the voice and recognized his girlfriend from the diner.

"I tried going to your house and you weren't there. I can't believe I ran into you here. Aren't you supposed to be working out with Lance? I didn't think you even liked coffee."

The man stared at his girlfriend as if he didn't recognize her—or perhaps like she was a piece of abstract art he would never understand—before shaking his head. "I canceled. Aren't you supposed to be with Chad? I didn't expect to see you again until next week."

Edith made a show of glancing at her wrist, hoping nobody noticed she wasn't wearing a watch, and stood. "I'm just going to . . . yeah."

She scurried away, grabbed the plant, shoved the last bite of scone into her mouth, and dashed out the exit, vowing from henceforth that not only was she going to eat healthy, but she wasn't going to spend another second thinking about Mr. Dreamy Blue Eyes, aka Paul *Hubba-Hubba and Unavailable* Newman.

Unfortunately, she had a feeling that vow was going to be much tougher to swallow than the scone.

CHAPTER SIX

"Who was that?" Angela asked, plunking her purse on the table. Coffee splattered over the rim of his mug.

"Uh . . ." Henry sopped up the coffee with a napkin. How did he still not know her name? "Not sure."

Angela narrowed her gaze for a moment as if assessing the truth in that statement. He must have passed her test. She shrugged, then flopped into the chair across from him. "Didn't you get my messages?"

"I guess not." Henry tried focusing his attention on Angela and not the woman walking away. She waved good-bye to Julie, scratched Chester behind the ears, leaned over to grab something from the floor—

"Are you listening?"

"Huh? Yeah. Of course." Henry forced his gaze on Angela. "You said, 'You'll never believe this. They loved us.'"

Angela's fingers flew across the screen of her phone. "Of course they loved us. They want to fly us on their private jet—their private jet, Henry!—to Chicago." She held up her phone and showed him a picture of a jet.

Henry murmured some sort of acknowledgment.

"If everything goes like we think it will, they're going to fly us out to their villa—I told you that they have a villa, right? It's gorgeous!" She swiped across several pictures. "I bet these don't even do it justice. They want us to photograph *everything* leading up to the wedding. I leave in like, two minutes. I'm only here to grab some coffee before we fly out. I'm glad I was able to see you. Oh, by the way, what did you want to talk about?" She looked up from her phone. "You sent me a message yesterday that said we needed to talk."

Oh yeah. Yesterday he was going to break up with her. Then this morning he wasn't.

"Henry?" Angela said, thumbs paused above her phone. "Was there something you needed to tell me? Because there's actually something I've been meaning to talk to you about."

He searched out the window, gaining a glimpse of blonde hair under a flash of red. *Forget her.* He looked back to Angela. "Why don't you start?"

"Don't take this the wrong way, but—" Angela dropped her phone in her purse. It must be serious if she was putting her phone away. "I think we should use this time apart to figure out where our relationship is going. I'm not saying this to make you panic."

Henry shook his head. No panic here. If anything, a weird sense of relief.

"I know you want to get married and start a family. I do too."

Okay, a bit of panic now. "I'm listening," he said, aiming to keep his voice steady.

"For some reason it's never felt like we've been on the same page." Angela stood and grabbed her purse. "That's why I think we just need to take this time to regroup, come back together, and decide whether to get married or break up. Sound like a plan?"

"Uh, sure." Get married or break up. Nothing life-altering about that decision.

"Great." Angela stood next to his table a moment. Henry didn't know whether she was waiting for a kiss or a high five. How did a man say goodbye to a woman who was soon to become either his fiancée or his ex-girlfriend?

Her phone pinged, saving him from having to do anything. "That's probably Chad, wondering where I am. Bye, Henry." She patted his shoulder and spun away with phone in hand, heels clacking, fingers tapping.

Hours later, Henry sat in his blue Chevy pickup. He rolled the front windows down to catch a breeze before cutting the engine. The clouds from this morning had moved on about the same time Angela had. He tried not to read too much into that.

Now evening sunlight beat through the windows, a gentle heat soaking into the skin on his forearms. It felt good after spending the afternoon in the air-conditioned trailer-office he shared with his office manager, Peg, who would find the Arctic too warm for her liking.

Henry stared out the windshield at an open field over-grown with weeds. Beyond it lay a dozen acres of wooded land and a future that seemed even further out of his reach than when he'd first stared at it fourteen years ago. *"We'll build a house here. Raise a family. Get some chickens, horses, goats, whatever you want, Maggie. Someday this will be ours. I promise. We'll make this work."*

Other than putting in an offer for the land two years ago, which was soundly rejected, Henry had never come any closer to making it work. No wonder Maggie had run. She must have known all along a future with him would never amount to more than a field of weeds.

Last Henry had checked, the land was still for sale. He didn't know why he tortured himself coming out here when he would never be able to afford it. All he knew was some-thing about this place had always felt right. Familiar. Like it already belonged to him.

Sort of the same way he felt whenever he saw *her*. Which was crazy. She didn't belong to him anymore than this land did. Why couldn't he be content with what he did have? A family business to run. Angela. A woman willing to marry him and start a family. He should have dropped down on one knee in the coffee shop and proposed before she left.

Somehow the idea left him restless. Before he could spend too much time figuring out why, he pulled Edith's letter out of his shirt pocket. He'd found it on the kitchen island after he swung by the house on his way to work. He hadn't noticed it earlier, so she must have set it there while he was at the coffee shop. Once again, they probably just missed each other.

He unfolded the paper covered in handwriting becoming as familiar to him as his own, as peacefulness settled into his bones like the sun on his skin.

Dear Henry,

You want to know about my husband? I must say, it's not something I usually like to talk about. But for some reason I don't mind telling you. Maybe because you're such a good listener. You let me talk without so much as a single interruption. Now that's the sort of quality that will always make a girl swoon. Although a pair of gorgeous eyes sure doesn't hurt either.

But in answer to your question about how long we were married, I better start at the beginning. (You're probably already regretting you asked. Too bad.)

We were high school sweethearts. As soon as I turned sixteen and my dad gave me permission to date, Brian was on my front porch asking me to the movies. He was the first and only guy I ever dated. We were inseparable. I married him two weeks after I turned eighteen. To describe my parents as unhappy about it would be like describing a great white shark as a fish.

Looking back, I understand now why they were so disappointed. I'll spare you from all the boring details (I know what you're thinking—too late) but growing up, I had big dreams. Dreams my parents listened to me talk about nonstop. Dreams that included traveling the world and helping people in areas nobody else wanted to go to. My dreams never included marrying straight out of high school.

But that's what I did. My parents tried warning me I'd be throwing my dreams away. They tried convincing me to wait until at least after college. I just figured they were being overprotective. We fought about it. A lot. They eventually said if I was old enough to get married, I was old enough to not need them. They were so mad, they didn't even come to the wedding.

Right away I discovered my dreams were going to require a few adjustments. Especially when Brian informed me he wanted to pursue a law degree. Not only that, he wanted to start a family right away. So for the next few years, while he went to school, I worked. Waitress, teacher's aide, nanny, whatever would pay tuition and put food on the table. Whenever I brought up traveling or my own education, he didn't see the point since we were trying to start a family.

He used that excuse for years.

Eventually Brian's career took off. An uncle to a good friend owned a law practice and helped Brian quickly climb the ranks. I didn't have to work anymore to support us. But nothing was happening like we'd hoped at home. My doctor assured me I was healthy and that it was only a matter of time. But the more time went by, the more pressure we each began to feel. And the more pressure we felt, the more we wanted to avoid it.

That was our way of fighting, I realize now. Instead of raising our voices, we became polite. Painfully so.

Before long, Brian was spending more and more time at the office. He'd come home late and leave early. Me? I'd go to bed early and sleep in late. Our marriage was sinking, but neither of us wanted to be the one to admit it. That would be too impolite.

In all this time I never talked to my parents. Never tried. But one afternoon my dad showed up unexpectedly. I saw his car in the driveway after I'd been out getting groceries, but I was too afraid he'd see what a mess I'd made of my marriage. Too proud, really. So I drove on past.

I can't tell you how much I regret that decision. He died two weeks later from a heart attack. Not a day goes by I don't wonder what he came there to tell me. When I went to his funeral—alone—my mom wouldn't even acknowledge me.

Not sure what else to do at this point, I decided to get my nursing license. In the back of my mind I knew if our marriage did end, I was going to need something to fall back on. I had no idea what to expect from Brian if it really did come down to divorce. There's always a job to be had in health care, I figured.

So while we continued our quiet charade of a marriage, I became a registered nurse. Once I had my license, I went to work in the emergency department. I loved it. I picked up every shift I could, trying to build a nest egg for myself. Now it wasn't a question of if the marriage would end, only a question of when.

Until the night one of Brian's partners from work called me.

I had never spoken to this man before, and I didn't know what to tell him when he asked me if I had noticed the changes going on with Brian. A stranger I had never met had to inform me that my own husband was falling asleep at work, having difficulty concentrating, and taking pills around the

clock for headaches. I had no idea. Apparently
it had been going on for months.

The man I was married to, the man I was
supposed to be sharing my life with, had a
rapidly growing brain tumor, and not only
had I been clueless, I had been planning
to leave him. What kind of wife was I?

His initial prognosis gave him one to two
years. He made it fourteen months. As much
as it pains me to say this, those were some of
the best days of our entire marriage. We were
talking again. We were sharing again. We were
together again. And when he died, I can say
in all honesty I loved him again.

You want to know how long we were married?
There was a time I would have told you, too
long. But now my answer is not long enough.

What about you, Henry? You just got me to
say things I don't normally go around telling
people. Now it's your turn. What's kept you
from marrying all these years? Surely there's
been at least one woman who's caught your eye,
if not your heart. What's holding you back?
Take it from me, life's too short to watch from
the sidelines. If you find your Goldie Hawn,
you go after her. And then you better tell this
old soul all about it.

Your friend, Edith

PS—(You know I can't ever stop without at least one PS.) I just remembered you asked where I was going after this summer. It's a little village in South Africa. Okay. Enough. My hand is cramping. I'm calling it a night.

Henry slowly folded Edith's letter and slipped it into his front shirt pocket, the paper crinkling against his chest.

She must have still been rather young when her husband died. He hadn't expected that. He wondered if she had ever come close to remarrying. And South Africa? What was she going to be doing in South Africa?

He could think of at least a dozen more questions for her.

But it looked like if he wanted to find out more about the interesting woman living under his roof, he was going to have to provide a few answers of his own.

CHAPTER SEVEN

Hot, humid air smothered the early morning like a flannel blanket. Edith lifted her bangs from her sweaty forehead, then let them drop. She should have worn a headband. Or better yet, never decided to take up running again during tropical heat conditions. She stopped and bent over with her hands on her knees. Oh, man. Her twenty-year-old self would have been appalled if she'd known how out of shape her thirty-year-old self would turn out.

But then who really cared what her twenty-year-old self thought? Edith stood, still catching her breath as she started walking down the sidewalk. Let her twenty-year-old self be appalled. Her twenty-year-old self hadn't had a clue. What Edith's thirty-year-old self wouldn't give to go back and teach her twenty-year-old self a thing or two about life. Though wasn't that the truth for anybody? Edith hoped so. She'd hate to be the only one looking back thinking how differently she would have done things if only she'd known—

"You okay?"

Edith swiveled her head, stubbed her toe on uneven sidewalk, and stumbled several steps forward, catching her balance just before she did a face-plant into a mailbox. "Of course." She patted the mailbox and raised the red flag as if that's what she'd meant to do all along.

"Just checking." One of Henry's neighbors from across the street, a middle-aged woman with dark-auburn hair, wearing sea-green scrubs, clicked the key fob to her blue Honda Civic. "Your face looked all contorted and weird. Thought maybe the heat had gotten to you. I'm Cheryl, by the way."

Edith shook her hand. "Don't mind the sweat. I'm Edith. You're a nurse?"

Cheryl followed Edith's gaze to the name badge clipped to her scrubs. "Oh. Forgot to take it off. Yeah." She unclipped the badge and dropped it into her purse. "Just moved here a few months ago. Took a job at the nursing home out on the edge of town."

"Night shift?"

"Night shift, day shift, double shifts, whatever shifts they'll let me work for the time being."

"Sounds busy."

Cheryl lifted one shoulder. "When you've got four kids and your ex doesn't like to pay his child support on time, you do what you do to get by, you know? Thankfully my oldest daughter pitches in and helps out. I should probably head inside and make sure she's up. Yesterday she overslept."

The front door opened and banged shut. A frazzled red-haired, freckle-faced girl hopped down the length of the three porch steps. Her feet drew her up short and her eyes widened at the sight of Edith. Edith's probably did the same at the sight of her.

Edith snapped her fingers, searching her brain. "Gabby," she said triumphantly when the name came to her so quickly. "Nice to see you again. I didn't know you lived across the street from us." As if she and Henry were an *us*. Maybe the heat was getting to her. She opened her mouth to amend her statement when Cheryl cut her off.

"You two know each other?"

"We met at the diner. She, uh—" Edith's hand moved to her thigh, the muscle twitching at the memory of the EpiPen needle. "Helped me out. Sort of."

Whether the girl's cheeks flushed with pride or embarrassment, Edith couldn't tell. Gabby's eyes drifted across the street and back to Edith. "So you and the man from the diner . . . you've gotten to, um . . . know each other?"

"Huh? Oh. Yeah." Edith remembered now she had asked Gabby who he was. Gabby must have seen them bump into each other yesterday morning at the coffee shop. One of the curses of small-town living, she supposed. "I guess you could say we've gotten to know each other a little bit. I mean, not really. Just superficial interactions."

Gabby's eyes widened. Cheryl's narrowed. Edith's stung with sweat.

"Which is fine with me," Edith said, wiping her eyes. "I mean, he's nice, don't get me wrong, but I'm only here for the summer. Doesn't matter how easy he is on the eyes, I'm not interested in starting anything up."

Cheryl's eyes darted across the street. "Sounds like you already have."

"What? No." Had Cheryl seen them together too? "Goodness, we're just being friendly."

Mother and daughter shared a quick look. Edith had a feeling more had taken place in this conversation than she was aware of. Or maybe she was just dehydrated and delirious.

Cheryl took a step back. "Well, Gabby's got to get to work, and I better check on the rest of the kids. It was nice meeting you . . ."

"Edith."

"Edith," Cheryl repeated. Her gaze swept across the street. "And what did you say your, uh, friend's name was?"

Her friend? Edith followed her gaze. Oh. Apparently they were done talking about the man from the diner. Fine by her. "That's Henry," Edith said, pointing to his house.

"Henry. Okay. I'll have to remember that. Like I said, we've been here a few months, but I've been working a lot and haven't had a chance to meet many people outside of the nursing home. But it's nice to put a few names to some of the faces at least. Edith and Henry. Edith and Henry," Cheryl mumbled, giving Gabby a quick hug. "Have a good day," she said to her daughter. "What time do you think you'll be home?"

Edith backed away, letting the mother and daughter converse in private. *Edith and Henry.* Now Cheryl was talking about them as if they were an *us*. How funny.

She crossed the street and let herself into Henry's house.

She'd have to tell him about it in the next letter. He'd get a kick out of it. "We better watch ourselves, Henry," Edith said with a laugh as she closed the front door. "We're going to set the neighbor's tongues wagging if we're not careful."

———— ♥ ————

Hi Edith,

   Just checking in and making sure my uncle Henry is treating you right. My house should be ready soon. Although, I don't know, if you keep spoiling my uncle with banana bread and butter pecan ice cream, he might try to keep you!

Kat

———— ♥ ————

Hi Kat,

   Ha-ha, yes. I've noticed your uncle has a bit of a sweet tooth. He's not diabetic, is he? I didn't think to ask ahead of time. You want to hear something funny? I'm pretty sure the new neighbors across the street think your uncle Henry and I are a couple. Isn't that a hoot! Maybe we should stage a big breakup in the front yard once your house is ready.

Edith

———— ♥ ————

That's hilarious! Have you told Henry? You should. I've always told him he needs a strong woman in his life. And yes, I definitely think you should put on a show for the neighbors. I give you full permission to smack my uncle across the face whenever it's time to move out. Can't you just see it? "You took the best years of my life, Henry." Then smack!

———— ♥ ————

More like, "You took the last of the butter pecan ice cream, Henry." Then smack!

———— ♥ ————

Oh, Edith. I love you. If there weren't such an age difference, I'd say you and my uncle were perfect for each other.

———— ♥ ————

I know. I always used to say I was born in the wrong generation. Oh, well. Take care, Kat. It's been fun talking to you. I'll let you know how the "big breakup" turns out.

———— ♥ ————

Can't wait!

CHAPTER EIGHT

"I want something clean. But not too clean. White, just not overly white. A gentle sort of white. Like . . . like . . . Maria von Trapp. When she marries the captain. Pure but still spunky. That's all I'm asking. Do you understand what I'm saying?"

Henry stared at the strip of paint color samples he held in one hand while massaging his knee beneath the office desk with his other. The rainy weather was wreaking havoc on his joints today. "You want your kitchen walls to look like Maria von Trapp on her wedding day."

"No, I want them to *feel* like Maria von Trapp on her wedding day." Mrs. Newberry leaned across the desk to tap her finger on the bottom color named lily of the valley. "Right now, it feels like the baroness. Cold. Impersonal. Unaffectionate toward children."

Okay. Henry dropped the sample strip on his desk and leaned back, his wooden roller chair creaking beneath his weight. Was he due for more Tylenol yet? His knee ached. And now thanks to Mrs. Newberry, his head ached.

Where on earth was Peg? She usually dealt with Mrs. Newberry for him. "I'm a little tied up the next few days—" he ignored her huff of displeasure—"but how about I come out later in the week? We'll see what we can do about making your walls come alive with the sound of music."

"That's all I'm asking."

Sure. Until next week when she decided her walls needed to feel more like the opening number to *Hello, Dolly!* Henry held back his thoughts with a tight smile as he shifted forward in his seat, more than ready to stand and escort Mrs. Newberry out the front door.

"There was one other thing I wanted to mention as well."

Henry sank back in his chair.

"The knobs on the kitchen cabinets."

"The ones I switched out last Tuesday?" he asked, palming his forehead to massage his temples.

"Yes. They're just so *round*." She wrapped a plastic hair wrap over her gray bob and tied it beneath her chin. "Do you have anything less, I don't know . . . circular? Maybe something a little more oval? I don't want squares. I know that."

"Right." He'd already switched those out two weeks ago. "I'll take a look at it along with the paint color."

"That's all I'm asking." As she started to rise, the door to the office opened and a hooded figure stepped inside. The moment he tossed back the hood of his rain jacket, Henry froze and Mrs. Newberry popped the rest of the way out of her seat with a squeal.

"Why, look who it is!" She dropped her umbrella and clasped her hands together in front of her heart. "What a wonderful surprise. And we were just talking about you too."

"You were?"

"We were?" Henry and his brother, Nick, both spoke at the same time.

"Yes." Mrs. Newberry grabbed Henry's brother by the hand. "Oh, Nicky, whyever did you have to retire? Things just aren't the same without you. Not that you aren't doing a wonderful job, Henry. That's not . . . I didn't mean . . . I just meant—"

"I know what you meant." Henry rose from his seat with a grimace as Mrs. Newberry continued gushing accolades over his big brother. After pouring some coffee, Henry gripped the pot in one hand and held out the mug in his other. "Still take it black, *Nicky?*"

Nick had always favored their mother in looks and personality. Which was why Henry knew his brother would never be so rude as to admit in front of Mrs. Newberry one of the things he despised most in the world, second only to black coffee, was being called Nicky.

"No thanks," Nick answered. "Cardiologist says I need to cut back on my caffeine."

"Cardiologist?" Mrs. Newberry's mouth gaped open. She swung a petrified look from Nick to Henry, then back to Nick. "I didn't know you were having heart troubles."

"Nothing serious. My heart just gets a little too excited

when I have caffeine. Nothing to be concerned about. I promise."

"Well, I am concerned. I'm very concerned. Is this what forced you into early retirement? I knew there had to be more to the story. Why a pillar of this community would just up and move away, I never understood. But now I see. Yes, I see."

Henry rolled his eyes as he plunked the coffeepot back on the burner. He kept the mug of black coffee for himself and limped back to his desk. Mrs. Newberry sure hadn't shown any concern during his five surgeries or countless hours of physical rehab, but goodness, the great Nicky Hobbes has one irregular heartbeat and let's add him to the prayer chain.

"Nothing more to the story, I assure you." Nick retrieved Mrs. Newberry's umbrella from the floor. "Marybeth's parents are getting up there in years and requiring a little more help to get around. The timing just seemed right to give up the company so we could move to be closer to them."

"Oh, but that must have been so tough. What with this company being in your family for so many years."

Nick handed her the umbrella. "It still is in the family."

"It is? Oh yes. Henry." Mrs. Newberry wrinkled her nose and laughed like Nick had made up a joke. "Oh, Nicky. It was so good to see you again. Tell Marybeth I said hi. And you know . . ." She opened her umbrella while standing in the doorway, the steady pitter-patter of rain falling from a gray sky behind her. "It's never too late to come back. This town will always keep a light on for you." Her laughter faded with the closing of the door.

Nick turned back to face Henry with the type of stare down that should only belong in a spaghetti Western at high noon when a rustling from the corner broke the sudden tension. "Is she gone?"

Both Henry and Nick spun to find Peg sliding out from behind a fake miniature tree propped in the corner of the office.

So that's where she'd gone. "How long have you been hiding?" Henry demanded.

Peg pushed one of the leafy branches aside. "For about as long as Alice has been here plus twenty seconds. Thank goodness she still uses that ridiculous purple polka-dot umbrella or I never would have seen her through the window in time. Thank you," Peg added as Nick offered her a hand.

"Can't believe how dusty that tree's already gotten," she said once she'd maneuvered past the large pot, dropping his hand to swipe off her pants.

"It's an interesting touch," Nick said.

"It adds ambience. Didn't I tell you for years this place needed ambience? Next thing I think we need is a couch. Don't you think that would look nice along the wall there?"

Nick shrugged and Peg tossed up her hands. "Should have known better than to ask one of the Hobbes boys. Never could convince a single one of you to even put a decent sign out front. I swear, you're more alike than you want to admit." She moved over to her desk chair and sat with an ungraceful plop.

"So what brings you back, Nick? Or should I say Nicky?" She tossed a wink at Henry.

"You shouldn't. Ever." Nick perched on the edge of

Henry's desk, arms folded. "Talked to Kat the other night. She mentioned the leak and the mold. I thought I'd swing by and check in on the place. Help put her mind at ease." He shrugged, no big deal.

Henry finished swallowing his sip of coffee. Yeah, he didn't believe that for one second. And judging by the angled brow on Peg's face, she didn't either. "Kat should have asked me if she was worried. I could have saved you the drive."

Nick shifted his shoulders nonchalantly. "Kat knows you're busy. I'm sure she didn't want to bother you."

Uh-huh. Because that really sounded like Kat. Not wanting to inconvenience her uncle in any way. "You're checking up on me, aren't you?"

"Here we go," Peg mumbled.

"What makes you think I'd be checking up on you?" Nick stood and faced him.

"Why else would you be here?"

"I told you. Kat wanted—"

"No." Henry thunked his coffee down on his desk. "I'm talking about here. This office."

A rumble of thunder sounded over the trailer. "Maybe because my brother works here, and sometimes brothers—I don't know—like to see each other?"

"So then why didn't you call ahead of time? What if I'd been busy?"

"It was an impromptu trip." Nick strode to the window and looked out. The rain beat down harder.

"It's a six-hour drive. You had plenty of time to give me a heads-up."

Nick released the blinds, turning. "And why exactly would

you need a heads-up? You got something going on you don't want me knowing about?"

"What? Like driving the family business into the ground? Hate to disappoint you, but we're still turning a profit."

Peg made a small sound and Henry shot her a warning look. It might be a small profit—switching out cabinet handles didn't exactly make for big paychecks—but they were still putting food on the table.

"You want to know why I came back? Fine. I'll tell you. It's not the profit I'm worried about. What I'm worried about is the integrity of this business."

"You've got to be kidding me," said Henry. Even Peg couldn't mute her snort on that one.

"I may not run it anymore, but that's still my name attached to it. Dad's name too. You're carrying on more than a business. You're carrying on a family legacy. I thought you understood that by now."

Henry had started to pick up his coffee but slammed the mug down. "What are you talking about?"

"I'm talking about your personal life."

Henry belted a humorless laugh. "And what concerns do you have about my personal life, considering I have no personal life?"

"Really? So you're not still dating Angela?"

Peg shifted in her seat and eyed the fake tree in the corner as if she wanted to hide behind it again. Henry was certain the only thing keeping her from bolting outside was the storm. His brother seriously drove six hours to ask him about Angela?

"What's it to you if Angela and I are still dating or not?"

Henry grabbed his mug and marched to the sink. After dumping it out, he refilled it with hot coffee just to give himself something to do.

"I went by the house today."

"So?"

"I went inside."

"So?"

"Wow." Nick shook his head. "You really don't ever grow up, do you? You're still the same dumb idiot making the same dumb idiot mistakes you made fourteen years ago. But hey—" he clapped his hands—"I applaud you. Your acting abilities have improved tremendously. I almost believed you were ready to settle down and be an honest man. I mean, I left you in charge of this place, didn't I?"

"Are you ever going to tell me what this is about?"

"Yeah, I'm kind of wondering the same thing." Peg shrugged when Nick twisted to look at her. He'd probably forgotten she was there, observing the whole thing. "What? You can't expect me to leave now. Besides, I'm pretty sure there ain't a thing about either one of you I don't already know. I used to change both of your diapers, remember?"

Nick twisted to face Henry while still speaking to Peg. "Well then, I'm sure you already know Henry here has someone living with him."

Henry and Peg shared a quick look. She appeared just as confused. Good. Then he wasn't the only one not getting it. So what if he had an old lady living upstairs in his house?

"Stop the act, Henry. I went upstairs to see what it looked like since you'd remodeled. I saw your bedroom. And unless you've taken to wearing bras recently, you're not sleeping alone in that bedroom."

This would be laughable if it wasn't so insulting. Peg cleared her throat and opened her mouth to speak, but Henry held up his hand. "No, Peg. Let him finish. What else do you know?"

"I know this woman isn't Angela. When I stopped by the bakery for a scone, Julie said she overheard Angela talking about some wedding gig and has been out of town ever since."

"Well done, Sherlock."

"Just how many girlfriends do you have, Henry?"

"Okay. This has gone on long enough." Peg stood. "Nick, I know what you're thinking, but—"

"Peg—" Nick lifted a hand to cut her off—"I don't mean you any disrespect, but the truth is you've always turned a blind eye when it comes to my little brother. So while I'm sure you mean well, I don't want to hear it."

"B-but you should," Peg sputtered.

"Nope." Henry dumped his full mug down the sink. Let his brother think what he wanted. "You heard the man. He doesn't want to hear it. And honestly, neither do I."

Henry didn't bother with grabbing an umbrella or rain jacket. Just headed straight for the door. "Have a safe trip back. Tell Marybeth I said hi. And, Peg, if anybody calls, tell them I'll be out of the office the rest of the day making dumb idiot mistakes and living a life filled with my usual fornication."

He slammed the door shut and jogged down the steps as fast as his knee would let him, which wasn't too fast. The rain had plenty of time to pound over his head. Soak into his shirt. Seep into his bones.

Maybe if it rained hard enough, it would wash away the sickening feeling that his brother's words contained an element of truth. No, he wasn't shacking up with anybody at the house. But why hadn't he given his brother an honest answer about Angela?

Because maybe Nick was right. Maybe Henry hadn't changed at all.

———— ♥ ————

Edith hunched her shoulders and tucked her head. The initial downpour had been a welcome relief, something to cool her off. The current bolts of lightning flashing over her head, on the other hand . . .

Her breaths puffed in and out as she dodged a puddle. Not that it mattered since her running shoes and socks had already sopped up every drop of precipitation. Another crash of thunder sounded above her. Edith's footsteps faltered. Next thing she knew, the pavement was an inch from her face. Muddy rainwater splashed in her eyes, coating her knees and palms.

"Perfect," she mumbled, climbing back to her feet and wringing out the hem of her waterlogged shirt. So much for a nice, peaceful afternoon jog.

She hadn't planned to wind up in the cemetery when she started her run, but when she passed the open gates and saw the paved path weaving in and out of gravestones, it looked like the ideal place. No traffic. No people. Smooth roads.

And thankfully plenty of trees. Edith sought shelter beneath a row of large maples. Mud squished beneath her as she shook out her arms.

Before she could lift her foot, a quick flash of lightning followed several seconds later by a blast of thunder had her more concerned with hugging the tree than stretching her thighs. It wasn't that she was scared of storms, exactly. She just had a healthy respect for them. And she wished now she'd chosen to respect them from inside the shelter of Henry's house.

Although if she had, she wouldn't have caught a glimpse of Henry earlier.

Edith wrung out her ponytail. Too bad that's all it was. A glimpse. Part of her couldn't believe they'd been living under the same roof for the better part of two weeks and had yet to meet in person. Which was why she'd made a point of asking around to find out where Henry worked so she could stop by to see him this afternoon during her run.

But by the time she got to his office trailer, the storm had already rolled in. She had just rounded the corner when she caught sight of him marching down the steps and straight to his car. He drove away before she could get a real good look at him. Tall with thinning gray hair maybe? He moved quicker than she would have expected from a man who required physical therapy.

An older woman had flagged him down to hand him a jacket through his window before he drove away. Edith caught her just as she was stepping inside the office and asked if that was Henry who had driven away.

"What's that, dear?" the woman shouted over the rain.

"I was asking about Henry," Edith shouted back.

"Henry?" The woman held her arm over her head, trying to shield her hair from the weather. "Sorry, honey. He's not here. Is there something I can help you with? Why don't you come inside?"

"Oh. No. I'm good." Edith didn't want to keep the woman out in the rain any longer, so she waved. "I'll try another time."

Maybe tomorrow. They were bound to meet eventually. This town was only so big. Shoot, the house was only so big.

The rain softened. The next rumble of thunder sounded farther away. Storm must be moving on. Edith could probably finish her run. Wasn't like she could get any wetter. She squished her way across the grass to the pavement, breaking into a jog.

At the end of the path she rounded a curve past a large monument. A lone figure stood over a grave. His head shot up and his eyes connected with hers.

Paul?

Her steps faltered. One of these days she should probably learn his real name. But that might give the impression she was interested in him. Which she was. And she didn't want to be.

Edith slowed, not sure whether to keep running or stop and say hi. What was the proper etiquette in a cemetery? She thought about Brian and the few times she'd visited his grave. And yeah, she had always preferred to be left alone.

Except Paul Newman was walking toward her, staring straight at her in the rain that had slowed to a soft pitter-patter. His button-down shirt rolled up to the elbows dripped with water, and his dark jeans looked heavy with the weight of the rain. He wore a pair of brown work boots. Edith bet his feet were nice and dry at least. More than she could say for her own.

Rain drizzled down the sides of his face into his shirt collar. "Hey," he said, coming to a stop a few feet away from her.

"Hey."

He shoved his hands into his pockets and looked her over from head to toe. "You look good. You do something different with your hair?" .

Edith blew out a breath she didn't know she'd been holding and smiled, wringing out her ponytail again. "Tried a new conditioner. I wasn't sure if anybody would notice."

The corners of his lips tipped in a small smile. Up close, his blue eyes were rimmed in red. She glanced past him to the graves. She really shouldn't intrude. "Sorry to—"

"So you're a runner?" he said, dropping his gaze down the length of her.

"Kind of. Not like I used to be. I used to run marathons. Now I just . . ." She looked down at the trails of muddy water snaking down her legs, dripping into her grimy socks. She didn't even want to think about what her face looked like.

"Train for mud runs in cemeteries?"

"It's a special niche in the running community. Hasn't quite taken off yet."

"I'm sure it's just a matter of time." Paul's smile didn't quite reach his eyes. Edith bounced another look off the grave he'd been standing over. He twisted, following her gaze.

"My parents," he said, turning back to face her.

"I'm sorry. I didn't mean to intrude."

"No intrusion." The rain might have stopped completely, but Edith couldn't tell when a gust of wind blew raindrops from the surrounding trees down on them. Edith shivered. Paul swiped a palm across his face. "So tell me, Liddell, what else do you do, besides run? We didn't really get the chance to finish our conversation the other morning."

"Liddell?"

"Oh, come on." Paul's shoulders sagged with exaggerated disappointment. "You can't call yourself a runner and not know who Eric Liddell is."

"Technically, all I said was I used to run."

Paul groaned. "I'm disappointed in you." He lifted his arms and began mimicking slow-motion running while singing *da-da-da-da-dun-dun* in a very off-key tune. So off-key it took Edith a moment to recognize the song.

"*Chariots of Fire.*"

"*Chariots of Fire,*" Paul said. "Eric Liddell."

"I remember now. It's been a long time since I've seen it. You can stop making that motion now. You can definitely stop singing. I remember."

He sang louder. "*Da-da-da-da-DUN-da-DUN-da-DUN . . .*"

"I said I remember."

"*Da-da-da-da—*"

"You're just making noise now."

"*Dooby-dooby-doo.*"

"Lord, have mercy."

He stopped singing, but his smile reached all the way to his eyes now. And Edith felt fairly certain hers reached to the top of her head. Which was why she should get moving again. Before they started sharing more than a smile. Before they started sharing real names. Phone numbers. Free evenings. Their hearts.

"Well . . ." Edith looked at her wrist. She really needed to invest in a watch someday. "I should finish up my run. Nice bumping into you."

"You too, Liddell. Maybe we'll see each other again."

She waved and took off down the path. *Not if I can help it, Paul Hubba-Hubba Can't-Sing-Worth-a-Lick Blast-Your-Blue-Eyes Wish-I-Could-Get-You-out-of-My-Head Newman.*

CHAPTER NINE

Later that week, Edith attempted to smother a jaw-cracking yawn. Maybe she wasn't as accustomed to working night shifts as she thought. Or rather, accustomed to staying awake all night to water and feed a house full of plants as she thought.

"We're not working you too hard, I hope." Sharon winked and held up the coffeepot. Early sunlight filtered through the window curtain above the kitchen sink, brightening up the already-cheery yellow walls and white cabinets. "Need a cup?"

"No thanks. I think today I'll go straight home and crash." Edith got up from the kitchen table and grabbed her bag.

"Sounds good. Anything happen overnight I should know?" Sharon leaned back against the counter and sipped her coffee.

"Gladys dropped off two more ferns. Pretty sure they're both artificial."

"Sounds about right," Sharon said. "Try to get some rest. One of these days or nights, somebody's going to need us. I feel it in my bones."

All Edith felt was bone-tired. She waved goodbye on her way out the door. She'd made a habit of stopping by the coffee shop on her walk home. Every morning she was met by the black kitty cat. Every morning she heard Opal berate Julie over the unsanitary conditions caused by the black kitty cat. And every morning Edith left the shop full of caffeine, full of scones, and full of disappointment the man she wasn't supposed to be hoping to see again never showed.

Edith paused at the corner of Main Street and Prospect. Green- and white-striped awnings shaded the sidewalk down Main Street, where shop owners swept away dirt with Amish brooms and adjusted their Open signs. If that wasn't quaint enough, the curved streetlamps bearing colorful flower baskets tipped the scales.

For such a weird little town, it sure was awful cute.

Even the stretch of boulevard leading to Henry's house, lined with oak trees and maples, made her feel like she ought to be wearing a polka-dot dress and riding a bicycle with a flower basket in front.

She sighed. Oh, but she was tired. Too tired for coffee. Certainly too tired for disappointment. And most definitely too tired to wonder why she couldn't stop thinking about a man she didn't know, who wasn't available, and one she would be leaving at the end of summer anyway.

The boulevard was the smart way to go—even without the dress and bicycle.

A minute later, the soft ding of a bell announced her entrance into Julie's coffee shop. What could she say? She was a creature of habit. Plus, she needed to see Chester the cat. Make sure he was alive. It had nothing to do with anything else. Or anybody else.

But shoot, since she was here, she might as well sit for a quick spell and read Henry's letter. Besides a few short notes between them, mostly about whose turn it was to buy ice cream, they hadn't shared a lengthy correspondence since the letter about her husband. Edith might have worried she shared too much and made Henry uncomfortable, except he said in one of his notes he needed a little time to mull over his answer to her question.

The formality of placing his latest message to her in an envelope made her think he'd finished mulling.

"The usual?" Julie asked from behind the counter, face flushed as always.

Edith looked up from where she'd been absently scratching Chester's ears. She gave Julie a tired smile and said, "Yep. Hit me with the usual."

Seated a few minutes later at the round table in the back, Edith opened the envelope and began to read.

Dear Edith,

First of all, let me say how honored I was that you would share a bit of your story with me. I understand how painful some of those memories must be for you. Thank you for not telling me to blow it out my ear like I was afraid you might.

Now I suppose fair is fair. My turn. You want to know why I never married? I'll be honest. I've tried answering this question at least a dozen times over the past week. Each time I thought I had the answer, I ended up crumpling the paper and throwing it against the wall.

You're right. A girl did catch my eye and my heart. I could tell you all the details, but in the end, I guess the answer is actually pretty simple.

The girl didn't want me.

Henry

CHAPTER TEN

"Let me get this straight," Lance said, raising his voice to be heard above Frank Sinatra's croons. "You're baring your soul to an old lady who's living in your house but you've never actually met. You've got the hots for a lady you've met but don't know anything about. And you're still going out with a lady who drives you crazy every time she talks, which is all the time."

Henry grunted through another set of leg lifts. "Yep, that about sums it up."

"Sounds to me like a bum knee is the least of your problems." Lance pointed to the leg lifts. "Twenty more."

Henry completed another set and collapsed onto his back. "How come I never see you pushing anybody else as hard as you push me?"

"Because nobody else here needs it as much as you. Plus, it would kill them." Lance smirked and tossed him a towel. "So what are you going to do about the mystery woman?"

"I don't know."

"Angela?"

"I don't know."

"Edith?"

"Marry her. She seems the least complicated of the three."

Lance laughed. "See? I knew you had a thing for old ladies." He handed Henry a water bottle. "Your knee's getting stronger. I think you'd be okay if we cut back your sessions to just a couple times a week now. Unless you think you might miss me too much."

"That's a risk I'm willing to take," Henry said. "Does this mean I can start climbing ladders again?"

"Not if you have any more tackle football games on your schedule."

"That was just the one time."

"And look where it landed you." Lance pointed to the blue floor mat as he pulled out a green resistance band. "Just keep doing your exercises every day."

"Yeah, yeah, I know." Henry eased down on the mat and took the resistance band from Lance. "You sort of nag like an old lady, you know that?"

"Must be why you like me so much."

After a shower and a bite to eat, Henry drove down to his office. "Hey, gorgeous." He swooped in to give Peg a quick peck on the cheek on his way past her desk.

She stared at him with wide eyes. "Did something happen to Fred?"

"What? As far as I know, your husband is fine."

Peg's look of horror switched to confusion. "Then what's going on? You never act this way."

"What way?" Henry eased into his desk chair.

"Nice."

Henry scowled. "I'm always nice to you."

"Not when you're barking at me about the heat."

"What heat? There is no heat."

"It's summer. Who wants heat in summer?" Peg hollered. "I swear, if I didn't love your folks the way I did, I'd throw you out on your ear first chance I got."

Henry couldn't keep his lips from twitching, picturing the five-foot-one woman trying to even reach his ear, as he shuffled through the pile of papers on his desk. "I'm sorry."

Peg opened her mouth to start another tirade but then stopped. "You're sorry? Oh no. Something did happen. Is it your knee? They planning to cut your leg off or something?"

"You'd like that, wouldn't you?" Henry tapped the papers against his desk until they were a nice tidy package. "Well, don't worry. I'm going to be out of your hair soon enough." He put a paper clip on them and tossed a few pens into a cup holder before he rose. "Lance said I can hit the ladders again."

He grabbed his thermos and planted another kiss—this time on the top of her little permed head. "So turn the temperature all the way down to single digits for all I care. I'm out of here. If anybody comes looking for me, I'll be downtown in the historical district, taking measurements."

"Oh, Henry," she said in a singsong voice. "I think you're forgetting something."

"What?" Henry paused, one hand gripping the doorknob.

She looked at him expectantly. "You did forget, didn't you?"

Henry looked over to the calendar on the wall, saw the date circled in red, and groaned. "No."

"Yes." Peg smiled and he could all too well imagine what she must have looked like as a little girl in pigtails, taking joy in a brother's misery. "So you're going to need to pick up that monkey suit of yours from the dry cleaner's and give yourself plenty of time to get all gussied up. Cocktails start at five o'clock sharp. No being late. Not to this one." She aimed a pink polished arthritic finger at him. "And don't forget the checkbook."

"Can't we just mail them a check?"

Peg's glare took the temperature of the room down another twenty degrees. Henry held his hands up. "I'm kidding." Sort of. He knew part of his dad's legacy in this town was due to his generous nature, not just his painting and carpentry skills. His brother had carried it on until he retired, and now it was Henry's turn. He just wished the legacy didn't require wearing a tuxedo. "Did we donate something for the silent auction?"

"We most certainly did." Peg's lips twisted to the side in what he recognized as her attempt not to smile—or gloat.

"What did we donate?"

"The usual."

Free estimates and 20 percent off shouldn't make her eyes sparkle that much. "Anything else?"

"Only something sure to bring in a generous bid." Her shoulders shook. "A dance with you."

He'd ask if she was joking but her rosy cheeks and schoolgirl giggle told him she wasn't. "I can't dance." He was still getting used to walking.

"What were you expecting to do downtown in the historical district?"

"Uh, *not dance.*"

She swiped her palm through the air. "If you've been given the all clear to get out of the office, I'm sure you can handle waddling back and forth for one little song tonight. You know how many women in this town would kill to get wrapped up in your arms? Why, Gladys alone would take out a second mortgage just for the chance."

"Isn't Gladys wheelchair-bound?"

"You can sit on her lap." Peg cackled. "She'll spin you around."

Henry rubbed his forehead. He supposed he should be glad only the geriatrics of this town found him attractive. At least he stood a chance of keeping up with one of them on the dance floor.

The phone rang. "Well?" Peg paused in reaching for it. "What are you still doing here? I thought you said you were getting out of my hair." She threw him a wink and answered the phone.

"Hobbes Painting and Construction," Henry heard her say as he closed the door behind him, not feeling quite as chipper as when he had entered. The annual community benefit gala was not what he had in mind for his first day out of the office.

Edith walked into the banquet hall of Valley View Country Club and discreetly tugged at her bodice. Maybe she should have chosen the more conservative black dress. This red one showed off her every curve—curves she had practically forgotten she had until the young shop owner saw her in the dress and said, *"Yowza!"*

Between that exclamation and the extra 30 percent off, Edith hadn't been able to resist.

Now, as Edith cast a shy glance around the room, she hoped she wasn't overdressed. Although, with a neckline that dipped further than she was accustomed to, she might be underdressed more than anything.

"Edith." Sharon's eyes lit up as she strode toward her. "You look amazing."

"Is it too much?" Edith asked. "I wasn't sure how formal tonight was."

"It's perfect." Sharon squeezed her hand. "I should make you give the speech tonight. We'd probably get all the donations we need for the next five years."

Edith yanked her hand out of Sharon's. "I don't do speeches. Ever. I'm a nervous sneezer."

Sharon laughed, but Edith wasn't joking. "C'mon," Sharon said, leading her across the room. "Let's grab a drink. There's a few people I'd like to introduce you to before the dance starts."

"Dance?"

"Oh yes. And with a dress like that, you better be wearing your dancing shoes. The boys are going to be lining up to twirl you across the floor, I can guarantee you that much."

Edith's stomach rumbled with an equal share of nerves and hunger. "What about dinner?" She swiped two odd-looking concoctions from a server's tray and popped them into her mouth. Her tongue nearly shriveled at the amount of salt. She grabbed a glass of water from another tray and emptied half of it.

In the time it took to swallow, Edith lost track of Sharon. The room became crowded with more people. From somewhere the heavy live beat of a drum started up, and she recognized the tune of Benny Goodman's "Sing, Sing, Sing."

Boy, this town sure didn't mess around when it came time for a party.

Before the song finished, people young and old flooded the dance floor. Edith's feet itched to do a little "Jump, Jive, an' Wail" of her own. How long had it been? Since high school, at least. Brian had always hated dancing. It had nearly taken an act of Congress to convince him to dance with her while they were dating. Once married, not even an executive order could force him onto the dance floor.

Edith stepped out of the way of a server. They both did a double take. Dressed in a starched white button-down shirt with a black bow tie, carrying a tray almost as big as herself, Gabby, Henry's redheaded neighbor, eyed Edith from head to toe. "Yowza," the girl murmured before moving on.

Edith smiled. *Two yowzas in one day. Can't beat that.*

"Ah, miss, please say that smile's for me."

A short older gentlemen who put her in mind of Mickey Rooney held his hand over his heart. Edith's smile grew wider. The words popped out in a flash. "It is if you ask me to dance."

He beamed and held out his hand. After setting her empty glass aside, she grabbed on and didn't let go. It was all she could do to keep up during "In the Mood." By the time

"Boogie Woogie Bugle Boy" ended, she must have burned more calories than she had in a year and been dipped, twirled, and spun by every man within a sixty-mile radius.

Well, not every man. None of her dance partners looked like the quick glimpse she'd caught of Henry the other day in the storm. And she hadn't seen Mr. Hubba-Hubba either.

Maybe Sharon would know if either of them were here tonight. Maybe Sharon would also know how much longer before dinner.

Edith declined the next offer to dance. Fanning herself, she let her gaze wander across the room, searching for Sharon's silver-sequined gown in a sea of dark colors. What she found was a familiar pair of blue eyes staring back at her from across the room.

The intensity of his gaze paired with the dashing figure he cut in his dark tuxedo made her stomach give a flip that had nothing to do with hunger.

"Yowza," Edith whispered.

CHAPTER ELEVEN

Henry caught Peg shooting him another dark look. "Stop jiggling the water glasses," she whispered, smacking his leg beneath the table.

He leaned back and tried to relax. Ever since he saw *her*, Henry hadn't been able to keep still. If that red dress hadn't knocked the air out of him, watching her twirl, laugh, and dance like a girl of sixteen certainly did.

Who was this woman? And why did she keep disappearing? Like an oasis in the desert, there one minute and gone the next.

And now for the past two hours, he'd been forced to sit still like a choirboy in church when he felt more fidgety than a toddler on a sugar high. As far as he was concerned, his company could donate whatever equipment, labor, or money the people here wanted, just so long as somebody told him who that woman was.

The table started shaking again.

"I swear you're going to find yourself with two busted kneecaps if you don't knock it off." Peg sent him a sidelong glare. "I know people."

Henry forced his leg still and his attention back to the speaker.

"In conclusion, I just want to say a heartfelt thank-you to all of you who have given so generously to our crisis nursery center. It's because of your donations we exist. So thank you. And now . . . let's get back to dancing!"

Applause filled the room and Henry leaned forward. Crisis nursery center? Wasn't that where Edith volunteered? Maybe she was here. When the applause died down, Henry stood, anxious to continue his search for the woman in the red dress before he worried about finding Edith.

"Henry—I was hoping to catch you."

Henry suppressed a groan and clamped his lips together in what he hoped came across as a smile. "Hi, Sharon. Nice speech." His eyes drifted above her head to a flash of red. Just a tablecloth.

"Thanks. I was hoping to introduce you to one of our volunteers before dinner but didn't get the chance. How's your leg doing?" Sharon asked.

"Good as new." He shifted his weight onto it and winced. "Practically."

Sharon laughed. "Yeah, really looks like it. You sure you're going to be up for that dance you promised?"

"I can manage. Hey," Henry said, snapping his fingers,

"do you by chance know if Edith Sherman is here tonight? She's been staying with me, and this is going to sound crazy, but we've never met."

"You're kidding me." Sharon grabbed his arm. "That was who I wanted to introduce you to. She's wonderful. I didn't know how we were going to fill so many scheduling holes this summer, but then God just dropped her on our doorstep. An answer to prayers, that's what she is. But I didn't realize she was staying with you. She told me she was living upstairs in the house of an older gentleman."

"Well, I can see how the word *gentleman* would throw a person off."

Sharon gave him a playful punch on the arm, making Henry smile. "So what does she look like? Maybe I saw her earlier without even realizing it."

"Oh, honey, believe me, if you saw her tonight, you'd have known it."

Henry's heart rate slowed to a deafening thud, sensing the words to come.

"She's the blonde-haired woman wearing the red dress. And she's the one you're going to be dancing with."

———— ♥ ————

Sharon hadn't been kidding about needing her dancing shoes. If either of Edith's heels made it through the night without blistering, it'd be a miracle. Edith checked the time. About another thirty minutes before she needed to cut out for her shift at the crisis house.

Band members—someone said it was the high school jazz

band—began warming up their instruments, ready to start another set. Edith could see the Mickey Rooney look-alike craning his neck in search of a dance partner, probably her. The image of him doing the Charleston during the first round of dancing flashed before her. Elbows jutting, feet swiveling front to back. "I still got it!" he'd yelled—right before he sent an entire tray of hors d'oeuvres sailing into the air.

Edith giggled and decided now might be a good time to duck out after all. She could do with a bit of fresh air before she started her night shift.

After slipping out the back exit, she kicked her shoes off, immediately relishing the cool soft grass between her toes as much as the caress of night air on her skin. A narrow path glided away from the banquet hall, and Edith meandered next to it.

The light of the full moon guided her. The muted brassy sound of big band music, competing with the tune of cicadas, followed her. She folded her arms over her stomach, a sense of peace battling with a restless desire to run. Did she need to remind herself she wasn't a part of this community? This town was nothing more than a stepping-stone while she crossed from the shores of her past to the banks of her future.

But, golly. Who knew stepping-stones could be so much fun?

The turf beneath her feet grew scratchy and stiff. Without realizing it, she'd wandered onto a putting green. A flagpole stuck out from the center. A breeze lifted the flag and sent goose bumps rippling down her arms. She should have grabbed her sweater from the car. Oh, well. It was probably about time to head back anyway.

"There's going to be a lot of broken hearts if you're done dancing for the night."

"Ah!" Edith spun around, yanking the flagpole with her as if she were preparing for a jousting tournament. "Expose yourself."

A deep throaty chuckle reached her before a figure stepped out of the shadows. "Pretty sure that would get me arrested in this town."

Edith fumbled with the pole, a nervous laugh squeaking out when she recognized who it was. "It's you. I saw you. Earlier, I mean. When I was dancing. Not that I was looking for you. I wasn't looking for you. Don't you dance?"

Blowing the bangs from her eyes, she finally managed to shove the flagpole into the hole. When she looked up, his uneven gait was ambling up the putting green. "Right." She winced. "Your leg. Sorry. Of course you don't dance."

The glow of moonlight captured his face scrunching up in that self-deprecating manner of his. "Yeah, I don't think anybody will mistake me for Fred Astaire again." He stood close enough the breeze carried a hint of his aftershave—a clean spicy scent that pulled her in closer. Close enough to peer up into blue eyes that had darkened beneath the starry sky to a shade of cobalt.

"Fred Astaire *again*?" She released a breathless laugh. "Goodness. You must have been quite the dancer."

"Practically a legend."

"I wish I could have seen that."

His fingers brushed against hers on the pole. Edith dropped her hand as if a match had burned it. She was playing with fire, all right.

"I-I should get going. I have to work tonight." She searched for where she had dropped her shoes. There, by the edge of the putting green. "See you around."

"What about your dance?"

Something in his voice—desperation?—made her pause. "My dance?"

He shoved his hands in his pockets and shrugged his shoulders. "You won the silent auction bid. Fair's fair. I owe you a dance."

Edith felt her throat working hard to swallow. Silent auction bid? *Oh.* That's what Sharon had been wagging her eyebrows about earlier. But why would she put Edith's name on the bid?

"I think there's been a mistake." And there was about to be another one if she couldn't figure out how to make her feet start working again. Instead of running away from him, they remained glued to the turf.

A familiar rich, fluid melody brought on by clarinets and saxophones floated in the air, swirled around them. Really? "Moonlight Serenade"? Could there be any other song in the world that turned her heart to mush more than this one? "I really need to go."

"One dance." He held his hand out. "The song isn't that long."

"Happy Birthday" would be too long in his arms. "I'm not so sure this is a good idea," she said, unable to stop herself from sliding her hand into his.

"My knee can handle it."

It wasn't his knee she was worried about.

But it wasn't like she was agreeing to marry him. Shoot,

she wasn't even agreeing to date him. She could handle one little dance. Couldn't she? Edith reached for his shoulder as his palm slid around her waist. She could.

"All right. But just the one."

He smiled and the space between them disappeared. They swayed, hardly lifting their feet. She told herself it was because she didn't want to jostle his knee. Not because she was using this as an excuse to simply be held.

An unexpected pressure built behind her eyes. When was the last time she had been held, come to think of it? Her throat tightened and her nose burned. A shuddery sigh escaped from her lips. To muffle the sound of a sob, she pressed her face into his shoulder. Warm, strong hands slid around her back, securing her against his chest.

She didn't know when the music had stopped. Probably around the same time they had stopped with the pretense of dancing. One of his hands moved up to cradle her head against him.

"You okay?" he whispered.

No. She'd married Brian so young. And then they'd drifted so far apart. She thought maybe she'd forgotten what it was like to be held by a man, but now she realized she hadn't forgotten. She just never knew.

"Aww shucks." A voice interrupted them the same moment a bright beam of a flashlight blinded them. Jumping a step back, Edith held her hand up to block the light. She recognized the Mickey Rooney look-alike, as well as some other members of her new fan club. "Should've known Hobbes would get her all to himself. Come on, boys. Looks like we're back to dancing with our wives tonight."

The men offered some good-natured groans, then immediately began talking about golf. "Usual tee-off time tomorrow?"

"Wait—" Hobbes took a step toward Edith. She was glad the darkness hid her flamed cheeks as she spun away and gathered her shoes. *Hobbes. Not Paul Newman. Hobbes. Wake up, Edith. This isn't some pretend fantasy. He's a real person.*

A real person who'd looked at her as if he really did want her all to himself.

Stop. The last thing she needed was to be getting ideas when she was supposed to be chasing her dreams. South Africa. Adventure. A new story. Not this . . . *whatever* this was.

Edith ran all the way to her car. And she made sure not to look back.

———— ♥ ————

A few hours later, Edith hung her dress on the top of one of the wooden doorframes at the crisis center. She had brought a change of clothes with her to the benefit so she could come straight here afterward. The silky material slid over her fingers as she ran her hand along it.

What had Henry said in his letter? Don't let a pair of blue eyes keep you from chasing after your own bit of adventure?

Yeah, well, what about a set of strong shoulders? A self-deprecating smile that turned her insides to mush? Or a weird sort of connection she'd never experienced with anyone else before? What about that? Could that be enough?

With a sigh, she released the material and tiptoed out

of the room. No. And her great-great-aunt Edith would be ashamed of her for even considering it.

Edith shuffled down the stairs and headed to the kitchen to put on the teakettle. No more thinking about the man called Hobbes. Not tonight. Not ever. Only thoughts of the future. Three years in South Africa. After that, who knew? South America? Europe? India? South Africa was only the beginning. She had to remember that.

The clock on the microwave showed a little past midnight as she set the kettle on the burner. Maybe some popcorn to go with that tea.

Movement behind the kitchen window caught her eye. She jumped and clamped her hands over her mouth to stifle a scream, then slowly worked up the courage to peek behind the curtain.

A face appeared. This time she did scream. Then gasped as recognition settled in.

Edith ran to the back door, unbolted the lock, and jerked open the door. "What in the world are you doing here?" she whisper-shouted. "You scared me to death. You shouldn't be here. It's the middle of the night."

Steve held his hands up. "What did you expect me to do? You weren't answering my calls. This was the only way I knew how to talk to you."

Edith palmed her face. How had he even found her? "Steve, I didn't answer because there is nothing left to say. Now please go. I'm working."

"No. Not until you promise to talk to me. You may not have anything to say, but I have plenty to say." Steve crowded into the door, and Edith blocked his entrance.

"Stop. You really can't be here. I mean it. This is a crisis nursery center." She didn't know why she added that last part, but it did make him pause.

His eyes darted to the ceiling. "You mean there's a bunch of babies up there?"

Now she knew why she'd added that last part. Steve reacted to babies the way Edith reacted to blue cheese. He took a step back, scratching his neck. "Tell me when we can meet. I'm not leaving until you give me a place and a time."

Edith's cheeks burned and her hands shook in frustration. "Why are you doing this?"

"Because I think you're running away from something we could have together," Steve said. "Plus I need you."

"You do not need me, and I am not running away. I told you I'm moving on. I already have," Edith said.

"What does that mean? Are you saying there's someone else?"

Edith inhaled a deep breath. That wasn't what she'd been saying at all, but sure. She blew out her breath. If that was the only way to make him see that there was no hope of a relationship between them, then fine. "Yeah, actually. I've met someone."

"Who?" Steve demanded.

"Who? I don't know who. I mean—I know who. Of course I know who. I just mean you don't know who. Him. Him-who." Edith shoved her bangs to the side. The teakettle began to whistle. "Just go away."

"Not until you at least give me a name."

"Ugh. You are so—" The whistle pierced louder. Edith spun toward the stove. Spun back to Steve. "No."

"A name," Steve said, blocking the door when she tried to close it. The teakettle screeched.

"Henry," she blurted, unable to stand the sound a second longer. "His name is Henry, okay? Now go." She pointed her finger out the door, then raced to take the kettle off the burner. The whistle disappeared, replaced by a gentle bubbling. So much better.

"How?"

Edith whipped around. "How what?"

"How did you meet this *Henry*?"

"None of your business." She sighed, seeing how he refused to budge until she gave an answer. "Fine. We met through a mutual acquaintance, okay? I'm staying at his house this summer. Happy?"

"You're already living together?" The veins in Steve's neck bulged.

That's it. Edith was done. She pointed to the ceiling. "Do you want to wake the whole house? Because if you do, you are not leaving until you rock every one of those living creatures upstairs back to sleep."

Steve's face paled. Though now that she thought about it, his color hadn't looked that great to begin with.

"I want to meet him," Steve said. "You owe me that much. I want to know who this man is that you're moving on with after my brother and shoving me aside for."

Edith shrugged her shoulders helplessly. "His schedule is really busy."

"I'll wait. As long as it takes." Steve gave her a challenging look. "Arrange a meeting. Otherwise I'm not going anywhere."

Then he disappeared out the door into the darkness.

CHAPTER TWELVE

Henry stared at the ceiling. The same image that chased him to sleep last night greeted him first thing this morning.

Edith.

Like a stack of Polaroids, his mind flipped through every one of their interactions. The evening at the diner when he thought she looked like Goldie Hawn. The morning he spoke to her at the coffee shop. The rainy day in the cemetery. Last night in the banquet hall. Beneath a starlit sky. In his arms.

He groaned and rubbed his palms down the front of his face. Why didn't he tell her who he was? He'd meant to. Wasn't that why he'd followed her out to the golf course?

Okay, so maybe the hopes of getting that dance had sent him chasing after her as well. But who could blame him?

That dress! No wonder half the town had stood in line to dance with her.

Henry stepped to the bathroom sink and splashed cold water over his face.

Except it wasn't just about the dress. It was about her. Edith's own words had pushed him to follow her. *"Life's too short to watch from the sidelines. If you find your Goldie Hawn, you go after her."*

Well, he'd found her. And she'd been sleeping in his bed for the better part of three weeks.

Henry dunked his face beneath the cold running water. How had he not known? And what was he going to do now that he did know?

He reached for a towel and wiped his face dry, staring at himself in the mirror. He had to tell her. That's all there was to it. She was under the illusion she was living one floor above a docile old man. She deserved to know she was only one staircase away from a young hot-blooded male whose thoughts about her were anything but docile.

Henry finished using the bathroom just as the front doorbell rang. By the time he threw on a T-shirt to go along with his pajama bottoms, a fist was pounding on the door. "What in the world?" Henry muttered. Better not be Chelsea telling him she'd thrown his newspaper on the roof again.

Henry opened the door. Before he could speak, a man forced his way into the doorway, aiming a finger at his nose. "Are you sleeping with her?"

Henry took in the man's bloodshot eyes. The disheveled hair. The stench of cigarette smoke rolling off his wrinkled clothes. "I think you've got the wrong house, pal."

The man peered past Henry's shoulder. "Are you telling me Edith's not living with you?"

Edith? This guy was here because of Edith?

Henry stared at the man, weighing his response. "I don't see how that's any of your business."

The man jabbed his finger against Henry's chest, talking through a clenched jaw. "Edith is my business. And I want to know if you two are together."

"Sounds like a question you should be asking her."

"I did. Now I want to hear what you have to say."

Henry didn't like the possessive look in the man's eyes. It kindled his protective nature until it grew into a full blaze. "I'm going to kindly ask you to leave. If I have to repeat myself, I won't be so kind about it."

Henry was pretty sure he'd stolen that line from an old Western, but hey, it sounded good, didn't it?

The man smirked at him. "Believe me, I know exactly the sort of game you're playing. Just like I know Edith. In fact, I know her a lot better than you ever will." He narrowed his gaze. "She'll come back to me." He backed onto the porch, pointing his finger vaguely at the house, appearing to be talking more to himself than to Henry. "This ain't what it looks like."

"Or maybe . . ." Henry folded his arms across his chest and leaned against the doorframe in what he hoped came across as a nonchalant stance instead of what it really was—a much-needed move to relieve pressure off his bum knee. "It could be exactly what it looks like."

A challenge sparked in the man's eyes. "Prove it."

"Prove what?"

"That you're not just going after the same thing I'm after."

"And what would that be?" Henry actually didn't want to hear the answer to that. He held up his hand. "I think it's time for you to go."

"Couldn't agree more." The guy shoved his hands into his pockets as he turned and sauntered down the front porch steps. "I hear a cup of hot java calling my name. Should I save you a seat? Or do you mind if I keep it a private affair between Edith and me? Because I couldn't help but notice you never answered the question about whether you were a couple or not. Sort of makes it sound like she's still up for grabs."

Henry glared at the back of the man's head until it disappeared down the street and around the corner in the direction of the coffee shop.

Henry slammed the door closed. He didn't know who that man was or what was going on, but he knew trouble when he saw it. Limping as quickly as he could, he changed out of his pajamas and brushed his teeth.

He checked his reflection once more on the way out. "All right, baby blues. I'm counting on you to keep me from getting slapped."

Although maybe a good slap upside the head was what he needed. Why else would he be doing this unless he was crazy?

The feel of Edith dancing in his arms, pressed against his chest, washed over him. His breath hitched and his pace quickened. He knew why he was doing this.

Because Edith was too special to be up for grabs.

♥

Edith sat at her spot by the back window of the coffee shop. What could she say to Henry that wouldn't make her sound like a complete idiot?

Dear Henry,

I need you to find me a younger version of yourself (do you know Hobbes by any chance?) who can pretend to be my boyfriend for a little while in order to keep my dead husband's delusional brother from coming near me. Thanks. I owe you a gallon of butter pecan for this one.

She ripped the paper into shreds. "What am I doing?" she muttered. After taking a drink of coffee that had turned cold, she tore out another sheet of paper from her notebook and leaned over it.

Dear Henry,

"Writing love letters?"

"Ah!" Edith crumpled the paper in her hand. "What are you doing here?"

Steve sat down in the chair across from her, his face pale and wan despite the cocky grin. "Getting a cup of coffee, just like you."

Edith slammed her notebook shut. "I'm not comfortable with you being here."

Steve held his hands up in mock surrender. "Very well."

He stood and moved to the table next to hers. Sat down. "This more comfortable for you?"

"What do you want from me, Steve?" Edith worked to keep her voice quiet, not wanting to make a scene. Especially since she recognized a number of people from the banquet last night. The Mickey Rooney look-alike waved at her from across the room whenever she glanced his way. Wasn't he supposed to be playing golf this morning? She waved back to him. Again.

"Edith, are you listening to me? I said I need you to come home."

Edith rubbed the headache building along her forehead. "Yes, I heard you. Now it's time for you to listen to me. That's not my home anymore. How many times do I have to tell you? I've moved on."

"With Henry."

"With . . . my life."

"And that doesn't include Henry?"

He was trying to trap her with her words. Brian would use the same sort of lawyer tactics on her whenever he wanted to win an argument, and it always drove her nuts. So Edith would make her words crystal clear this time—even if it was a lie.

"I am moving on with Henry. I am in love with Henry. I want to spend the rest of my life with Henry." Oh, dear. Her voice must have risen because people everywhere were casting her wide-eyed glances. Probably confused as to why she had fallen in love with her geriatric housemate.

She ducked her head and gathered her notebook, her pens, her last shred of dignity. "You know what? I need to go."

"Too bad," Steve said, waving his palm toward the window. "Because your boyfriend's just about here."

"What?" Edith twisted, searching for the tall man with the thinning gray hair she'd glimpsed last week. She shook her head. "I don't see him. I only see—" Her breath caught. "Oh no," she whispered. She couldn't tell if the weird sensation in her face was due to all the blood rushing toward it or away from it.

Hobbes. The artist formerly known as Hubba-Hubba. He limped past the windows and entered the shop, looking as intense and handsome in a T-shirt and jeans as he had last night in his tux.

And he was staring straight at her. Why was he staring straight at her? Not only that, he was walking straight toward her. Almost like a man on a mission. Why was he a man on a mission? What was the mission?

Edith stood—a feat considering how her legs wobbled. "Hi." Before she could utter another word, he scooped her into his arms and kissed her. Soundly. On the mouth. Long enough for her to taste the mint of his toothpaste. Edith's shoulders relaxed. She rather enjoyed the taste of his toothpaste.

A whistle and a few catcalls sounded. *Oh, my goodness.* Edith broke the kiss, ducking her head as a light spattering of applause echoed throughout the coffee shop. What had gotten into her? What had gotten into *him*? She lifted her gaze.

"Hi," he said, his eyes crinkling around the edges, first with wariness as if gauging her reaction, then with amusement, her stunned reaction fully gauged.

Steve cleared his throat and Edith jumped. She'd forgotten

he was there. Hobbes turned toward Steve, keeping Edith tucked against his side with one arm, while reaching out with the other. "Henry. Don't believe I caught your name."

Henry? Why was he pretending to be Henry? Edith forced herself to take slow, even breaths.

Steve stood, his chair scraping against the wood floor. "Steve Sherman." He grasped Henry's hand and squeezed, his grip appearing as tight as the clenching of his jaw.

"Nice to meet you," Hobbes said, dropping Steve's hand and tugging Edith closer, "but I should probably get Edith home. She's worked all night. I'm sure she's ready to get some rest." He flashed Edith a confident smile. The one she returned felt tremulous at best.

"Ready?"

Hardly. Edith jerked her head in a nod.

Steve's voice followed them to the door. "I guess I'll be seeing you two around then."

He would?

Hobbes kept Edith close as he glanced over his shoulder to Steve. "We're not going anywhere."

They weren't?

Julie stood at the counter, mouth hanging open. Even Opal paused in berating the existence of Chester the cat long enough to watch Hobbes lead Edith out the door in silence.

They walked down the sidewalk without saying another word. Edith didn't know where they were headed, so she just stayed tucked against Hobbes's side and kept moving. He led her a few blocks over before pausing and looking around.

"Follow me." He grabbed her hand and pulled her into

an alley behind a brick hardware store. They came to a stop on a graveled area between a dumpster and a row of shrubs.

Once they were secluded, he let go of her hand and stepped back. The confidence from the coffee shop had disappeared, replaced by a nervous smile. "Quite the morning, huh?"

Not trusting her voice to work, Edith wet her lips and did the first thing that came to mind. She kissed him back.

CHAPTER THIRTEEN

Henry had planned to tell her the truth. Lay it all out for her. Set the record straight. But it was sort of hard to do with her lips all over his mouth. Again.

Okay, so maybe the first time had been his idea. And what a good idea it was. Except now it was giving him a lot of other ideas. Ideas he shouldn't be thinking.

"Whoa," he said, breaking away from their kiss. He released his grip on Edith and stepped back. "Whoa," he said again.

Edith touched her swollen lips with the tips of her fingers, then covered her mouth with her entire palm before pulling it away. "I am so sorry," she said, looking horrified. "I didn't mean to do that."

"You didn't?" Henry asked.

"Well, I did. But not like that. As if I was . . . you know, mauling you." She shoved her long bangs away from her forehead. "I was just trying to say thank you. That's all."

"Right. I know. And that was just me saying you're welcome.'"

Edith smiled, still a bit flushed and breathless. He shoved his hands in his pockets and forced himself to take a few steps back before he was tempted to tell her *you're welcome* all afternoon.

Cardboard boxes poked out of the top of the dumpster. "So," Henry said, nudging a wooden pallet with one of his boots. "Who exactly is Steve? And why is he here?"

"My late husband's brother. And he's here because . . ." She shook her head and blew her bangs from her eyes. "I don't know. He's delusional?"

A finch landed in the shrubs. Edith stared at it, giving Henry the chance to study the face he'd been losing sleep over since the first moment they met. All this time that face had belonged to Edith.

Edith.

"Why did you do what you did back there? At the coffee shop? Why did you . . . ? How did you . . . ?" The finch flew away, and Edith met his gaze. "What's going on?"

Henry cleared his throat and tugged at his shirt collar. *Tell her.* "Yeah, about that." *Tell her.* "Funny story." *Tell her!* "Henry called me." *Coward.* "Yeah, um . . . Steve went to his house this morning, looking for you, and Henry called me afterward."

"Oh no." Edith groaned. "Poor Henry. I did not mean for this to happen. Is he okay? Steve didn't, I don't know, scare him or anything, did he?"

"Heck no. Henry's a tough guy. Everybody knows he

doesn't scare easy." Except when faced with a beautiful woman he didn't want to lose.

Edith started pacing the small space next to the shrubs, which sent two more birds fluttering away. "You know what? I'm going to go find Henry right now and explain everything. The last thing I want to do is drag that dear sweet old man into this mess."

"He's a good guy, isn't he?"

"The best. He leaves me the sweetest notes. I'm half in love with him. He reminds me of this cute little old man who used to go to my church. Well, my parents' church. After I got married, I sort of stopped going. My husband was never really into church. But recently I've started going again. Anyway, none of that matters."

Edith grabbed her bag that must have fallen onto the ground during their kiss. She hiked it onto her shoulder. "Right now all that matters is I find Henry and tell him I'm moving out."

"You sure? That seems—" *Rather reasonable considering the sixty-year age gap between us has been removed, so we probably shouldn't continue living together since all I can think about is kissing you, and oh yeah, I'm Henry, by the way—*"rash. Maybe you should think it over."

"What's to think over? Henry doesn't need this sort of drama. *I* don't need this sort of drama. I'll find somewhere else to stay until Steve leaves town. Kat's house has got to be almost ready. Do you know Kat?"

"Everybody knows Kat."

"Right. Small town. Keep forgetting." Edith started to march past.

"Hey, look," Henry said, latching on to her elbow and spinning her back to face him. "I can guarantee Henry doesn't want you to leave." *Ever. Definitely not today.*

"Really?"

"Of course. That's why he called me this morning." Henry could see his lies snowballing in front of him. But it was worth it, right? To protect her from Steve? He'd do a little soul-searching later on whether that was his real motivation. "Henry cares about you, Edith. I know he does. Why do you think he came up with this whole idea of me pretending to be your boyfriend?"

"He did?"

"After Steve came to his house, he was really worried about you."

Edith groaned and started pacing again. "I never should have let Steve think I had a boyfriend. And why on earth did I say Henry's name? This is such a mess. I just didn't know what else to say when Steve wouldn't leave last night."

"What do you mean he wouldn't leave last night?" His protective instinct roared to life, suggesting his real motivation *was* to protect Edith from Steve. Which meant she should definitely stay in his house until Steve left town. Which meant he should definitely wait to tell her he was Henry. Right?

"Don't worry. Steve left once I threatened him with babies. But how long can I continue to do that?"

"Threaten him with babies?"

"He's going to figure out the truth eventually. I don't have a boyfriend. The house is full of plants. *Ugh.* Why can't I just get on a plane today and fly to South Africa and never return? Is that too much to ask?" Edith continued rambling and pacing.

Henry palmed his stomach. The thought of Edith never returning hurt worse than a kick to the gut. And felt way too familiar. He should tell her the truth. Now. Before she pulled a Maggie on him and left him in the dust.

"It isn't Paul, is it?" Edith had stopped pacing and was staring at him.

Henry shook his head. "You've lost me. Who's Paul?"

"I never knew your name when we met before, so I just always called you Paul in my head. Well, Paul Hubba-Hubba Newman if you want to be exact," she murmured before clearing her throat. "So what's your real name? I assume Hobbes is your last name?"

"It is." A glimmer of hope lit inside Henry's chest as a slow smile tilted his lips. So he was the blue-eyed man that had reminded her of Paul Newman, was he? *Hubba-hubba.* He'd spent all this time thinking about his infatuation with her, but he'd neglected one major thing. This woman was wildly attracted to him. She'd said as much in her letters. More than that, she was—how did she put it?—*"half in love"* with him.

"Why are you looking at me like that? What are you doing?" She eyed him warily as he slowly approached her. "Are you going to tell me your name? You're making me nervous."

He was making *her* nervous? If she only knew.

He forced as much calm into his voice as he could and willed his hand not to shake while he brushed a strand of hair behind her ear. "I thought you already knew. My name is Henry."

Her forehead wrinkled with confusion. "I don't . . . I don't understand."

"Until Steve catches a one-way ticket out of here, I plan on being the new love of your life. And let's just say for now, the new love of your life goes by the name Henry Hobbes."

———————— ♥ ————————

The first time Edith woke up, she wondered if it had all been a dream. But the way her lips still tingled, no way the kiss she and Henry shared by the shrubs had been a dream.

Henry.

It was weird calling him that. But he was right. Why take the chance of calling him the wrong name when he was supposed to be playing the part of Henry? Boyfriend Henry. Not old Henry, who was the real Henry.

The whole thing left her brain muddled. Or maybe it was her sleep schedule that had muddled her brain. She rolled over and drifted back to sleep.

The second time she woke up, it was because she heard the sink running downstairs. Why did she hear the sink running? She bolted upright. What time was it? Was someone in the house?

Afternoon sunlight snuck past the window blinds. Henry—old Henry—was never home at this time. Steve wouldn't be so bold as to enter a stranger's house uninvited.

Would he?

Edith crept down the stairs and peeked around the banister. She heard a man humming to himself in the kitchen.

Steve wasn't the humming type, so she inched farther, eventually tiptoeing to the edge of the kitchen.

"Hey, Edith."

She flinched and jumped around the refrigerator, aiming an accusatory finger at Henry. "You shouldn't scare people like that. What are you even doing here?" Edith asked, trying to sound stern even though she couldn't keep the delight entirely out of her voice. Henry—hubba-hubba boyfriend Henry—was here. In the house. Scrambling eggs on the stovetop and rummaging through the refrigerator like he owned the place.

He tossed a spatula into the sink and clicked off the burner. "Hope you're hungry. And I hope you like eggs."

"I am hungry. And I do like eggs. But what are you doing here?" she repeated.

He used his chin to point to a letter on the kitchen island. "That's for you. Henry said it should explain everything."

Edith grabbed the letter, aware of the way this Henry watched her from the corner of his eye.

Dear Edith,

I hope you don't mind a little meddling in your life. Please forgive me if you do. It's just that I've grown to really care about you in the short time we've been living together and corresponding. And the way that man Steve spoke about you had me very worried.

When I realized that you had led him to believe you were involved with a man named Henry, I decided to play along and get the young man you see standing before you involved. You can trust him, Edith. He'll take good care of you. I'll come back when the time is right.

Your friend, Henry

This didn't make sense. Edith folded the note and set it back on the table. "He left? I don't understand. Does he really expect you to stay here and keep pretending to be him?"

Henry slid the scrambled eggs onto a plate. With his back to her, he asked, "Are you okay with that?"

"Am I okay with that? Are *you* okay with that?"

"Why wouldn't I be okay with that?" Henry handed her the plate and a fork.

"Because you're having to uproot your life to babysit some lady you don't know all because her dead husband's brother has some weird fixation on her and doesn't know when to move on with his life already." She shoved a forkful of eggs into her mouth. "Mmm. That's good."

"Thanks. And, Edith . . ." Henry handed her a glass of orange juice, his gorgeous blue eyes locked on hers. "I don't mind. Not one bit."

Blast those eyes. She dropped her focus back to the eggs on her plate before she did something silly—like blush. Out of the corner of her eye she saw him wipe his hands on a dish towel. "I need to head back to work."

"Of course." She waved him away with her fork. "Don't feel like you have to watch over me. Really. Do your thing. This whole Steve thing is going to blow over in a few days—if he even sticks around that long." She hoped, anyway. Edith shoveled in more eggs. She hadn't realized how hungry she was.

"Lock up behind me. I should be back later this evening. Do you work tonight?"

"No." Edith washed her bite down with a swig of orange juice. "Sharon insisted I take the next few days off even though I told her that's crazy since the whole reason I'm here is to help out. But she wouldn't budge on it."

Henry nodded, then hesitated next to the doorway of the kitchen. He scratched behind his ear and squinted toward the window. "There's a lot of windows in this house."

"Is that a bad thing?" The look on his face suggested it was.

"I'm just thinking, based on what I've seen so far, I wouldn't put it past Steve to try spying on us." He cocked his head toward the window above the sink. "He could be watching us right now."

"I doubt it." Edith took another sip of her orange juice.

Henry scratched behind his ear again, appearing to mull over a decision. "But better to be safe than sorry, don't you think?"

"Sure." She could close all the blinds if it made him feel better. That's what that devilish look in his eye was about, right? The blinds?

Henry pushed off the doorframe and strode toward her. She paused with her orange juice halfway to her mouth. He took it from her hand and set it back on the table before swooping in for a quick kiss. Much too quick.

When he leaned back, enough for her to see the subtle

curve of his mouth, she didn't know if the heat in her belly was because she wanted to slap the smile off those lips or kiss them off.

"Just in case," he said with a wink.

Edith nodded, afraid if she talked, it would only come out as a squeak. When the back door closed a moment later, she dropped her head into her hands and begged God to make Steve leave town that very minute. She couldn't keep up this charade.

Especially since she wasn't sure which part was the charade—them pretending to be a couple or her pretending like she wasn't falling head over heels for a stranger.

Her appetite gone, Edith dumped the rest of the eggs in the garbage. She refused to let anything keep her from going to South Africa at the end of the summer. Her life wasn't here.

Even if she left a tiny piece of her heart here after she left.

CHAPTER FOURTEEN

Later that evening, Henry pressed his thumb against the doorbell, banged the knocker, then pressed the doorbell again. After the third round of *buzz-buzz-knock-knock-knock-buzzzzz*, the door cracked open.

"Henry?" Lance opened the door wider. "What are you doing here?"

"Do you have a minute?"

Lance scratched the back of his head and darted a glance back into the house. "I'm sort of on a date. We're getting ready to eat dinner. Is this something that can wait?"

"I kissed Goldie Hawn."

"I'll be just a minute," Lance hollered over his shoulder as he stepped outside, closing the door behind him. "Continue."

"Except she's not Goldie. She's Edith. Now we're pretending to date and I'm pretending to be Henry, so I had to send
the real Henry away, even though there is no real Henry
because I'm the real Henry. But she doesn't know that, and
before you say I should have told her the truth, I *know* I
should have told her the truth, but you didn't see that Steve
guy. He's bad news. I don't trust him. You wouldn't either. So
now I can't tell her the truth, because if I tell her the truth,
she's going to get mad I didn't tell her the truth. Then she
might go away. And I don't want her to go away, but that's
crazy because at the end of summer she's going away anyway,
you know?"

Lance opened his mouth to speak, but Henry rushed on.
"Problem is I like her, Lance. I mean, I *really* like her. All I
want to do is keep kissing her. And not just because she's
a bombshell—oh, man, that red dress—but she's the type
of woman I could see sharing the rest of my life with. Am
I insane? I have to be. I barely know her. But the thing is,
I do know her. She's told me things and I've told her things,
so there's this strong connection between us. But she doesn't
know that. She thinks she's got a connection with *Henry*.
What am I supposed to do?"

Lance blinked. "Who's Steve?"

"Her husband's brother."

"She's married?"

"No. He's dead."

"Steve?"

"Her husband. Have you been listening? What kind of
therapist are you?"

"A *physical* therapist. And for the record, I didn't know

we had a showing-up-unannounced-with-personal-problems relationship."

"Well, we do. Now are you going to help me with my problem or not?"

"What problem? Sounds to me like you've got a bombshell living in your house who you've been getting to smooch left and right. You call that a problem?" Lance grabbed the door handle. "Now if you'll excuse me, there's a lovely lady sitting in my kitchen and I'm hoping to land a few smooches of my own, so . . ."

"That's it? That's all you've got for me?"

"Yeah, man. That's all I've got for you—as both your physical therapist and your friend. You still wanna talk, head down to the corner pub. I'm sure crazy Al would love hearing you ramble about dead husbands and old lady bombshells. Shoot, he's probably the only one in this town who could make a lick of sense out of anything you just said. Good night." Lance closed the door.

Henry ambled back to his pickup truck. Well, fat lot of good that did. Not that he'd really been expecting to receive any earth-shattering advice. More that he just needed to collect his thoughts a minute before he got back to his house. Before he got back to Edith. Before he got back to wanting to kiss her again.

It wasn't as if he didn't already know what needed to be done. He needed to tell Edith the truth. And he would. Just as soon as Steve was out of the picture. That way even if she hated him for lying, she'd at least be out of harm's way.

When Henry pulled into his driveway, pink-tinged streaks of orange brushed across the horizon. He let himself in through the front door, surprised when the smell of home-cooked food wafted from the kitchen. He'd been planning to throw in a frozen pizza.

"Hey." Edith stuck her head out from the kitchen. Cute little worry lines formed between her eyebrows as she blew her bangs out of her eyes. "Have you had supper already?"

"No. Usually I grab a bite on the way home, but tonight I went over to see a friend about . . . something."

She brushed her bangs to the side and the wrinkles along her forehead smoothed out. "Good. I made some chicken and rice casserole. It's ready if you're hungry."

"Starving."

Edith dished out two servings and they sat together at the kitchen island. Other than the scraping of their forks, they ate in silence, shooting each other the occasional polite smile. "This is really good," Henry said.

"Thank you."

Silence again. Henry wasn't used to sharing a meal with someone like this. Whenever he and Angela ate together, he chewed and Angela talked.

Angela. Henry wished he could swallow his guilt as easily as the casserole. He hadn't given her one second's thought. No, wait. That wasn't right. He had given her one second's thought, and in that one second, he berated himself for not ending things with her already, then decided it was easier on his conscience if he didn't give her any more thought.

Edith wiped a napkin across her lips. "So that woman I've seen you with a few times. Is she your girlfriend?"

Henry sputtered on his water. Was Edith a mind reader?

He cleared his throat. "Uh . . . no. No. *No.* I wouldn't have kissed you or started pretending we were—" he motioned his hand back and forth between them—"you know, if she and I were still . . ." He flopped his hand in the opposite direction, as if Angela were the refrigerator.

He really needed to set aside some time to have that conversation he'd been avoiding with Angela, didn't he?

Henry picked at his last bite of chicken. "We've dated on and off the past couple of years. Her parents own a farm near here. After people started using their barn for weddings, Angela started her own wedding photography business. It didn't take long for it to take off. She's good at what she does. But as she got busier and busier, we began connecting less and less." And the fact that Henry hadn't minded one bit should have been a giant red flag.

"I'm sorry." Edith poked her fork at the few remaining grains of rice on her plate. "Breakups are tough."

Henry stood and dumped the rest of his scraps in the garbage. "What about you?" he asked, desperate to change the subject. "Clearly you have something special going on with Steve."

"Ha. That was part of the reason I came out here for the summer and why I'm looking forward to leaving at the end of it. Ever since my husband died, I haven't wanted to form any new attachments. I just want to be me, living my life on my own terms for once. No ties. No connections. No—"

"Steve?"

Edith let out a breath of laughter. "Definitely no Steve." She took her plate to the sink. "You know, growing up, he wasn't a bad kid. He was a couple years behind me in school.

I think he always had a bit of a crush on me. But unfortunately for him, the only crush I ever had was on his older brother."

She rinsed her plate, then began filling the sink with water. "To be honest, Steve never showed his face much in all the time I was married to Brian. It wasn't until Brian got sick and was near the end that it suddenly felt like Steve and I were around each other all the time. I can't say he ever crossed the line, but I started to notice how he'd find little ways to be touching me. You know—a shoulder squeeze here, maybe a little back rub there—things like that. And if he wasn't touching me, it felt like he was always watching me."

Edith paused. "Am I talking too much?" She reached for Henry's plate. "Sometimes I get carried away. Here, let me wash."

Henry kept the plate. "How about I wash and you finish the story." He could use something to do with his hands right now, besides thinking of ways to use them on Steve. "And don't worry," he said to lighten the mood, "I'll let you know when you're talking too much."

Edith wrinkled her nose at him and looked so adorable that Henry plunged his hands into the sink water just to keep from pulling her close. "So what happened?" Henry asked after he'd washed off their plates.

"Huh? Oh." Edith's face remained somber as she grabbed a towel to start drying. "Well, eventually my husband died. We knew it was coming. He'd been sick for a while. Cancer," she explained.

"I'm sorry."

"Thank you." Edith became quiet. For a long minute

Henry didn't think she planned to say any more. But then with a wave of her hand, she said, "Anyway. After Brian was gone, Steve kept finding reasons to come over to the house. He'd bring by dinner. He'd take out the garbage. One evening I came home and found him cleaning out the gutters. It was all nice things, and I really did appreciate the way he was trying to help out, but at the same time, it was too much."

She opened a cabinet and returned the dried plates. "Before long he was there all the time. And if he wasn't there, then he was calling all the time. It was like we were married. And that's when I realized, after everything I'd gone through with Brian—all the struggles, all the heartache—the last thing I wanted was get tied down in another marriage. Not when I was free to do as I pleased for the first time in my life."

Henry worked hard to keep his face impassive. He drained the sink, then toweled his hands dry as he leaned back against the counter. "So you decided to go to South Africa."

"I decided to go to South Africa. It's somewhere I've wanted to go for a long time. Especially this particular area of South Africa. Once I connected with an organization that was taking on volunteers, well, one thing led to another, and that became the plan." Edith hung her towel back on the stove. "But as you can see, Steve is not a big fan of the plan."

Yeah, well, neither was Henry. It was all he could do not to crush her to his chest and beg her to forget all about the plan. But then he'd be as bad as Steve.

Henry cleared his throat and shifted his weight. "Well, I'm proud of you, Edith. It takes a lot of guts to do what you're doing." He swallowed the words threatening to spill out and instead said, "Don't let anyone hold you back."

"I'm trying not to," she said quietly, holding his gaze. She suddenly narrowed her eyes and crinkled her nose. "What is it with you two?"

"What do you mean?"

"You. And Henry. The real Henry. I tell you guys things I've never told anybody else, and I don't know either of you. Especially you."

Henry dropped the hand towel onto the counter behind him. He folded his arms across his chest and feigned a smug smile. "You read what Henry wrote. I'm a good guy. What else do you need to know?"

Edith rolled her eyes and folded her arms in a mirror imitation of him. "Oh, I don't know. Maybe who you are, what you do, why you're helping me—things along that nature."

"You want to know what I do? Fine." Hopefully she didn't notice how he'd skipped right over her first question. "I own a painting and construction company."

"Oh." Her brow wrinkled in thought a moment before smoothing out again. "And do you like it? Owning your own company?"

Henry shrugged, searching for how to answer that. "The office side of it isn't exactly what gets me out of bed in the morning. Or the painting. But yeah, I like construction. I love being a contractor. I love carrying on my family's business. It's just . . ."

"Just what?"

"I don't know. Boring, I guess."

Edith's brows rose as she unfolded her arms and leaned against the counter. "Boring how?"

"The projects we've been getting. It's all little stuff. Remodeling a kitchen. Upgrading a bathroom. Adding on a new deck. I want to build something from scratch. Something unique. Something that's a challenge."

"So why aren't you?"

"Can't do projects you don't get hired for. That's the problem with having a small crew." *And a town that doesn't completely trust you.* "Everybody watches HGTV these days and thinks a house can be built in a week. But it takes time. Back when my dad started, the average square footage of a house was about 1,100 feet. His four-man crew could get one up in ninety days. But now, people want houses twice that size and they want it built in less time. I can't promise that. The only thing I can promise them is the same level of craftsmanship this company has always provided." A promise that seemed to carry less weight the moment his brother retired.

Henry sighed and leaned against the counter next to Edith, their arms grazing. "So lately I've been stuck taking on the projects we can manage on a shorter deadline, and well . . ."

"You're bored."

"So, so incredibly bored," he said, slumping sideways until it looked like his elbow on the counter was all that held him up from the pressure of boredom trying to flatten him into the ground.

Edith laughed over his theatrics the way he hoped she would. "So is that why you're helping me then? Because you're bored out of your mind and have nothing better to do?"

"Oh no. I have a far better reason for why I'm helping you." Henry angled in front of her, pinning her back against the counter.

"Oh?" Edith asked, chewing her lip, clearly in a failed attempt not to smile. "What could that possibly be?"

He palmed the counter on each side of her, his thumbs grazing her shirt at her waist, as he lowered his face close to hers, close enough to smell the scent of coconut in her hair from her shampoo. Close enough to see the tiny golden flecks in her brown eyes before he dropped his lips next to her ear. "Because I like the way you say thank you," he whispered.

She playfully punched him in the stomach and Henry groaned. Right before he left the kitchen laughing, about as far away from bored as a man could be.

CHAPTER FIFTEEN

A distant ringing sound woke Edith the next morning. It took a moment for her to get her bearings and realize it must be the landline in the kitchen. She stretched with a yawn. Well, whoever it was could leave a message.

Since she'd had the last few days off from work, her sleep schedule had gotten all out of whack. She padded down the creaky wooden stairs and into the kitchen for some coffee. An empty cereal bowl sat in the sink. Looked like Henry had already eaten breakfast and disappeared for the morning.

The phone started ringing again. Oh, for goodness' sake. Edith yanked the phone off the wall cradle just to make it stop ringing. "Hello?" her voice croaked.

"Oh. Um, hi," a female voice said and then hesitated.

"I may have called the wrong number. I'm trying to reach my uncle Henry."

"This is the right number." Edith tried to clear the morning frog out of her voice. "You aren't Kat by any chance, are you?"

"Yes. Wait. Are you Edith?"

"That's me." Edith stretched her arm out, trying to reach a glass from the cupboard so she could drink some water and hopefully not sound like the bass singer from a barbershop quartet.

"Oh, wow! How are you and Henry getting along? Any big breakups in front of the neighbors?" she asked with a laugh. "I'm so sorry about the last-minute changes with my house, by the way. That's actually why I'm calling. My landlord said the mold is just about taken care of. *Finally.* You should be able to move in soon. I meant to call the other day, but with the time zone difference, I could never find a good time. So is Henry there? I just want to say hi if he's not too busy. I know he's got his therapy around this time."

"Yeah, sorry. He's not here."

"Oh. Well. Tell him I'll try again this evening."

"No. I mean, he's not here at all. He left town. I'm not sure when he'll be back."

"Really? Did he say where he was going? I just talked to my parents yesterday and they didn't say anything about Henry coming to see them. I'm the only other family he has, and I'm out of the country."

"Oh" was all Edith could think to say. She rubbed a hand across her stomach, nauseated that she had caused this sweet old man to abandon his own home. A sweet old man who should be at his physical therapy sessions, not wandering lost and alone somewhere. "Kat, I think it may be my fault—"

"This is amazing," Kat's voice interrupted on the other end of the line.

"Amazing?" Edith asked, not sure she understood correctly.

"Henry hasn't done something spontaneous since . . . I couldn't even tell you when."

"You're not worried about him then?"

"Well, it's a bit strange he didn't say where he was going, especially when he's got a business to run. But he's a grown man after all. And even with a bad knee, it's not like he can't take care of himself."

"A bad knee?" Edith asked.

"Yeah. Bozo thought it would be fun to play tackle football with the high school team during the alumni game. Took five surgeries to get him back on his feet again. That's why he's been getting physical therapy."

"Right," Edith said, having trouble picturing her version of Kat's uncle Henry playing tackle football. Or running a business. "I didn't realize Henry was still working. Isn't he close to being retired?"

Kat snorted into the phone. "In his dreams, I suppose. He's only thirty-two."

Edith moved the fist clenched against her stomach up to her chest and splayed her fingers across her lungs, willing them to expand against the sudden vise. "What sort of business is it that he runs?"

"Painting and construction. You probably walked past it and didn't even realize it. He needs a better sign. It's a few blocks off Main Street. Hobbes Painting and Construction. Not exactly the most creative title." Kat laughed into the phone. "I told him he should change it, but that's Henry for you."

Edith let out a strangled laugh. "Yep. That's Henry for you."

"Hey," Kat said in a sudden conspiratorial manner, "you don't suppose he has some secret girlfriend he's running off to see, do you?"

Edith was grateful she didn't have that water now. She would have sprayed it across the kitchen island.

"You've been staying with him. Have you seen any signs of a new love interest? Other than you, I mean." Kat laughed.

"Ha-ha, yeah. Other than me."

"Man, I hope so. That Angela floozy strung him along for way too long. I kept telling him to cut the string and save himself, but you can imagine how well he takes love advice from his niece. Though really, with only being two years apart, we've always been more like brother and sister."

"I see," Edith said.

"Here I called to say you were about free to move into my house. Now I'm half tempted to tell you to stay put and find out what Henry's hiding." Kat giggled. "I'm kidding. Mostly." She giggled again. "Well, I better get going. If you hear from Henry before I do, tell him to give me a call. Otherwise, like I said, the house should be ready soon. *Mi casa, su casa.* It was nice talking to you, Edith."

"Likewise."

"And can I just say before I go how wonderful I think it is that you're staying so active. And not just being active in one of those Red Hat Societies, but really getting out there and doing something worthwhile. Not that the Red Hat ladies aren't worthwhile. Oh, man, I didn't mean that. You're not a Red Hat lady, are you?"

"Nope."

"Oh, phew. Okay. I'm gonna go now before I put my foot in my mouth. Bye, Edith."

Edith set the phone back in the cradle and stared out the open kitchen window.

A wind chime plunked a hollow wooden tune. A cardinal picked at seeds from a hanging bird feeder in the backyard. The smell of freshly mowed grass lingered from the neighbor's yard. Edith hardly noticed.

She could only see Henry—the Henry she knew on paper and the Henry she knew in person—transforming in her mind to become one man. Henry was . . . *Henry*.

So why did he lie about being Henry?

She rubbed her forehead. This was already starting to give her a headache. She grabbed a couple of Tylenols out of her purse and swallowed them dry.

Then she hurried back upstairs to her room and pulled up Kat's original email. She read it. Then read it again. Yes, he was an uncle. Yes, he needed physical therapy. Yes, his name was Henry. But clearly there was no mention of him being a little old man.

Edith looked through the notes and letters Henry had written to her, reading them now with a different perspective. And that's when it hit her. His admiration for the women of her generation. His concern over her using the back steps and breaking a hip. Kat's comment just now about the Red Hat Society.

Edith slapped a hand over her mouth. She could see it now like three cherries lining up on a slot machine—Edith, widow, volunteer work. *Ping, ping, ping.*

All that time Henry had assumed *she* was old.

Edith placed her cool hands against her flushed cheeks, not sure who she felt more embarrassed for—Henry, who must have died when he realized he was sharing cartons of ice cream with the woman who saw him choking on his own saliva the first time they ever met. Or herself, who not only aired all her dirty laundry in front of him on paper but couldn't keep her lips off him in person.

Oh, Edith had a pretty good idea who she was more embarrassed for.

"This isn't good," she whispered. "This is the opposite of good. This is . . . this is awkward." Just thinking about it made her break into a sweat.

Unless I don't tell him.

Edith pushed away the thought, only to pull it right back again. What would happen if she didn't tell him? She thought through the scenario. They carry on the charade of being a couple. Steve eventually leaves. Edith moves into Kat's house and finishes out the summer. Henry goes back to being Henry. No harm, no foul.

Now what happens if she does tell him? Things get awkward. Steve sees through the charade. Confrontations ensue. And her entire first summer of independence falls apart quicker than wet toilet paper.

Edith flopped onto the bed. How had this summer gotten

so complicated? She came out here to get a jump start on her new life with no strings attached. And yet somehow her and Henry's lives were more entangled than an unorganized fisherman's tackle box.

But going to South Africa was still the right choice, wasn't it? It had to be. She was chasing after her dream. A dream that involved serving others. How could it not be the right dream? Besides, she'd tried the marriage route—and proved without a doubt that was not a route worth traveling again.

True, her marriage to Brian had been an uphill climb against the wind from the very get-go. Perhaps being older and wiser now would ease some of those struggles, but why risk it?

She'd made peace with her past. Her life with Brian might never have inspired a Shakespeare sonnet, but at least it had ended in forgiveness. And really, wasn't that enough?

A pair of blue eyes filled with humor and kindness flashed before her, pleading otherwise. But Edith swiped the image from her mind.

One heartbreaking marriage that ended in peace would have to be enough. She didn't have the courage to want more. Which left her one choice. She'd keep quiet. Kat's house should be ready soon. No reason to let Henry know she knew what he knew and should have already known by now. Yep, everything would be fine. Except for one little thing.

Steve needed to go.

CHAPTER SIXTEEN

Sweat trickled down Henry's temple as he darted away from Gabby, his neighbor across the street, who was currently dressed up as Uncle Sam and riding a unicycle.

"Hey, nice balance," Henry called after her right before she nearly collided with Lance, who apparently was also Uncle Sam, only on stilts. Lance staggered sideways to avoid Gabby, who was now spinning in circles like an out-of-control dog chasing its tail.

If ever there was a silver lining to jacking up his knee, this had to be it. Henry watched Gabby bang into two popcorn vendors and a snow cone machine while Lance attempted to sing Bruce Springsteen's "Born in the USA" through a megaphone as he handed out pamphlets advertising tonight's fireworks display at Kennedy Farms—as if anybody in town needed a pamphlet to remind them of the annual Fourth of July event that had been taking place for as long as fireworks had been invented. He laughed when Lance lost his balance and toppled into the town square's giant fountain. Right next to where Gabby had made a splash landing two seconds before.

Henry added his applause to the rest of the flea market crowd, cheering mostly for the fact his knee injury had given him a bona fide excuse not to attempt unicycles or stilts this year. Lance and Gabby weren't the first Uncle Sams to wind up in that fountain.

Dabbing the sweat from his brow, Henry returned his attention to the real reason he was out and about today. "Where are you, Steve?" he muttered, scanning the town square in search of the little pest.

The guy gave him the creeps. He was always so . . . sweaty. Granted, right now Henry was too. But Steve wore his sweat on top of a weird sickly pallor that reeked of desperation. And that sort of desperation was creepy. Henry had no intention of letting him near Edith. Not alone, at least. Which was why Henry was following him.

Or rather why Henry *had* been following him until he lost sight of him during the Uncle Sam debacle.

Henry spun in a circle. The repetitive sounds of carnival rides and music carried from a block over. Steve didn't seem like the type who got his kicks from a spin on the merry-go-round. Shoot, Steve didn't seem like the type who got his kicks from anything. Well, other than drinking orange soda and bugging Edith.

A guttural growl sounded behind Henry. He turned and

spotted the orange soda can on the ground first. Then Steve. But thankfully Steve didn't notice Henry. Bent over with his eyes scrunched shut and Niagara Falls dripping down his forehead, Steve probably didn't notice anything.

Henry ducked behind a flea market stand displaying an assortment of bird feeders and birdbaths. After another grunt, Steve straightened and mopped the sweat off his face with the bottom of his shirt.

"Hey," he said to a young boy walking past about to take a bite of his snow cone. "Do you know Edith Sherman?"

Henry nudged a step closer, using a spaghetti squash birdhouse to block his face.

"Huh?" the boy responded, blue liquid sliding down his fingers and dripping onto the sidewalk.

"Blonde hair, brown eyes. New to town."

"Ohhh." The boy slurped from the rim of the cup, speaking with his mouth half-full. "You mean Henry's girl."

Henry couldn't keep from grinning.

"Yeah, just saw her at the medical tent. She fixed my arm. It was bleeding all over." The boy lifted his elbow to show off his lifesaving Band-Aid.

Steve inhaled a slow breath, clearly not impressed with the boy's battle wound any more than probably hearing Edith referred to as *Henry's girl*. "Where's this medical tent?"

"Down the street from the car show."

"Where's the car show?"

"Down the street from the library."

"Where's the library?"

The boy squinted one eye in thought. "You know where Tall Danny lives?"

"No."

"Well, it's down the street from his house."

Henry tried not to laugh. Especially when his new little best friend waved at another boy and yelled, "Yo! Tall Danny! This guy wants to know where you live," and the other boy yelled back, "Down the street from the library. Why?"

"Forget it," Steve muttered, shoving past the boy and making it half a dozen steps before he gripped the back of a park bench and closed his eyes. Almost as if he were about to pass out.

Henry set down the birdhouse. Was he seriously about to pass out?

Before Henry could decide whether it would be best to catch him or let him fall, a voice Henry would recognize anywhere broke through the vague chatter of milling people.

"This man. Right here." *Peg.*

Wearing a red, white, and blue straw hat, star-shaped sunglasses, and a *God Bless America* sequined T-shirt, she marched up to Steve and jabbed him in the back with her pointer finger.

Henry reached for the birdhouse again.

"I saw it with my own eyes." Peg jabbed Steve in the chest when he turned to face her.

"Saw what?" Steve rubbed his chest, nearly losing his balance against the park bench.

"You. Littering." Peg pointed to the ground where Steve's crumpled orange soda can lay in the grass. "There's the evidence. Do something, James."

Henry should have brought popcorn. Because sure enough, there was James, dressed in his dark police uniform.

Whether the miserable look on his face was due to the heat or the fact that his career choice had led him to moments like this was a toss-up.

"Now look here—" Steve started to say before his face contorted in a blend of heavy perspiration and agony.

"Hey, buddy, you okay?" James asked. "You don't look so good."

"Of course he doesn't look good," Peg said. "He looks guilty. Now knock off the buddy talk and arrest him."

Steve clutched the bench with a growl.

"Hear that, James? He's getting feral. Arrest him."

"Come on, Peg," James said. "It's the Fourth of July festival. We're all here to have a good time. Let's not make a mountain out of a molehill."

"Do you see a mountain, James? Because I don't see a mountain. I don't even see a molehill. All I see is a piece of contamination soiling my community's beautiful town square." She propped both her fists on her waist. "And then there's the matter of the pop can on the ground."

Steve pushed away from the park bench. "Now look here, ya old lady—"

"Hey—" James lifted a palm to Steve's chest. "I don't want to hear you finish that sentence with anything other than 'It was nice meeting you.' Then I suggest you pick up the can, throw it away, and go about your business."

"That's it?" Peg's red- and blue-starred bracelets jangled up and down her forearms. "You're not going to fine him?"

"Peg, you know that's too much paperwork for me to do over one little soda can," James replied.

"Soda can? I'm talking about the defamation of my character. He called me old."

"Both of you—" James stepped between them again with his palms up—"leave. Now." He aimed a finger at Steve. "After you throw away the soda can."

Steve grabbed the crumpled can and slammed it into a blue trash receptacle. "Stupid Barney Fife cop," he muttered, storming off in one direction as Peg stormed—albeit much slower—the opposite direction muttering her own opinions about the situation.

"Should've gotten at least five years in the slammer."

———— ♥ ————

It wasn't hard to keep tabs on Steve after he left the flea market. All Henry had to do was follow the trail of offended faces Steve left in his wake. "Where's the library? Tell me. Now."

"It's closed for the Fourth of July," five people told him—much to Henry's amusement—before Steve must have figured out he needed a different approach. Something with less barking perhaps.

"Excuse me," Steve said to a young woman pushing a stroller. Henry didn't recognize her. She could be visiting relatives in town, here for the festivities. "I'm looking for the medical tent."

She shrugged. "Sorry, I don't know where—"

"The car show then," Steve cut in, his raised tone suggesting he was already losing patience. "Do you know that? Does anybody in this town know anything?"

"I saw a bunch of cars a couple of blocks over."

"Wonderful." Steve shoved past her and kept walking—staggering? Henry wasn't sure what to call Steve's current mode of transportation. But somehow, even with all the teetering, it carried him two blocks farther to where rows of classic cars lined both sides of Main Street.

Any other time, Henry would have admired the collection. Right now all Henry admired was the way Steve managed to see everything in the world but the banner at the end of the road that read *Medical Tent* in giant bold letters.

"Can either of you tell me where to find the medical tent?" Steve said to a couple of old-timers peering inside a 1950s Porsche. One was short and squat, the other tall and slender.

Henry found a shady spot beneath one of the store awnings and leaned against the brick building, almost feeling sorry for Steve. The guy couldn't have found two people less likely to give him a straight answer. They were Westshire's very own Abbott and Costello. Now that Henry thought about it, he wasn't sure anybody called them by their real names anymore.

They must not have heard Steve over their whistling sounds of admiration for the Porsche. "Yes siree. That is a cherry. An absolute cherry," the shorter of the two, Costello, said. "I tell you it could make a man's heart nearly stop."

"You can say that again," Abbott replied.

"I tell you it could make a man's heart nearly stop."

"Saw that one coming."

"Hey—" Steve raised his voice, finally getting their attention—"I need you to point me to the medical tent."

"See, what did I tell you?" Costello elbowed Abbott in the ribs. "He feels the same way."

"As he should." Abbott pointed to the car. "Did you know this is the same model James Dean was driving when he crashed and died?"

"Oh, that was heartbreaking." Costello removed his green John Deere hat and covered his heart. "I'll never forget what a tragedy that was. Such a beautiful car."

Abbott groaned. He wasn't the only one. Though Steve's groan held more of a growl. "The medical tent?"

"Now you want to speak about a real tragedy," Abbott said, ignoring Steve. "Jayne Mansfield."

"Oh." Costello made the sign of the cross. "You're right. That was a tragedy. No joking about that."

"Or Grace Kelly."

"Oh, Grace. Beautiful Grace. Who could ever forget her in *Rear Window*?"

"Or Jimmy Stewart."

"Yeah. Wait. What?" Costello smacked Abbott with his hat. "Jimmy Stewart didn't die in a car crash."

"I didn't say Jimmy Stewart died in a car crash."

"Well, then why did you say 'Jimmy Stewart'? We were talking about actors who died in car crashes."

"We were. Then we started talking about *Rear Window*. Jimmy Stewart's in *Rear Window*."

"So what if he's in *Rear Window*? Everybody knows he's in *Rear Window*. But do you know how many combat missions he flew during World War II? Eh?" Costello replaced his hat and made a show of straightening it just so. "Bet you don't know that one."

"Why would I know that one? You'd have to be a weirdo to know that one."

"Twenty."

"My point exactly."

Steve pounded his fist on the hood of the car. "The medical tent! Where is it?"

Both men stopped talking and stared at Steve. Stared at his fist. The hood. Steve again. "You feeling all right, buddy?" Abbott asked. "You're looking a little peaked. Doesn't he look a little peaked?"

"Definitely peaked," Costello said. "You ask me, he should go to the medical tent."

Abbott pointed down the street. "Head that way, pal. Henry's girl will fix you right up."

"Edith," Steve said, the name barely making it past his ground jaw. "Her name is Edith Sherman. And she's not *Henry's girl*. She's my sister-in—"

"Well, hey, hey! Why didn't you say so in the first place?"

"How about that?" Both men spoke over each other, shaking his hand.

"I didn't know Edith had family in town."

"Isn't that wonderful?"

"That's wonderful."

"Your sister's quite a dancer."

"And a real beaut."

"Speaking of beauts . . ."

They returned their attention to the classic cars.

All right. Looked like this show was over. Henry pressed away from the brick storefront, ready to confront Steve and find out what he wanted from Edith. But a hand latched on to his wrist.

"There you are," Peg said. "We have an emergency. Here."

She shoved a paintbrush dripping with white paint into his hand. "Go fix it. Now."

"Fix what?"

"The sign at the edge of town that says 'Welcome to Westshire.' One of the O'Reilly boys got to it, so now it says 'Welcome to *Worst*shire.' And I'm not even going to say what the little potty mouth did to the sign advertising the fireworks tonight."

Knowing Peg's definition of "potty mouth" and the O'Reilly boys' affinity for bathroom humor, Henry had a fairly good idea what sort of explosions were being advertised on that sign. He glanced to where Steve ambled down the sidewalk toward the medical tent. "Thing is, I'm kind of busy at the moment."

"Doing what? Holding up the wall? This will only take a minute. Besides, this festival brings in tons of outside visitors. You want us to be the laughingstock of the entire county? Go. Fix it. Be the town hero."

Paint dripped down his pants and pooled on his shoes. Sure, because this was what a town hero looked like.

CHAPTER SEVENTEEN

Edith lifted her hair away from the back of her neck, aiming the little handheld fan over her skin for a minute before dropping her hair. Sweet mercy. Sharon hadn't been kidding when she said today was going to be a scorcher.

Edith shoved the fan under her shirt. Barely ten in the morning and her bra was soaked in sweat. Lovely. It would be a miracle if she didn't send anybody into the emergency department for heatstroke. Other than bandaging up one scraped elbow and passing out several notepads with the crisis center nursery address at the top, the morning had been uneventful.

"Edith."

Ugh. Uneventful until now. Edith turned off the fan. "Steve." She twisted round to face him. "Steve," she said again with a gasp. "You look awful. What's wrong with you?"

Sweat poured down his flushed face, his hair sat plastered to his forehead like a wet mop, and his eyes blinked without focus. "What's wrong with me? What's wrong with *you*?" He pressed his palms flat on the table and leaned forward. "What kind of game are you playing? You don't belong here. This town, these people . . . c'mon. Get real. Who are you kidding?"

Edith plunked the fan on the table and lifted a shoulder. "Who says I'm kidding anybody?"

He straightened, leaving behind two sweaty palm prints. "Henry. If that's not a joke, I don't know what is." He wiped his shirtsleeve across his forehead, for all the good it did. Sweat dripped off his face onto the table. "Brian may be gone, but you're still a Sherman. It's time to come back home and act like it."

"Act like I don't matter again? No. Your family doesn't need me. They never did. You shouldn't have come here." Edith reached down to a cooler filled with ice and water bottles. She yanked one out, twisted the cap off, and thrust it at Steve. "And for crying out loud, drink some water before you keel over. You cannot survive on orange soda when the heat index is over a hundred."

"My parents miss you."

She snorted. "Right. I'm sure they're beside themselves in grief." The heat must be getting to Steve if he thought Edith was going to buy that for a second. "Your parents made it pretty clear how they felt about me. Take this." She jiggled the water bottle.

He pushed it away. "They weren't happy you guys eloped straight out of high school. It wasn't personal against you."

"Really? Because it felt personal. In fact, the words they said to me after the funeral felt very personal."

"Their son had just died. Cut them some slack."

She chucked the bottle back into the cooler. "What about before their son died, then, huh?"

"What are you talking about? My parents were great to you. They paid for half of Brian's law degree."

"They coerced him into giving up the future we had planned by paying for half of Brian's law degree. He didn't even want to be a lawyer. At least not right away. We were going to join the Peace Corps together. We were going to travel to South Africa together. We were—"

"Stop." Steve held up a hand. Swayed a little. "It doesn't matter. The past is in the past. Just come home. We can . . . we can . . ." His sways grew more pronounced. Like he was standing on the deck of a ship in turbulent seas.

"Steve? Oh, sheesh." He was going down. Edith lunged across the table to grab hold of his shirt. If she could maybe guide his torso onto the table . . . He staggered a step back. She missed. He collapsed.

"Perfect," Edith muttered as she hopped over the table and crouched down next to him. His color looked worse, the flush in his cheeks replaced by a gray pallor. And he'd smacked his head. A tiny pool of blood leaked from the back of his scalp. "Great."

At least he had a pulse and was breathing. It could be worse. Like he could still be standing and talking.

Oh, she was terrible. Edith reached for her back pocket to grab her phone and call 911. Except she didn't have her phone. Now she really was terrible. She'd left it charging at the house this morning. What kind of medical tent worker did that? One who clearly wasn't planning on needing it.

"Hey." Edith waved her hands back and forth over her head and yelled toward a group of men at the car show.

A couple lifted their hands and waved back. Then returned to looking at the cars.

"Ohhh," a woman's voice, filled with delight, sounded behind Edith. It was Julie, the owner of the coffee shop and bakery. She wore a hat with an attached fan on the brim. "Sharon had said you were going to be doing some rescue demonstrations. I'm glad I didn't miss it."

"This isn't—" Edith tried saying, but Julie's shouts drowned her out.

"Hey, everybody! Get over here if you want to see Edith show us how to save a life!"

"Oh, is it starting already?" A group of women nearby started clucking and shooing each other over to Edith's medical tent. "I didn't think that was until later this afternoon."

"It's not until later this afternoon," Edith said, but a sharp whistle pierced through her words. Julie again. She kept whistling and shouting while Edith kept saying, "You guys, this isn't pretend. It's real. We need to call 911."

"Don't start yet," Julie scolded. "A few more are still coming. Hustle up, boys. Hustle up."

"This is what *hustling up* looks like when you're ancient, don't you know." A group of men from the car show made it to the gathering crowd circled around Steve's body. "Well, hey, look who it is," the shorter of the men said, elbowing a tall, slender man next to him. "Edith's brother."

"That's your brother?" Julie said to Edith, then looked at

the women around her. "I didn't know that. Did you know that?"

"No. Listen. He's not my brother."

"Of course he's not her brother," the tall, slender man said with a wink. "Now let her stay in character so she can continue the performance."

"This isn't a performance," Edith said.

"Sorry. I meant the demonstration." The tall man nudged the squat man next to him. "She's really getting into this, isn't she?"

Steve moaned and everybody started shushing each other. "Ooh, quiet. Shh-shh. It's starting."

"What's starting?" Henry appeared, slightly winded, at the edge of the crowd. He was holding a paint bucket and paintbrush, and the front of his pants was covered in white paint. He dropped the bucket when he noticed Steve on the ground. "Is he okay?"

"No," Edith said. Finally. Someone who would listen to her. "Will you please call 911?"

Henry pulled out his phone.

"I didn't know this was audience participation," a voice murmured.

"How fun," a woman responded. "Kind of like that murder dinner theater last spring. Remember that? I solved the case. Remember that?"

Steve's eyes fluttered and another moan slid out of him. "It's okay, Steve," Edith told him. She ripped open a gauze bandage from the first aid kit and pressed it to his head. He groaned.

"Do we need to shock his heart?" the tall, slender man asked. "I had that done to me once. Whoa, Nelly, felt just like getting kicked in the chest by a horse. And I would know. Had that done to me once too."

"You sure that horse kicked you in the chest and not the head?"

Some people laughed. Julie flapped her hands at them to be quiet. "You're going to distract Henry from his lines."

Henry ignored them, giving the location to the 911 dispatcher. "Downtown. Corner of First and Main. Yeah, he's breathing. He's moving. Looks like he might be starting to come around now."

Oh, he was coming around, all right. Edith struggled to hold him in place. If he tried to stand, he would most likely pass out again. "Nice and easy, Steve. Take a moment to get your bearings."

He sat up, pushing Edith away from him.

"Did I miss the part where she performed CPR?" a woman asked.

"Steve. Listen to me—"

"Ambulance is on the way," Henry said, crouching awkwardly next to Edith with his bad leg stretched to the side. He grabbed Steve by the shoulders. "Take it easy, pal."

Steve's eyes locked on Henry's. "You." He growled and started struggling against him. "You can't have her."

"What did he say?" an old man asked.

"He said, 'You can't have her,'" the tall man said, imitating Steve's growl.

"Can't have who?"

"Edith."

"Why can't Henry have Edith? I thought they were already together."

The short, squat man stepped forward, using a corn dog to point back and forth between Henry and Steve as they struggled against each other on the pavement. "Yeah, but see, Steve's her brother. And he's always been real protective, see."

"Oh yes." The woman who had bragged about solving the murder dinner theater jumped forward. "Ever since their parents died of the consumption, it's just been the two of them. Orphans. They used to survive by hiding on trains." She snapped her fingers. "With the circus! They traveled with the circus!"

"You guys," Edith said, pointing to Henry and Steve. "Do you not see what's happening here?" Steve and Henry were latched on to one another in a weird sort of battle that mainly involved lots of rolling and grunting.

The crowd backed up to give them more space. "Remember when the circus came through here years ago? I was probably no more than five."

Edith inhaled a deep breath and released it. Where was the ambulance? Any longer and Henry was going to need it too. She spotted a police officer. He thankfully noticed the commotion. His footsteps faltered for a second, as if not sure what he was seeing, before taking off toward them at a run.

"What's going on?" he demanded as he parted the crowd.

"Oh, neat. James is in on this too." Julie clapped her hands. "Sharon has really outdone herself this year."

"Hey, break it up, break it up." The officer crouched down, trying to separate Henry from Steve. "What's the meaning of this?" When he got a look at Steve, he grabbed him by the shirt. "I should have known I hadn't seen the last of you." He hauled Steve to his feet.

"Let go of me. I haven't done anything." Steve staggered and took a swing at the officer.

The women in the crowd gasped. "Arrest him," someone shouted.

"Taser him," Julie shouted.

"This is better than Netflix," a boy slurping on a snow cone said.

The sound of sirens grew closer. "Think they'll let us push any buttons? Maybe lie down on the gurney? That might be fun," Julie said.

Edith knelt next to Henry. He was still sitting on the pavement, his bad leg straight in front of him, the other bent with his arms propped against it. A frown and a few scrapes spotted his handsome face. "Are you okay?"

"I'm fine."

"Are you sure? Do you need help getting up?"

Two EMTs nudged her aside. She recognized the man from her first night at the diner. "We'll take it from here," his partner, a female paramedic with a tight bun, said. "Are you in pain?" She wrapped a blood pressure cuff around his left arm.

"I'm not—"

"Quiet," she said, wearing a stethoscope and pumping up the cuff on his arm.

The EMT on the other side, Frank if she remembered correctly, held up two fingers in front of Henry's face. "How many fingers do you see?"

"Two. But I'm not the one who—"

"Quiet," the woman said again.

Henry glanced at Edith before dropping his gaze and

shaking his head. Was he mad? Well, why wouldn't he be? "Excuse me," Edith said, tapping Frank on the shoulder. "He's not the one we called an ambulance for."

"You sure? He looks a little rough. I'm not sure all that paint is going to come out of his pants either."

Air deflated from the blood pressure cuff. "Blood pressure's high."

Yeah, Edith imagined hers was a little on the high side too. "That's the man we called an ambulance for." She pointed at Steve, who continued to dodge and weave around the officer with about as much stealth as an inebriated boxer.

"I have rights," Steve said, his speech slurred.

"Yes, you do. They're called the Miranda rights. And I'm going to state them to you right now." The crowd applauded when the officer pulled out his handcuffs.

"You try to handcuff me and I will end you." Steve lunged forward, taking another swing and missing by several feet.

"Taser him! Taser him!" voices shouted.

Steve's body suddenly grew rigid, his eyes rolling backwards—the crowd gasped—and he thumped to the ground. The paramedics heaved Steve onto the stretcher and loaded him into the back of the ambulance to thunderous applause.

"Great show. That was almost better than the circus," one man said.

"Sharon ought to make that an annual event," Julie said, nodding her head in agreement before waving over her shoulder and leaving.

The rest of the onlookers started to disperse as well. The two men from the car show walked past Edith on their way back to the cars. "Your brother is quite the actor, isn't he?"

the shorter man said. "The way he transformed his face. Amazing. Almost like he really did get Tasered. Wow. Good stuff."

"I'll say," the taller man responded. "He almost reminded me a little of Steve McQueen. Now that guy—*he* was quite the actor."

"Remember *Bullitt*? That 1968 Ford Mustang?"

"Only every time I close my eyes." They tapped the brims of their hats. Edith gave a half-hearted wave back, watching them disappear down the road.

What just happened?

"This town, Henry, I tell you, it grows more and more—" Edith spun in a circle. "Henry?" The medical tent sat empty. His paint bucket and brushes abandoned. Where did he go? He wouldn't just leave like that, would he? Without saying something?

Edith stepped back beneath the tent and picked up the fan. Blew it against her face.

This town grew more and more *what*, she didn't know. Or maybe she didn't want to put a name to it. Like she didn't want to put a name to her feelings toward Henry. It shouldn't matter if he had left. She was leaving him, leaving this town, soon enough anyway. It didn't matter.

So why was there an ache in her chest telling her it did?

CHAPTER EIGHTEEN

The familiar sound of IV pumps beeping and monitors alarming greeted Edith at the entrance to the ICU. Which room was it again? 203? She peeked past the curtain to room 203 and, finding Steve, slipped into his room.

With his color back to normal, his long sandy eyelashes resting peacefully against his cheeks, he looked more like the innocent boy she remembered back in high school.

Okay, maybe not innocent. He was a Sherman after all. Maybe more like good-natured. At the very least, a far cry from the sweaty beast taking punches at an officer yesterday afternoon. Edith looked down at the restraints circling his wrists, attached to the bed frame. Another one was strapped to his right ankle.

"Good gravy, Steve. What kind of mess have you gotten yourself into?"

His chest rose in a steady rhythm, in sync with the ventilator. According to the nurse she spoke to over the phone, they'd had no choice but to sedate and intubate him when he came into the emergency department like a rabid lunatic.

Overnight, he'd had another savage episode. But apparently he'd also passed a kidney stone large enough to warrant a birth announcement in the local paper, so no wonder he'd looked awful this past week and had been behaving like a wild man. The smack on the head didn't help matters either. But thankfully it was only a superficial laceration. They were able to close it with a few staples.

Hopefully today would be a better day. And hopefully Edith was nowhere nearby when they took off his sedation to get him off the ventilator in case today wasn't a better day.

"Excuse me." The officer from yesterday—James, was it?—stepped into the room. Yes. James. Edith could see his name embroidered on his uniform. Embroidered? She glanced again. Definitely embroidered. With white daisies serving as bookends.

"I know." He sighed, dipping his chin to follow her gaze. "My mom thought if any criminals saw a mother's touch on my uniform, they might be less inclined to shoot me." He shrugged. "The things we do for family, even when it doesn't make a lick of sense."

His gaze settled on Steve. Edith stepped back to give James room for what he needed to do. Was this where he formally charged Steve for . . . ? Well, whatever Steve was getting charged for. Assaulting a police officer, disturbing the peace. Edith had even heard some rumblings around town about some serious littering charges.

"I'm dropping all charges," James said.

"I understand." Edith's head popped up. "Wait, what? Why?"

"Because we do things for family. Even when it doesn't make a lick of sense."

"I still don't understand."

"My mom thinks the world of you. Sharon," he added when Edith continued to stare at him.

"Sharon's your mom?" Of course. Now Edith could see the resemblance. But that still didn't explain anything.

"Considering all you've done to help out at the crisis nursery home and considering your brother didn't really hurt anyone—other than himself—my mom begged me to let it go."

"I'm sorry, but did you just say my brother?" Edith held up a palm. "Right. Okay. About that."

A knock interrupted them, and a young blonde-haired woman wearing large black-framed glasses and a nice pantsuit popped her head past the curtain. "Sorry to interrupt, but are you Edith Sherman?"

Edith nodded.

"Perfect. I'm Suzy, the social worker. Steve kept screaming your name before he got intubated yesterday, so I feel like I know you already. Do you mind if I ask you a few questions about your brother? And is it okay if we appoint you as his surrogate and decision maker?"

"Yes." Edith did mind.

"Great!" Suzy's phone started ringing. "Sorry." She dug it

out of her pocket. Held up a finger. "That was mostly all I needed for now. This is Suzy," she said, turning and walking away from the room.

Edith started to follow her, then spun back to James. "Why do I feel like she just appointed me to be his surrogate?"

"Probably because you just agreed to be his surrogate."

"No, I said yes. But I didn't mean yes. I said yes, meaning yes, I mind, which is way different than *yes*."

"Riiight." The walkie-talkie clipped to James's shoulder squawked with static.

"We've got a reported burglary call coming from Alice Murphy's house," a woman's voice said. "Based on the description, I'm fairly certain her husband just forgot his keys and is trying to get in the back door again."

James sighed. "I'm on my way." He nodded goodbye to Edith and disappeared out of Steve's room.

Edith longed to do a disappearing act of her own. Or better yet, make Steve disappear. He was not her problem. Wait. He *wasn't* her problem. What was she even doing here? And why didn't she think to give anybody his parents' number yesterday? Maybe the heat had gotten to her more than she realized.

Edith dug out her phone and searched her contacts. Thankfully she'd never deleted his mom's phone number. She'd certainly deleted his dad's after that last conversation they had at the funeral. Ah, here it was. She wrote down his mom's number beneath the word *SURROGATE* in all caps, then slid it to the social worker, still on her phone next to the nurses' station, and sprinted for the exit.

"Good luck, Steve," Edith muttered. "And good riddance."

———— ♥ ————

Outside the hospital and halfway across the street to the visitor parking lot, Edith's phone rang. Good gravy, if it was already the social worker trying to dispute Edith passing the buck on the whole surrogacy issue . . . "Hello?"

"You sound out of breath. Did I call at a bad time?"

It didn't sound like the social worker. But it also didn't sound like anybody Edith knew. A car tooted its horn to suggest Edith should ponder the identity somewhere other than the middle of the road.

"I'm sorry—who is this?" Edith waved an apology to the driver and scurried out of the way.

Her sandaled foot tripped on the curb just as the woman responded, "Kaya Reddy."

"Argh," Edith growled, clutching her big toe.

"This is a bad time."

"No. No, this is a great time. Hi, Kaya. I'm so happy to hear from you." Now she recognized the accented voice. Kaya was Ithemba's operational manager.

"Are you in labor? I can call back."

Edith huffed out a laugh, realizing yes, she might have started some purse-lipped breathing as she hobbled to an iron bench surrounded by a commemorative plaque and a small garden of flowers. "I'm fine," Edith said, massaging her foot. "I just stubbed my toe and wanted to die for a couple seconds, but the will to live is already back in full force."

Now it was Kaya's turn to laugh. "What a relief," she said in her South African accent, which always sounded to Edith's untrained ear somewhere between British and Australian.

"We hate it when our volunteers lose the will to live before they even get here."

"Yeah, I can see how that might be bad for morale." Now that the pain in her toe had ebbed to a dull throb, Edith lowered her foot to the ground. "So what's going on?"

"Mostly just checking in. Making sure you haven't changed your mind," she said, a soft tease in her voice.

"I assure you I have not changed my mind."

"Still no word on the passport?"

"Nothing yet. But a friend is supposed to forward it to me as soon as it arrives. Trust me, as soon as it is in my hands, I'm on my way. I'm not exaggerating when I say I'm so excited to volunteer for your organization I could scream."

Edith leaned back before remembering the bench didn't have a backrest. "Ahhh!" She toppled off backwards, landing in a patch of coneflowers and black-eyed Susans. Then screamed again when a bee tried flying into her ear.

"My goodness, you are excited, aren't you?" Kaya chuckled. "I just hope you maintain that same level of enthusiasm after you see your living accommodations. That will probably make you scream too. Especially if you don't like cockroaches. Are you still planning to stay more than three months?"

Edith crawled out of the flowers and staggered to a standing position several feet away, brushing the dirt off her rear end and praying nobody had witnessed her acrobatics off the bench. But based on the random applause from across the street and the "Way to stick the landing!" shout, she reckoned somebody had.

"Edith? Hello? Are you still there?"

"Yes. Sorry. Cockroaches. Three months. Wait, what? *Cockroaches?*"

"Can I take that as a no to staying longer than three months?"

"No. Yes. No. I mean, I want to stay longer. As long as I can. Years, even. Definitely more than three months. That's still my plan." Henry's handsome face and gorgeous blue eyes flashed in front of her vision. It was still the plan, right? She squeezed her eyes shut. "It is still the plan," she repeated, this time for her own benefit.

"Wonderful. Between you and me, sometimes it's not worth the effort to train volunteers when they're only going to be here a short while, but if you're willing to commit to *years*, then goodness. That really opens up some exciting possibilities. But we'll see how it goes after you get here. One day at a time, right?"

"Right. One day at a time." An ambulance drove past, lights flashing and siren blaring. Edith pressed a finger to her other ear.

By the time the ambulance rounded the corner toward the emergency department in the back, Kaya was saying her goodbyes. "We'll talk more later. My three children are excited to meet you by the way. They love visitors. We all do. No matter how long you stay, it'll be great."

It would be. So great. Edith dropped her phone in her purse, a heavy weight settling on her shoulders. So why didn't it feel great?

Edith glanced back at the hospital. Steve. That's why.

How could it feel great until she resolved things with him? It had nothing to do with Henry. Nothing to do with the fact he'd been avoiding her since yesterday. Nothing to do with the fact that she missed him and it had only been twenty-four hours and they lived in the same house, which made her wonder how much it would kill her when she hadn't seen him for over a year and they lived in different countries.

Yep, definitely nothing to do with that.

Shaking her head, Edith crossed the parking lot to her rental car. Maybe she was tired. Everyone had trouble feeling excited and great when they were tired.

She just needed a nap. That's all. Then she'd be ready for another night at the crisis house. And by the end of summer, ready to dive into the next chapter of her life.

Alone.

CHAPTER NINETEEN

The lavender twilight that had filled the sky past his office window earlier gave way to a deep indigo by the time Henry pulled into his driveway. None of the appointments today had gone as he hoped. The historical society was still hemming and hawing, not willing to commit, and the Realtor was even less promising. *We can fill out the paperwork with your new offer, but frankly, I think it's going to end up being a waste of time. That land isn't selling.*

"One victory, God. That's all I'm asking for." Something to prove he wouldn't forever be known as the guy who dropped the ball. Something to prove he could be the hero for once. Something to give Edith a reason to stay.

Henry turned off the engine and scrubbed his palms up and down his face. Probably seeing him roll around on the ground yesterday, unable to hold his own, wasn't that *something*. His knee might have been spared from getting reinjured, but his pride . . . yeah, that had taken quite the hit.

He grabbed a pile of folders and rolled-up diagrams from the passenger seat and let himself in the back door to his kitchen. The sound of voices from the living room and the smell of popcorn drew him up short.

The voices paused and a moment later Edith peeked around the corner. "Hey," she said. "I just popped some popcorn and started a movie. You want to join me?" She leaned against the doorframe in a pair of gray sweats and a black Pittsburgh Pirates T-shirt.

Henry drank in the sight of her like a dehydrated marathon runner who'd just found the last Gatorade bottle. When he continued to stare, Edith raised her eyebrows and straightened. "Henry?"

"Sorry." Henry dropped his armload onto the kitchen island. "You caught me off guard. I thought you were working tonight." *And planning to avoid me for the rest of your life.*

Okay, so maybe he'd technically been the one avoiding her. But only so he could avoid the fact she might be avoiding him since he looked like such an idiot yesterday.

He stepped to the refrigerator and pulled out a pitcher of iced tea, working hard to act normal when the inside of him was dancing like Snoopy in a Charlie Brown cartoon. "So you're not going in tonight, I take it?"

"Sharon called a little bit ago and said there was a mix-up with the schedules, so she didn't need me tonight. I just wish I'd known sooner so I wouldn't have slept all afternoon. Now

I'm going to be up half the night." She shrugged. "Basically have no choice but to watch movies and eat popcorn."

"I can see how your hands are tied."

She smiled, chewing on her lower lip as she played with the hem of her shirt. Henry spun away from her and drained his glass dry. Did she have any idea what she did to him? He dumped the cubes into the sink. "So how's—?"

"Join me."

They spoke at the same time. Henry had been about to ask about Steve, but he liked Edith's train of thought much better. "If you want," she rushed on when Henry didn't answer right away. "You don't have to. You're probably tired. Never mind. I get it if you—"

"What movie are we watching first?"

Her mouth relaxed in a smile. *The Long, Hot Summer.* At Henry's questioning look, Edith pretended to be in shock. "Paul Newman, Joanne Woodward, Orson Welles, Angela Lansbury." With each name spoken, the tone of her voice became more incredulous. "You've never seen it?"

"Never seen it? I've never heard of it."

Edith gasped and clutched her heart. "Well, sir, that changes tonight. Get your leisure pants on and meet me in the living room. I won't take no for an answer."

Henry was bone-tired. He hadn't had more than four hours of sleep any night this week. When he'd left work a little while ago, the only thing on his mind this Friday night was to get to his bed as fast as his weary legs would carry him and not wake up until sometime Sunday afternoon.

So when ten minutes later he found himself reclining on the couch—his leisure-clad legs resting on the coffee table, a bowl of popcorn resting on his stomach, and a beautiful woman resting at his side—he could only figure one thing.

He was falling hard and falling fast. And he didn't want it to ever end. Somehow he needed to convince Edith to shorten her stay in South Africa. And more importantly, convince her he was a man worth coming home to.

CHAPTER TWENTY

Edith lost Henry long before the opening song of *West Side Story* finished. To his credit, he had made it through all of *The Long, Hot Summer*. Probably because she forced him to eat another bowl of popcorn whenever he looked ready to fade. But it didn't look like popcorn or even the thrill of seeing Goldie Hawn in *Overboard* after this movie finished was going to stir him awake.

Edith moved the empty bowl from his lap and took in the severe angle of his neck on the back of the couch. No way that was comfortable.

"Henry," she whispered. When he didn't so much as stir, she rubbed a gentle hand along his upper arm. "Oh, Henry," she tried again in a lilting voice.

He inhaled a deep breath and shifted his head but settled

back into sleep. The light from the TV reflected across his features and Edith placed a hand over her mouth to stifle a giggle. With his dark hair tussled, his lips slightly parted, and a soft whistle coming from his nose with every exhale, she could easily imagine what he must have looked like as a young boy.

However, as her eyes lingered over the strong curve of his jaw to the steady planes of his cheeks, and with his bicep warm beneath her hand and his masculine woodsy scent enticing her closer, she was acutely aware how far Henry was from being a young boy. Underneath the innocent vulnerability of sleep, was a living, breathing man. A very appealing one at that.

Edith yanked her hand back from his arm. She scooted away on the couch and swung her eyes back to the TV, trying to shift her thoughts away from Henry and back to Tony.

He sang about something great coming. Edith rolled her eyes. "Sure, Tony. Something *real* great's coming for you." She shoved a handful of popcorn into her mouth. But as the man on the screen kept singing, Edith couldn't keep her eyes from peeking back to the man on the couch, before swinging back to Tony.

"I've spent all my life holding still," she mumbled around a mouthful of popcorn. "I'm tired of holding still, Tony. Don't you get that?"

"Is that a rhetorical question or do you expect Tony to answer?"

Henry's groggy voice startled Edith into flinging her bowl of popcorn from her lap. "You're awake!"

"Hard to sleep when the person next to you won't stop yammering," Henry said with a crooked grin.

"Well, it's hard to watch a movie when the person next to you won't stop snoring." Edith picked a piece of popcorn from her shirt and threw it at Henry.

"I don't snore. And that throw was terrible."

"Uh, pretty sure you do snore. Been listening to you whistle for the past twenty minutes." She threw another piece and it bounced off his shoulder. "Better?"

"What do you mean, whistle?"

"Like a grade-schooler playing the recorder." She sailed a piece past his left ear.

"Please tell me you never play darts for money. And everybody knows whistling is not snoring. Whistling is perfectly acceptable. Some might even call it manly."

Edith snorted, then clapped a hand against her mouth. Henry raised his eyebrows. "Did you just snort like a pig?"

"No," Edith said in indignation. "I guffawed—like a lady." They stared at each other for a beat before Edith burst into giggles and Henry was unable to stop a smile from taking over his entire face.

"And I'll have you know guffawing is perfectly acceptable. Some might even call it womanly." She set herself off into another fit of giggles.

"Wow. I'm starting to wonder which one of us here is actually the sleep-deprived one." Henry shook his head at Edith, though the corners of his lips and eyes betrayed his amusement.

Edith knew her face had probably turned as red as a ripe

tomato, the way it always did when she was laughing this hard. She fanned herself and turned her head to the side, finger combing her hair in an attempt to hide her face as she tried to regain some composure. It had been a long time since she had teased and laughed like this with anyone, especially a man. She and Brian hadn't had a lot to laugh about during their marriage.

Not sure now if her face was still warm from laughter or the sudden embarrassment in realizing how much Henry knew about her marriage, Edith continued to play with strands of her hair, desperate to look anywhere but at Henry. "Oh, hey, I've been meaning to tell you," Edith said, keeping her voice nonchalant. "Kat called."

When Henry didn't respond, Edith tossed him a glance. Any hints of amusement on his face had disappeared. "Uh, so yeah. She called just to say that her house is all squared away. I can move in anytime. So that's good news, right? Sleeping in your own bed again. Not having me underfoot anymore."

"What if I like having you underfoot?"

"Henry," Edith said with a soft laugh, trying to keep the mood light. But the longer he gazed at her, his blue eyes piercing her to the core, the less control Edith had of the mood or her emotions. "Henry," she whispered.

This wasn't going to end well for either of them. Didn't he see that? She was leaving. Soon. In a matter of weeks. Which didn't really explain why she was leaning toward him on the couch right now, did it? Focusing on his lips. Ignoring the warning bells going off in her head.

Warning bells.

"My phone." Edith jumped up from the couch. "Somebody's calling me. Upstairs. I hear it. Do you hear it? I hear it." She pointed at the ceiling. "I should go."

"Edith."

She paused at the bottom of the stairs, more winded than she ought to be for running all of six steps. "Yes?"

Henry held her phone up from where he remained seated on the couch.

"Oh." She waited for the smirk, the sarcastic remark, as she quietly slipped it out of his hand. What he did was a thousand times worse.

He turned his head and met her with those blasted blue eyes of his. "See you in the morning?" he asked, the quiet timbre of his voice tempting her back to the couch almost as much as the look in his eyes.

She took a step back, mumbling something like "Yeah. See. Morning. Night." Edith raced up the stairs, prepared to spend the rest of the night pretending to sleep, until her phone chimed with a voice mail alert. Whoops. She'd almost forgotten her phone really had been ringing. One glance at the caller ID and Edith's steps faltered on the top step.

Why was the hospital calling her?

CHAPTER TWENTY-ONE

"You're looking particularly chipper this morning." Julie beamed at Henry as she stood on her toes to hand him two coffees and a sack of scones over the top of the bakery counter. "I told Chester the first morning I saw you and that Edith-doll together, it was the start of something special."

Henry glanced at the black feline curled in his basket sound asleep. "Is that so?" He must be feeling chipper to encourage more of this conversation. Though he had to admit, after last night—watching movies with Edith, having her by his side, seeing her laugh, and yeah, almost kissing her again—he was feeling better than *chipper*. He was feeling like a man in love.

And apparently it showed all over his face. Julie couldn't stop smiling at him while shaking her head back and forth with both hands clasped over her heart. "I'm just so happy for you. She seems so sweet. And I know it's not—" she twisted her lips to the side and appeared to be searching the ceiling for the right word—"*ideal* to put the bed before the wed, but I know you'll do the right thing. I've been watching you for years, and you're not the type of man to take advantage of free milk without buying the cow."

Henry felt the eyes of every patron in the shop zero in on him. He recognized an elder from his church, his high school English teacher, the president of the historical society, among others. Even Chester's pale-green eyes blinked open, watching him with sudden interest.

"Um—" Henry would have tugged at his shirt collar if either of his hands were free. "I'm sorry. I think there's been a misunderstanding. Edith and I . . . we're not . . ."

"Together?" Julie asked with furrowed brows. "But I heard you the other day. You said you two were together. You *kissed* her. Even Chester saw that."

"Right. Yes. That . . . that did happen." Henry realized he hadn't paid yet. "Uh—" He set the cups and bag back on the counter, right now willing to leave everything, including his entire wallet, if it would keep Julie from talking any further. He lowered his voice. "We haven't really known each other all that long. She's only here for the summer."

Julie lowered her brows in confusion. "Oh. Then you're not living together?" She accepted the money from his outstretched hand and rang up the cash register, never taking her eyes off his face.

Henry wet his lips, then spent the next several seconds wobbling his head back and forth like a bobblehead doll while he attempted to motion yes and no at the same time. "Technically speaking, we have been living under the same roof. Yes. But nobody's been drinking any milk."

"Not even skim?"

Henry opened his mouth and closed it, not sure how to respond. Not even sure he should respond.

Julie shoved the cash register drawer closed and propped her elbows on the counter with her face resting between each palm. "Okay. I see. You're not one to kiss and tell. Very noble. But tell me this one. Do you love her?"

As tempted as Henry was to grab his coffee and scones and run away from this entire conversation, the open expression on Julie's face locked him in place. One quick glance around the shop and Henry might as well have been announcing game seven of the World Series, the way everybody leaned closer to listen.

Fine. If they were so interested to hear his answer, why keep it a secret? "Yes, if you must know. I think she's the most amazing, beautiful, kindhearted woman I've ever met. And yeah. I love her." He looked at the customers sipping on their coffees, now staring at him unabashedly. "I love her," he shouted, then laughed as a smattering of applause surrounded him.

"Good for you, Henry," someone shouted.

"She's a great dancer."

"And a good-looking cow," said another.

"Are we done now?" Henry asked, holding his arms out wide with the coffees and bag of scones in his hands. "Is the inquisition over?"

Julie giggled and wiped her hands on her apron. "I think

we've gotten enough out of you for one day. Tell Edith hi."
She aimed a wink at Henry. The menacing glare Henry aimed
back at her probably lost some of its effect sitting above the
goofy grin he was unable to hide.

When he got back to his house, Henry didn't imagine
Edith would be up yet, but he wanted to surprise her with
some scones just in case. He let himself in through the
kitchen door, humming "Tonight" from *West Side Story*.

Feeling like he'd already chugged his entire cup of coffee instead of the two sips he'd actually taken, Henry forced
himself to sit down at the kitchen island and get ahold of
himself. Now that he had declared his feelings for Edith in
front of a dozen town citizens, his body buzzed with anxious
energy over what to do next.

Hire a marching band. Form a parade. Start a conga line.
Beg her to stay.

Henry folded his hands together. Okay, maybe not
beg. He could do better than that. He just needed to find
the right words. Words like—"Whoa, where'd you come
from?"

Henry rose from his seat, expecting Edith to enter the
kitchen from the front, not slip in through the back door.
"I thought you were still upstairs sleeping." His smile faded
as he took in her puffy eyes and red-tipped nose. "What's
wrong?"

She offered him a wobbly smile, clicking the door shut
behind her. "What makes you think something's wrong?"

He was pretty sure it was a rhetorical question, and he
was even more sure the answer "Because you look awful" was
never the right thing to say to the woman you were trying

to win the heart of. So instead he said, "There's a scone and coffee for you if you want it," and sat back down.

"Thanks," Edith said in a subdued tone, edging further inside. "I have some good news."

He snapped his fingers. "I knew it. Soon as I saw you, I said to myself, now there's the look of a woman brimming with good news."

"Take it easy on me. I haven't slept yet."

A heavy tightness settled on his chest and made it hard to keep his voice light. "Must be some really good news then."

He grabbed her coffee cup, still hot beneath his fingers, and held it out to her. She moved closer, bringing a trace smell of her coconut scent along with her, and accepted the offer.

Up close, Henry could see faint shadows beneath her brown eyes. "On second thought, maybe you shouldn't be drinking coffee. Maybe you should just go to bed. Why haven't you slept? Did you go somewhere?" He hadn't heard her leave during the night.

"I drove to the hospital around four in the morning. Since then I've been walking and thinking." Edith pointed to the island. "I left you a note."

Sure enough, a folded slip of paper with *Henry* written on the outside stared back at him. "Is everything okay?" Stupid question. She wouldn't have gone to the hospital if everything was okay. She wouldn't have spent hours walking and thinking if everything was okay.

Something was wrong. Terribly wrong.

Edith lifted a shoulder and peered into the bag of scones. "Steve's gone."

Gone? Henry sank in his seat. He didn't know what to say. "I'm . . . I'm so sorry. Wow. I . . . Man. I never knew a kidney stone could be that serious."

Edith paused, one of her hands buried deep in the bag, as she closed her eyes in a slow blink, then broke off a piece of scone and tossed it at his head. "I said *gone*, not *dead*." But at least she was smiling. Which made him wonder why she had been crying before.

"So he's okay?" Henry reached for his coffee. He'd find the piece of scone that had sailed over his head later.

"Other than the fact he nearly splattered across the hospital parking lot last night, yeah, he's okay."

Henry sputtered on his coffee. "I'm sorry, what now?"

"They took him off the ventilator earlier in the day. Then I guess when Steve finally cleared up from all the pain medicine and sedation he'd been on and discovered his mom knew he was here in the hospital, he panicked and tried signing himself out against medical advice."

"Why would he panic?"

"Because apparently our boy Steve has a gambling addiction, and he recently sold a family heirloom to help dig himself out of a hole, thinking nobody would notice. Well, guess what, his mother noticed. And she's been trying to track him down ever since. Which is why he tracked me down."

Henry shook his head. "Because you have the heirloom?"

Now it was Edith's turn to sputter on her coffee. "No. Goodness, no. What would I want with a three-pound necklace inspired by the Atlantic puffin? Besides, I don't need a family heirloom. Before Brian died, he made sure I would be taken care of financially after he was gone. Which apparently Steve knew. Turns out, that's all he's ever been after. My money."

"He certainly had a funny way of going about it if that's all he was after."

"Steve has a funny way of going about a lot of things. Which is probably why he thought tying a bunch of bedsheets together and wrapping them around the toilet so he could climb out the window was a great escape plan when they refused to let him leave against medical advice without a ride."

"Please tell me you're joking."

"Believe me, after receiving phone calls all night from three nurses, two doctors, and one very irate engineer who informed me he was going to have to recaulk the toilet and spend the best years of his life sealing every window shut in the hospital now, I wish I was joking."

"Why did they call you?"

"Because they couldn't get ahold of his mother, and they still had my number listed as one of his emergency contacts. And I guess trying to climb out of a second-story window counts as an emergency in some hospitals. Go figure."

"So you drove to the hospital?"

"I did. I didn't know what I was going to do with him once I got there but turns out I didn't have to do anything. They hadn't been able to reach his mom because she was already on her way from Pittsburgh. She showed up approximately ten minutes before I did, read him the riot act, then dragged Steve out of the hospital by his ear. Literally. In fact several nurses made a point of letting me know his mother had *literally* dragged him out of the hospital by his ear. They seemed to take great pleasure in that."

"Kind of wish I'd seen it myself."

"Don't worry. I'm sure Peter, the engineer, won't mind reenacting it again. He actually plays the role of my former mother-in-law remarkably well."

"Wow. You had quite the night. All I did was sleep." Henry nudged the sack of scones across the table. "But hey, no matter how it happened, Steve's out of the picture. That deserves an extra scone for celebration, don't you think?"

She broke off another chunk of scone, adding it to the pile of crumbs she hadn't eaten from her first scone. "Exactly. Steve's out of the picture."

But she didn't look ready to celebrate. If anything, she looked ready to cry. Why . . . ? *Wait.* Henry sank back in his seat. With Steve out of the picture, what excuse did she have to stay with him? None. Not with Steve gone and Kat's house fixed.

Now Henry wanted to cry.

He stared at his coffee, searching for something to say. Something that wouldn't reveal his rising panic. The sort of panic that made tying bedsheets around a toilet and climbing out of a second-story window sound reasonable. "Are you sure Steve's gone?"

"I'm sure," Edith said in a quiet but brisk tone that warned him not to press. She ran her thumb along the edge of her coffee cup. "His mom called and left me a message. He won't be a problem anymore. At least not for me. I have a feeling Steve's always going to be a problem for someone." Her lips lifted in a half smile.

Henry's lips couldn't even manage a quarter of the distance. "Well, no one says you need to leave right away. You look exhausted. Why don't you get some sleep? We can talk about, you know, other stuff later. Much later. Just don't—" He clamped his mouth shut before he said *go*. What was his problem? Kat's house was only three blocks over. It wasn't like Edith was moving to the other side of the country.

No, that wasn't coming until the end of summer. When she moved to the other side of the world.

It was all Henry could do to squeeze air past his throat, especially when she said, "It won't take me long to pack. I might as well head over to Kat's soon as I finish. No point in staying here any longer."

"What about—?" Henry ran a palm over his mouth. "Dinner?" Surely that sounded less desperate than *us*. "There's no reason we can't still eat dinner. Together. Tonight." And the rest of the summer, maybe their lives.

"I don't think that's a good idea," Edith said.

"Why not? We both need to eat."

"I'm not talking about dinner." Edith set her coffee on the island, finally meeting his gaze. "Steve's gone. There's no need to keep pretending, so let's just stop pretending. *Henry.*"

He inhaled a slow breath. She knew. Of course she knew. She wasn't an idiot. He was the idiot. He blew out his breath. "Look, I know it was stupid. Me, pretending to be myself. I'm sorry. I shouldn't have—"

Edith held up a hand, bits of scone stuck to her fingers. "No need to apologize. We're good. Honest. In a way, it was fun. Pretending. But that's all it was, right?" She swiped her hands off with a napkin, then started backing out of the kitchen.

"Right." *No.* He stood.

"I better pack and get over to Kat's. I told Sharon I could fill in for the evening shift. So I should try to catch some sleep. See you around, Henry."

"Sure." *Say something.* "See you around." *Something better than that.*

But she'd already fled up the stairs. Henry grabbed the kitchen island for support. Once he heard the bedroom door close upstairs, he bowed his head, no closer to finding the right words.

CHAPTER TWENTY-TWO

Seriously. How hard was it to find one poblano pepper? Edith pushed her cart down the produce aisle, past a stand of peaches, and sighed. Apparently hard. When one didn't know what a poblano pepper looked like, Edith might go so far as to say it was very hard.

She sighed again—something she couldn't seem to stop doing ever since moving out of Henry's house a little over a week ago.

Henry. Edith smashed her lips inward before the thought of him provoked another sigh. *Just focus on finding the pepper.*

A wooden crate filled with bell peppers caught her eye. Now those she recognized. Green, red, yellow, yep, uh-huh, familiar. She had to be getting close. "Poblano, poblano . . ."

Edith scanned the labels on the crates next to the bell peppers. "Aha. Finally."

Last one too. She pulled it out of the container and held it in front of her face with a frown. Kind of small, wasn't it? Maybe they had more in the back somewhere. Edith dropped the pepper into her cart.

Forget it. Last thing she wanted to do was talk to anybody. Not when her goal the rest of the summer was to lie low—a feat even more difficult to accomplish in this town than finding a poblano pepper. The sooner she got back to Kat's house, the better.

Edith pushed her cart to the checkout lane. Why she thought she needed a cart for one pepper, she didn't know. "Find everything okay?" the cashier asked.

Not really, but Edith kept that to herself and nodded as she handed him the pepper. The young man adjusted his glasses and turned the pepper over in his hand. "Um, do you happen to know what kind of pepper this is?"

"A poblano," Edith said, digging into her purse for her wallet.

"Poblano? Oh no, honey, sorry to tell you, but that's not a poblano pepper." A middle-aged woman with a tight brown perm pushed her cart into the checkout lane behind Edith and held her hands up about half a foot apart. "A poblano is like this. That—" she pointed to the pepper in the checkout boy's hands—"is a jalapeño."

"It is?" Edith looked at the pepper, her cheeks warming. Surely she knew what a jalapeño looked like. "The label said it was a poblano."

Perm Lady shook her head. "Oh no. No, no, no. Definitely a jalapeño."

The checkout boy pushed his glasses further up his nose and squinted at the screen, mumbling to himself. "Oh. There it is." He punched some buttons and *$3.99* appeared on a screen.

An older gray-haired man in the next checkout lane guffawed. "*Three-ninety-nine?* For one poblano pepper?"

"It's not a poblano. It's a jalapeño," Perm Lady quickly corrected him.

"Either way, she ought to get a whole bag of peppers for three-ninety-nine. That's highway robbery."

Edith chewed on her lip. Three-ninety-nine *was* an awful lot to pay for one little pepper. The checkout boy seemed to agree. He kept hitting more buttons.

"It's too light to weigh." Gabby appeared, wearing a name tag and a red polo shirt containing the grocery store's name on the front. She continued speaking to the checkout boy as she bagged the older man's groceries. "You'll have to get the manager to punch in the special code."

The manager? Great. Edith twisted her bangs. The line behind her grew longer.

"What's the holdup?" a man with a bushy mustache asked.

"She's paying three-ninety-nine for one poblano pepper," the older man said.

"*Jalapeño*," Perm Lady said with a huff.

"Sure it's not a serrano?" Mustache Man said, craning his neck to see.

The checkout boy shrugged. "We can try that." He punched

more buttons. The price jumped to six-ninety-nine and every-body groaned, including the checkout clerk from the next aisle.

"Let me handle it," she said, ambling over to Edith's lane and yanking the pepper out of the boy's hands. "All right. Now what kind of pepper did you say this was?"

A cacophony of voices responded with different answers.

"Oh, just give the lady the pepper for free," Mustache Man hollered.

"And get arrested?" the checkout clerk said.

"As if anyone's going to arrest you over a pepper," Mustache Man grumbled.

"He might." The clerk's gaze swung pointedly to the back of the line, where James, dressed in his police officer's uniform, stood holding a basket of apples and frozen meals.

Mustache Man pointed his finger at him. "You didn't hear anything."

"Here." Edith reached into her purse. "Let me just pay the three-ninety-nine." She'd pay *thirty-nine*-ninety-nine at this point just to get out of here. Maybe. If she had the money. Her fingers clawed at the bottom of the purse. *Oh no.* Where was her wallet? It should be here. Why wasn't it here? Did someone rob her? Someone must have robbed her. Where would someone have robbed her?

Anywhere. It could have been anywhere. That was the thing about small towns. They lured you into letting your guard down, then *boom!* Stole your wallet the first second you weren't looking.

Where was James? She needed to alert him.

"Aha!" the clerk shouted in victory. "I figured it out. Your total is twelve cents."

"Twelve cents?" Mustache Man yelled. "My ice cream is melting for twelve cents?"

"I still say it's too much." The older gray-haired man from the other checkout lane adjusted the bag of groceries in his arms. "Honey, next time you want a poblano pepper—"

"Jalapeño!"

"Serrano!"

"—come over to my house. My wife's got a garden in the backyard. I'll give you the address. You can pick out a whole bushel of peppers for free. She'll even throw in some grape tomatoes."

"Cherry tomatoes," Perm Lady said. "Not grape. Cherry."

"What's it matter what you call the tomatoes so long as they taste good?"

As they continued arguing, Edith leaned toward the checkout boy. "I have a bit of a problem." She blew her bangs to the side. "This is going to sound crazy, but I think I've been robbed."

"What's she saying?" Gladys drove her motorized wheelchair to the back of the line.

"Not sure. Something about a robbery," Mustache Man yelled. Edith was starting to get the feeling he didn't know how to speak in anything less than a shout.

"A robbery?" Gladys spun her chair in reverse and banged into a display of potato chips. "James, do something."

The police officer rescued a stand of candy from toppling over. "Like what, Gladys?"

"Arrest her. She's obviously trying to steal that cucumber."

The doors to the grocery store slid open. Edith's feet twitched. Forget the pepper. How fast could she make it out of the store? She shifted her weight that direction, only to see Henry enter. Her breath hitched as his eyes connected with hers and he drew up short. His blue eyes flickered with some sort of emotion—one she didn't have the heart to name—before transitioning to an emotion she had no trouble naming. Dismay. His eyes had locked onto the scene taking place around her.

"James, are you going to arrest her or not?" The freezer door rattled as Gladys kept smacking her wheelchair against it in an attempt to reverse.

"Gladys, I'm about to arrest you if you bang into one more thing."

The gray-haired man shoved his receipt in Edith's hands. "I drew a map to help you find the house. Just go on around to the back and pick whatever you want. Do you like zucchini?"

"What's it matter if she likes zucchini?" Perm Lady said, tossing her palms up. "I grow yellow squash."

"That's my wife, by the way," he said, pointing at Perm Lady. "We discovered we get along better when we shop separately."

"Everything okay?" Great. Now Henry had limped over, looking all concerned and wonderful in his paint-stained T-shirt and jeans.

Edith opened her purse. "Not really. I need twelve cents and I can't find my wallet."

"The one under your arm?" Henry asked.

Edith glanced down. Her wallet. Tucked in her armpit. Right where she'd placed it as soon as she entered the checkout lane. She released a long exhale. Henry had already dug change from his pocket and handed over a dime and nickel.

"Keep the change, ya filthy animal," he told the clerk with a horrible gangster accent.

The young clerk laughed and pointed at Henry. *"Home Alone.* Nice."

Nice? Hardly. It was awful. Edith's lips twitched, desperate to tell Henry so. Desperate to hear him laugh. To hear herself laugh. Which was why she needed to get away from him. How did that one proverb go? Too much laughter makes the heart . . . confused? Something like that. "Thanks," Edith mumbled and bolted for the door.

"Edith."

What now? Edith looked over her shoulder. Henry held up her pepper.

Could she drag this scene out any longer? She scurried back, not even bothering with the cart. "Thanks," she said again. His fingers grazed her palm as he handed the pepper over, sending a spark of energy up her arm and down to her belly. Whoops. She made the mistake of meeting his eyes.

Lord, why did you make one man so handsome? Couldn't you have sprinkled it out a little more among the general population? She swallowed. "I need to go. I'm making a stew. I just forgot the pepper. But now I've got the pepper, so I should really add it to the stew. It's supposed to simmer for several hours. I'd hate for it to . . . you know, not simmer." *Walk. Away.*

Henry nodded. "Nobody likes an unsimmered stew."

"It's the worst."

His eyes crinkled at the edges. "It was good seeing you again. We should—"

"Good seeing you too." Edith took a step back. They

shouldn't. Whatever it was he wanted to say, they shouldn't. "I better get back to the stew. Now that I've got my pepper."

"Of course." Henry motioned to the door. "Don't want to keep a good stew waiting. Especially on a stifling hot summer day."

"You wouldn't know a jalapeño if it bit you on the nose," Perm Lady interrupted them before Edith could respond. She elbowed Henry out of the way and yanked the pepper out of Edith's hand, still harping at her husband. "The only reason you don't recognize it is because it's not wrapped with bacon."

"I still say it's a serrano," a voice shouted from the checkout lane.

Perm Lady rolled her eyes and twisted back toward the checkout. "If it was a serrano, would I do this?" She popped the entire pepper into her mouth, held her palms out in a there-you-have-it motion.

Edith gasped. "I can't believe she just did that. That was the last pepper."

"I know." The gray-haired man shook his head in wonder. "Isn't she amazing? That's why I married her."

"I'm not so sure that was a good idea," Henry added.

"What, marrying her?" The man turned on Henry. "Hey, pal, what are you saying?"

"I was talking about eating the serrano," Henry said.

"Oh? Well, maybe you didn't hear what my wife said. It's a *jalapeño*."

"It's not," Perm Lady croaked. Her face had flushed bright red, sweat popping out on her forehead.

"Ma'am?" Edith stared at the woman's face. "Are you okay?"

She clutched Edith's arm, her eyes bulging. Her husband was too busy arguing with Henry to notice her face had transitioned past the shade of tomato, heading straight toward eggplant.

"Uh, you guys?" Edith said.

"Ha, ha, ha, ha—" The woman began panting worse than a woman in labor.

"Hey, I googled it. I know what it was now." Mr. Mustache held up his phone. "It's a ghost pepper."

A ghost pepper? Oh, dear.

He turned his phone sideways. "Or maybe a habanero. Kind of hard to tell."

Either way. "Can somebody grab some milk?" Edith hollered. "It's going to be okay, ma'am." Maybe. If this woman stopped cutting off the circulation in Edith's arm. "You guys? A little help."

"The only person allowed to say marrying my wife wasn't a good idea is me. Got it?"

Henry lifted his palms and took a step back, triggering the automatic doors to open. "I think marrying your wife is a wonderful idea."

"Oh, really. So now you're saying you've got a thing for my wife?" The doors continued closing and opening and closing behind them.

"I would never have a thing for your wife."

"Why not? Something wrong with my wife?"

"Her entire throat is on fire for starters," Edith shouted as the doors closed, both men now on the outside of the store.

"Did somebody say fire?" Gladys zoomed over in her electric wheelchair, stirring up a flurry of plastic grocery bags behind her. "Where's the fire? I don't see a fire. James, do something."

"I am." James jogged over, holding a gallon of milk and twisting off the cap. "Try this."

"An entire gallon?" someone murmured. "That seems a little overkill. Did anyone even see him pay for it?"

Perm Lady grabbed the gallon, tilted her head back, and dumped it over her open-mouthed face in front of all the gathering onlookers.

"Oh, my—"

"Cleanup in aisle five."

"I still don't see the fire."

"This exact same thing happened two weeks ago."

The woman guzzled, sputtered, and coughed her way through the gallon of milk as if she were waterboarding herself. Finally she allowed herself to come up for air. "Ahhh," she wheezed out. "Better . . . Much better . . . I think . . . I might . . . live."

A flash of red curls streaked past the window, past Henry and the woman's husband still arguing outside. The automatic doors opened a second later. "Here, let me through." Gabby, winded, elbowed her way next to Perm Lady. "I ran out to my car and grabbed this."

"Grabbed what?" Edith asked.

Gabby crouched down, hiked her arm back—

Edith should have known. "Gabby, don't—"

Too late. She stabbed Perm Lady's thigh with an EpiPen.

Perm Lady shrieked, looked down at her leg. Looked at Gabby. Looked at Edith. Then dropped the milk carton, her eyes rolling back, as she slumped to the ground.

Edith felt everyone's gaze immediately swivel her direction. She was a nurse, after all. So she did what any nurse would do in that situation. She said, "James, do something."

CHAPTER TWENTY-THREE

Knock, knock, knock. Ding-dong. Ding-dong. Knock, knock.

"I'm coming. I'm coming." Henry hobbled to the front door, his knee stiff from overworking it these past few days. Anything to keep his hands busy and his mind off Edith. Seeing her in the grocery store had only rekindled his desire to be with her.

Too bad, once again, he'd managed to look like a complete idiot. After Mr. Locke had finished poking Henry in the chest and berating him outside the grocery store for having the hots for his wife, Henry didn't even want to go back inside and face Edith. Was it too much to ask that just once he come across as a competent and respected man in this town?

Despite all that, part of him still hoped it was Edith at the door. Maybe Steve had shown up again. Maybe Edith needed Henry again. Maybe—

His hopes burst faster than air from a whoopee cushion once he opened the door and saw who it was. "Hey," Henry said, sagging against the doorframe.

"Really? That's the greeting I get?" Lance shoved past him into the foyer. "After I listened to you prattle on all crazy-like about your love life?"

"Sorry. It's been a busy couple of days. You want something—" Henry waved his hand toward the kitchen, where Lance had already disappeared—"to drink? Help yourself."

Henry closed the front door. By the time he entered the kitchen, Lance was already holding a shot glass with the words *Virginia Is for Lovers* written across it.

Henry sank onto one of the kitchen island stools and watched Lance toss the dark amber drink to the back of his throat, swallow, then slam the shot glass down. "Ah, that's good stuff."

"That's iced tea."

"Well, I've got to be at work in ten minutes. What did you expect me to drink? Whiskey?"

"It's seven thirty in the morning. How about some coffee?"

"In a shot glass?"

"In a mug."

Lance shook his head, pouring himself another shot of tea. He held it in front of his lips a long moment, staring over Henry's shoulder and out the window. "This isn't the kind of conversation men have over coffee mugs." He tossed his head back and slammed the shot glass down on the table.

"Would you stop doing that? You're going to break the glass."

"I'm in trouble, Henry."

"What kind of trouble?" Henry got up and grabbed a plastic cup from the cupboard, switched it out with the shot glass, then grabbed a coffee mug for himself. He still didn't care much for the taste of coffee, but he'd gotten into the habit of it while Edith was living here. He had yet to break it. Or any desire to break it.

"The worst kind of trouble there is. Woman trouble."

Henry grunted. "I'm probably the last person you should be coming to for advice then. Have you tried Crazy Al?" He popped a K-Cup into the new Keurig machine he'd bought a few days ago and punched the ten-ounce button as Lance continued talking.

"It's not that having a kid is a deal breaker. I like kids. I *love* kids. And her kid is great. But she should have told me about her kid before I led her to believe I was a world-class athlete, you know? And definitely before we started smooching. A man says things to a woman—things that might get construed the wrong way—when they've reached the smooching stage of their relationship, if you know what I'm saying. And I think you know what I'm saying."

"I have no idea what you're saying." Henry retrieved his mug and leaned against the counter, taking a small sip.

"Baseball, man. Baseball." Lance sloshed some tea into his plastic cup and drank it all down in one swallow. He slammed the cup down with a muted clink. "That sound is not nearly as satisfying as the shot glass."

"What are you talking about, baseball?"

"The woman I'm dating. Things are moving fast. Getting serious. Everything's perfect except for one major thing. She thinks I know everything there is to know about baseball."

"Why does she think that?"

"Because I told her I know everything there is to know about baseball."

"Why—?"

"We were smooching!"

Henry set his mug on the counter and rubbed his forehead. "So she thinks you know a lot about baseball. So what?"

"I don't know anything about baseball. I live and breathe basketball. But do you think her kid plays basketball? Noooo. Her kid plays baseball. And guess who's got a bad case of shingles? Yep. Her kid's baseball coach. So who do you think she volunteered to fill in for the coach in the meantime? Yep! *This guy!"*

Henry exchanged the plastic cup back for the shot glass and filled it with tea. Handed it to Lance. "Go ahead."

Lance tossed the tea to the back of his throat. "Aaahhhh," he said as if it burned all the way down to his stomach. Then he slammed the glass down with a loud thunk. "So I need you, man."

"Sure. I'll give you a few pointers."

"Pointers? No. I need *you.* Tonight. Five fifteen. Northeast field. Diamond three. Wear something blue. You owe me."

Henry sputtered a drink of coffee. "For what?" He grabbed a paper towel and dabbed the front of his shirt.

"For rehabilitating you. You'd be wheelchair-bound if it wasn't for me."

"I'm pretty sure the orthopedic surgeon played a minor role in that process."

"Yeah? Well, was it your orthopedic surgeon's front door you showed up to the other night ranting like a lunatic about old ladies and mystery ladies and bombshell ladies? No. It was mine. Because we're friends. And friends help coach their friend's girlfriend's daughter's Little League baseball teams."

"Daughter? This is a girl's league?"

"See you at five fifteen. Don't be late. My smooching lips are depending on you," Lance called over his shoulder on his way toward the front door.

"That's disturbing," Henry called back. "You're disturbing."

"So are you, Henry. That's why we're such good friends." The door slammed shut a second later.

Henry glanced at his watch. Looked at his coffee-splattered shirt. He had time to change, but he'd better be quick. He shook his head and dumped the rest of his coffee down the sink. And he supposed he'd better wear something blue.

Coaching girl's baseball had to be better than coming home to an empty house.

—————— ♥ ——————

"How do I look?" Lance asked out the side of his mouth as soon as Henry arrived at the ball diamond at 5:15 sharp. "Do I look like a baseball coach?"

Lance was wearing a green visor hat, a blue polo shirt, tight white baseball pants that stopped at his knees, and a pair of stirrup socks. He'd painted a black stripe beneath each eye and wore a whistle around his neck.

"Ready for the big leagues," Henry said.

"The coach sent me the starting lineup. But he didn't send any playbook."

"There's no playbook."

"But there's signs, right?" Lance tugged on his right earlobe. "Steal first." He tugged on his left earlobe. "Don't steal first." He jiggled both earlobes. "Follow your heart and steal first if that's what your heart is telling you."

"Okay." Henry shoved the whistle into Lance's mouth. "How about you blow on that and tell the girls to use the bathroom before the game starts. Pretty sure that's our number one concern at this point." When Lance said *Little League*, Henry had pictured eleven- and twelve-year-old girls. Not four- and five-year-olds. He should have known better than to think Lance knew what he was talking about.

"On it." Lance blew the whistle. Then from somewhere he pulled out a megaphone. "Attention, blue team. Hit the latrine now or forever hold your bladder."

When none of the girls made a move to hit the restrooms, Lance lifted the megaphone again. "Everybody go potty."

He elbowed Henry as a dozen girls giggled and raced past them to the concession stand area, where the bathrooms were. "This is kind of fun. I sort of feel like Tom Hanks in *A League of Their Own.*"

Henry yanked the megaphone away. "You are not Tom Hanks. If anything, I'm Tom Hanks."

"Then who am I?"

"I don't know." Henry looked him over again. "The bus driver?"

Lance chirped on the whistle. "Technical foul, Henry.

One more and I'm kicking you out of the game." Lance's gaze swept past Henry and his voice lowered. "Oh, boy, she's here. Okay, stay cool. Don't be an idiot. She's walking this way. Check your fly. Make sure it's closed. Just be discreet about it."

"You always give yourself pep talks?"

"Me? I'm talking to you. It's your bombshell girlfriend. And your fly is definitely open."

"Huh?" Henry spun around. Sure enough, Edith was walking toward them. She smiled and tried brushing her bangs to the side. They immediately fell back across her forehead. Henry shoved the megaphone back at Lance and fumbled with the front of his pants, glancing down. "My fly is not open," he hissed.

"Got my megaphone back, didn't I?" Lance waved to Edith. Some of the girls were already returning from the bathroom. Lance lifted the megaphone to his mouth. "All right, blue team. Head to the dugout. First one there gets to be catcher." The girls continued walking. "Oookay, first one there gets an extra Popsicle."

The girls took off running. Walking backwards, Lance gave Henry a thumbs-up. "I think I'm already getting the hang of this."

Henry dug his hands in his pockets and took a step toward Edith. The first two rows of bleachers were starting to fill with parents and grandparents. "Hey."

"Hey."

They smiled at each other, waiting for the other person to say something more.

"What are you doing here?"

"How was your stew?" They both spoke over each other.
"Sorry. You first."

"No. You go."

Edith blew her bangs from her eyes. "The stew was good. Well, pretty good. Could have been better. It was almost like it was missing something."

"Hmm . . . like maybe a pepper?"

Edith's small laugh sent way too much heat through Henry's gut. Man, he missed her. So what if she was leaving at the end of summer? He'd deal with that later. He just wanted to be with her now. With whatever time they had. Even if he looked like an idiot.

"So what are you doing here?" Edith asked.

A chain-link fence ran next to them, separating the ball diamond from the bleacher area. He grabbed the bar running along the top of it. "See those girls out there? The ones warming up like a well-oiled machine?"

Edith made a show of scanning the ball field. "I see some girls doing cartwheels and others picking dandelions. Oh, and a girl wearing a catcher's mask backwards."

"That's my team."

Edith's eyes widened with exaggerated astonishment. "You're the coach?"

"Yep. And I don't want to brag, but so far this team is undefeated under my management." Henry made a show of hitching his pants. "I think this could be the year."

"Really? What's your team's name?"

"Blue team."

Edith pointed behind him. "What's that player's name?"

"Champ."

"You didn't even look at her."

"Don't need to. They're all champs in my eyes."

Edith clasped the fence, her fingers an inch from his own. Her smile made him want to close the distance. "You got suckered into this, didn't you?"

Henry leaned closer to her, dropping his voice. "You need to help us. Lance doesn't know baseball. I don't know little girls." He yanked down his shirt collar. "Plus, I'm pretty sure I have shingles. Isn't that contagious? Shouldn't I go home?"

"That's a mosquito bite," Edith said, poking her finger against his skin.

"So I might have Lyme disease. Is that what you're saying?"

"Not unless you're covered in ticks."

The scent of her coconut shampoo drew him closer. "Do you need to check me?"

Her lips curved in a delicious smile. "Do I look like Brad Paisley to you?"

"Nothing against Brad, but you look way better than he does." Henry couldn't stop staring at her. Whether she was wearing a red dress or a pair of jean shorts and a plain V-neck T-shirt, Edith was gorgeous. Henry opened his mouth to tell her so when a voice—amplified by a megaphone—blasted from the dugout.

"Would the two lovebirds stop flirting long enough so we can get this game started?"

Edith's hand shot away from his shirt. Laughter and a few catcalls burst from the bleachers. *Nice.*

"Good luck," Edith said, ducking her head.

"Yeah, thanks. I'll need it. You sticking around?"

"Uh . . ." She shrugged her shoulders, walking away, glancing halfway back. "Maybe. For a bit. I don't know."

Henry couldn't let her walk away. "Keep score," he blurted.

"Would Henry Hobbes please report to the dugout?" Lance's voice boomed out, eliciting more laughter. "Henry Hobbes to the dugout please."

Henry ignored Lance, keeping his gaze locked on Edith. "We need someone to keep the scorecard for us. Can you do it?" He could see Edith waffling. "Please?"

She blew her bangs from her eyes. "Sure. Why not?"

"Great." He waved her toward the dugout, feeling a small sense of victory. This was something at least. A start. Before the end of summer took her away.

CHAPTER TWENTY-FOUR

What was she still doing here? Other than making a huge mistake.

Edith batted a mosquito away from her face and slapped her arm. She was going to have to bathe in anti-itch cream after this evening. She should have walked the long route to Kat's house like originally planned. But no. Edith just had to cut through the park, didn't she? Just had to spot Henry. Just had to say hi.

And now she just couldn't walk away. Thirty minutes after the game had ended.

She smacked her leg. "Bloodthirsty mongers," she muttered.

"Tell me about it. Those girls about drained every last Popsicle out of me." Henry plopped a red-and-white cooler onto the empty bleacher seat next to Edith. "But don't worry. I managed to save you one. Hope you like banana."

"Blech."

"I'll take that as a sorta-kinda?" His mouth quirked up in a half smile, making his eyes crinkle at the edges. "Thanks for staying."

Oh yeah. This was definitely a huge mistake. She dropped her gaze and made like she was slapping another bug from her leg. "Good thing I did. What was the final score? Three hundred and twenty-three to five hundred and nine?"

Henry chuckled and sank next to her on the bleacher, his elbow brushing hers. "Something like that."

"To be honest, I was only sticking around for the Popsicle. Now that I know it's banana—" Edith pulled a face and leaned forward, pretending to leave.

"You know, you were a lot less high-maintenance when I thought you were an old lady."

Henry had grabbed hold of her hand, and Edith was doing her best to act like it wasn't a big deal. "I still can't believe we were both under the wrong impression about each other. I thought I was sharing a house with Walter Matthau. You know, from *Grumpy Old Men*."

"I thought I was sharing a house with Betty White from *The Golden Girls*."

Edith snorted. "Betty White," she mumbled. "You know who's to blame for all of this."

Edith and Henry spoke at the same time. "Kat."

They both chuckled and slid into a companionable silence. Edith slipped her hand out of Henry's, not because she didn't relish the contact. She did. But she was also hot. And sweating. And shouldn't be relishing the contact.

She discreetly swiped her palms against the denim fabric of her jean shorts. The sun had dipped low enough to paint the sky a mixture of orange and pink. Clouds stretched and ripped apart like cotton candy over the cornfields beyond the ballpark.

"I love that." Henry waved his hand toward the view. "I know it's not a majestic mountain or a sandy shore, but . . . I don't know. To me, it's beautiful. I like living here."

He leaned back and propped his arms on the bleacher behind them. "Do you miss Pittsburgh?"

"No. Not really. I guess it never felt like home to me."

"Even when you were married?"

Edith sighed and sank against the bleacher, Henry's arm behind her. "We were never supposed to stay in Pittsburgh. Our plan was to see the world. Or at least I thought it was. Turns out it may have just been my plan."

"Tell me about it."

"I already did." She bumped her shoulder against him. "In the letter. You pretty much know everything there is to know."

"No, I don't. Not nearly enough. I want to know more. Tell me why you want to travel. Why Pittsburgh never felt like home. Why you stayed to watch an entire peewee league game and why you're still here with me now. Especially if you don't like banana Popsicles." He winked.

Edith straightened. "I don't know, Henry. Honestly, I don't. Because this isn't what I want." She pointed to the sky and the cornfields. "You're right. It is beautiful and I get why you like it here, but . . . it isn't my story. It's yours."

Edith stood, feeling restless. Needing to move. "Did you bring any baseballs to go with that bat?" She pointed to the hot-pink bat propped next to the cooler of Popsicles.

"Lance left a bag of baseballs in the dugout. Why? You wanting to do some batting practice?"

"The mosquitoes are eating me alive just sitting here." It was as good an excuse as any. Certainly better than *I need to move away from you before I fall any further in love with you and make an even bigger mistake by staying here forever.*

Henry grabbed the bag of baseballs from the dugout and carried it to the pitcher's mound while Edith took a few practice swings at home plate. There was still enough sunlight to see for a while yet. She tapped home plate. "Bring the heat, Hobbes."

He sailed a pitch past her faster than she could blink.

"Oookay. Maybe a little less heat, more like room temperature. Somewhere in the tepid range."

He lobbed a ball over the mound. She swung and pinged it down the third baseline. "Hey! Did you see that? I hit a homer first try."

"You hit a foul ball."

"Tomayto-tomahto."

Henry tossed her another pitch.

"So," Edith said, swinging and missing the next pitch by a mile. "My parents had me young. Like, really young. Like my mom was only sixteen and my dad barely seventeen." She lifted her bat for the next pitch. "They ended up staying together and getting married a few years later, but let's just say they were super protective. I think they were terrified I'd end up repeating the same mistake they did."

Edith swung and missed again. "Would you stop throwing curveballs?"

"The only curve my pitches are making is downward. Because that's how gravity works."

Edith narrowed her gaze, then prepared for the next throw. "But I didn't want to live in a bubble." She clipped it foul behind her. "I wanted to explore, travel, live a life like my great-great-aunt Edith did."

Henry bent over to grab another ball from the bag. "Is that who you're named after?"

Edith leaned against the baseball bat like a cane, taking a moment to catch her breath. Who knew swinging a bat could be so strenuous? Heaven help her if she had to run the bases. "Edith McClintock. She was my dad's great-aunt. She lived to be nearly a hundred. I used to play cribbage with her once a month when we visited her in the nursing home. She told the greatest stories."

Henry tossed the ball up and down in his hand. "What kind of stories?"

"True stories. She was like a real-life Dr. Quinn, medicine woman. Except she never married. She became a doctor back when it wasn't super common for women to become doctors. Her dream was to become a renowned surgeon in Bellevue Hospital. And she might have too, except for this one experience she had on a trip overseas. Of all the stories she told, that one was my favorite."

Edith used the bat to scrape a line back and forth in the dirt. She was talking too much, wasn't she? Sometimes she got carried away. Why would Henry care about her great-great-aunt Edith?

"What was it?"

Edith lifted the bat to her shoulder and moved back to the plate. Shrugged. "It doesn't matter. Throw me another pitch."

"What? No way." Henry dropped the ball in the bag. "You can't set me up like that, then say—" he imitated her sauntering to the plate with the bat on her shoulder and shrugging—"it doesn't matter."

"First off, I do not talk or wiggle like that."

"There was a bit of a wiggle."

"And I didn't set you up. I just wasn't sure if you wanted me to keep talking about it or not."

"Why wouldn't I want you to keep talking about it?" Henry leaned down and grabbed a baseball.

"I don't know. It might be boring to you."

"Is it boring to you?"

"No."

Henry looked down to the ball in his hand, tossing it lightly a few times in his palm, before meeting her gaze again. "Then it's not boring to me, Edith." His voice had lowered in the same manner as the sunlight. Slowly. Softly. Like they were sitting at a private table for two, rather than standing out on a muggy mosquito-infested baseball diamond. How did he do that?

"So what was it?"

Edith stared at Henry. "What was what?"

"The story."

She blinked and tugged her shirt away from her stomach, needing a quick breeze. "Right. The story."

Edith spun toward the fence and started retrieving balls. "The summer right after she graduated with her medical degree, her grandparents took her on a trip to Africa under the guise of a graduation gift. Really they were trying to get her away from medicine and convince her to marry a wealthy friend of the family. He was supposed to *just happen upon* them and join their little caravan for the summer."

Edith used the bottom of her shirt like a sack to carry the balls to the mound and dumped them into the bag. "Nicely done," Henry said when most of them bounced off the bag and scattered in different directions.

Since he made no move to get them, instead sitting down on the pitcher's mound, Edith did the same. "So what happened?" he asked.

"What happened?" Edith smiled, remembering the way her great-great-aunt would recount the night that changed her life. "They went on a safari and somehow she got separated from everybody. One of those things where one group thought she was with the other group, and the other group thought she was with the first group. And she suddenly found herself alone. For an entire night. In the wilds of South Africa."

"Sounds scary."

"She was terrified. She said it felt like the night would never end. So she just kept moving. Even though it didn't make sense, she thought if she kept walking, she could somehow get to the morning faster."

"I can't explain it, little Edith. I just knew I couldn't let myself get stuck in the darkness. I knew it would kill me. So I kept walking. I kept searching for that first glimmer of light."

"Right before dawn broke, she was so lost she thought nobody would ever find her and if they did, it would be her bones after they'd been picked clean by a pack of lions." Edith held her finger up, the way her namesake used to at this point in the story. "But just as she was about to give up, the first tiny gleam of dawn crested over the horizon. And a softly singing choir of angels beckoned her to keep walking. Just a little farther."

"A choir of angels?"

"A softly singing choir. Get it right."

"My apologies." Henry's foot tapped her foot. It had gotten dark enough now she couldn't see his eyes beneath the brim of his baseball hat, but she didn't have to see them to know they were crinkling the way they always did when he smiled.

"But they were angels?" he asked.

"Well . . . not exactly. The choir turned out to be a group of village women gathering water. But when my great-great-aunt followed the sound, she walked down a tunnel of trees, the end looking like a big arch. And when she stepped through the arch and saw them singing beneath the first rays of daylight, they may as well have been angels. She said it was like stepping into a new life. She knew in that moment exactly what she was meant to do. She spent the next decades of her life using her medical background to do missions work all over the world."

"Wow."

"I know. Isn't it a great story?" Edith rose to her feet and used her palms to swipe the dirt off her rear end. "That's what I want more than anything." Edith held out her hand to help Henry up, his knee making the task a little more difficult. "That one story. That one adventure. Something that I can look back on and say *there*. The moment my life set off on a new trajectory. The moment I answered my calling. The moment my life really started to matter."

"Edith—"

"I know my life already matters, you don't have to say that, but . . ." Edith looked down at his hand still clasped around hers. "My life doesn't have a great story yet."

She dropped his hand and took a step back. Standing close to him on the pitcher's mound reminded her too much of dancing with him on the putting green. Reminded her too much of how his arms felt.

She needed to go. Before she grew any more tempted to stay. Before she repeated the same mistake she made with Brian. Giving up her dreams for love. Not that she loved Henry.

Okay, maybe she did. *No.* She didn't.

She backed up another step. Didn't matter. His life was in Illinois. Getting married. Raising a family. That wasn't the story she wanted. Was it?

No. She wanted adventure.

"Have you had supper yet?"

The last thing she needed was more time with this man. "Henry, I can't."

"Can't what? Eat?"

"Keep doing this," she said. "Acting like we're friends or . . . *more*. Don't you get it? I'm not staying. We can't be more. I'm leaving."

"For what? Three months? So what? You can come back."

"It's not three months. It's . . . longer. Three years maybe. I don't know." Edith shrugged, willing him to understand. "I need something more. I need—"

"You know what? I get it. You don't have to explain." Henry crouched down, corralling the balls into the bag. "This town isn't enough for you."

"That's not what I'm saying."

"Sorry. *I'm* not enough for you. Is that more accurate?" He zipped the bag and flung it over his shoulder.

"Henry, listen to me."

"I have. I heard you. You need a big story. You need a big life. And it's not here with me. You're not the first person to tell me that, so believe me, I get it. I really do."

Edith reached for his hand. "Would you just stop?"

He tugged his hand free and limped at a clipped pace toward his truck. "Thanks for keeping score tonight. See you around."

Edith watched him go, wanting to chase after him, wanting to sit in the dirt and weep. Wanting . . . she didn't know what. She settled for turning around and walking to Kat's house. It was for the best. They cared about each other too much to make a casual friendship work. Better to cut it off now. Let the healing process begin. Right?

Sure. Maybe if Edith kept telling herself that, she'd eventually believe it.

CHAPTER TWENTY-FIVE

Two weeks passed, carrying them into August, and Henry had neither seen nor heard from Edith. He didn't know if running himself ragged was a blessing or a curse. He only knew it hurt too much to think about her. So he would do whatever was necessary to not think about her. Even if it meant repainting Mrs. Newberry's kitchen every color of the rainbow from here until eternity.

A paper clip tinged off the side of his blue light glasses and landed on the blueprint covering his desk. He lifted the paper clip to eye level, then swung his gaze to Peg.

"I ran out of rubber bands," she said with a shrug. "And I need you to come look at this."

Henry slipped his glasses off and rubbed his eyes, weariness blurring his vision.

"Which do you like better?" Peg asked once he leaned over her shoulder and blinked at the images on her computer screen.

"I don't know. What am I looking at?" He slipped his glasses back on.

"The options for our new logo. Personally, I like this one." Peg enlarged the cartoon drawing on the right of the screen showing a pelican wearing overalls and holding a paintbrush.

"Logo? Since when do we need a logo? Our name is Hobbes Painting and Construction. If people can't figure out what we do by our title, then I don't think a bird is going to help matters."

"This is how you run a business, Henry." Peg spun her chair around to face him and leaned back with her arms folded across her chest. "You put your name out there. You get on billboards. You make a website. You come up with a logo," she said with emphasis on the last word.

"We've never needed to do any of that kind of stuff before. Besides, don't we already have a website?"

"Yeah, one my great-nephew could have designed." Her gaze flitted to a framed piece of notebook paper covered in scribbles, a prized possession from her three-year-old great-nephew. "Look, Henry, while you had your head in the clouds this summer, things have been happening. We've had two big projects swiped out from right under our noses by companies in the Quad Cities."

"That's fine. We're fine. The historical society project will keep us plenty busy."

"If they ever hire us. Supposing they do, it's still not going to keep us busy forever. I don't know if you even realize it, what with your head in the sand these past few weeks, but we're not exactly filled to the brim with projects these days—Mrs. Newberry's kitchen notwithstanding."

Henry stepped back to his desk and tossed his glasses down. "So which is it? Is my head in the clouds or in the sand?"

"Right now it's up your you-know-what," Peg said with a piercing glare.

"Gee, Peg, don't hold back. Tell me what you really think." Henry flopped into his chair and palmed each eye. She was right, of course. The business his dad had worked so hard to build was crumbling slowly, just like his hopes with Edith had, one brick at a time.

Maybe he should be glad his parents weren't around. After all these years, he still had a way of taking great opportunities and turning them into failures.

After a few silent seconds, he heard the groan of Peg's chair followed by the squeak of her orthopedic shoes as she treaded across the tile floor. "Henry," she said in a much gentler tone. He felt the warm press of her hand against his shoulder. "I'm sorry. I didn't mean to harp at you like that. Sometimes I forget you're my boss and not my own flesh and blood."

He lowered his hands and looked into the eyes of a woman who had known him since long before her face grew wrinkles and her hair needed to be colored to hide the gray. "It's okay. I need a good harping every now and again. Especially when my head is not in the right place."

"To be honest, I'm more worried about where your heart is these days."

"I'm sorry, did we just start filming a Hallmark movie all of a sudden?"

"No, you listen to me. I've known you since the day you were born. I've seen the choices you've made in your life—and yes, I've seen the mistakes too—but sometimes I wonder what it is exactly that's driving you. Since your mama died, I couldn't help but see the way you changed your life around. You pushed yourself and worked harder than a body is practically capable of, learning everything there is to know about contracting and construction. But what I've never been able to fully figure out is what for."

Henry shifted his shoulders in the chair. "I dropped the ball, Peg. Literally and figuratively. You know that."

"Oh, who cares about a football game from high school?"

"A lot of people, actually. My brother. My coach. That scout from U of I." Henry let out a humorless laugh. "Maggie."

"So your team didn't make it to state. So you didn't get any fancy scholarship. So your girlfriend dumped you. So what? That was a long time ago. You're a different man now."

Henry's throat thickened and he blinked several times to fight off the sting in his eyes. "Am I?" He didn't know. Maybe. He'd tried to be a better man ever since Maggie. Ever since she showed up on his doorstep, telling him she was pregnant.

He'd been foolish enough at the time to think dropping that football for the winning touchdown had been fate. Why bother with scholarships or college when he could have everything he wanted? A solid job in his hometown. A girl he loved. A family.

Too bad Maggie hadn't seen it the same way. Especially after she miscarried. Nothing Henry said could convince her to stay and marry him. She left town without looking back. And if Henry had any thoughts of following her, they fled the moment his mom died from a sudden heart attack.

"After Maggie left and my mom died, working my hide off was the only way I knew how to cope. The only way I knew how to redeem myself in this town. Honestly, it wasn't until Edith showed up that I realized how much I was missing and how much I still hoped for."

Henry rubbed his fingers across his cheeks. "Not that it matters. I'm pretty sure I messed that one up too." He straightened himself in the chair and cleared his throat. "Anyway. You think we need a logo, huh."

"Why do you say that?"

"Because you just said we do."

"No. Why do you think you messed things up with Edith? According to Julie, you two are smitten with each other."

"Yeah, well, Julie might know how to make the best scones in the county, but that doesn't mean she knows everything that goes on in this town."

"Hmm . . . except I have it on good authority from at least half of the town that you two weren't just playacting when that Steve fella was around. Shoot, Willy who runs the hardware store, why he says he even caught the two of you making out behind his dumpster one day."

He'd already cried in front of her. Was this woman really going to make him talk about his love life too? "I think the pelican would make a great logo."

Peg folded her lips inward and slapped his shoulder with

the back of her hand. "Fine. Be that way. But can I just say one more thing?"

"Have I ever been able to stop you before?" He got another slap to the shoulder.

"Don't be so hard on yourself. You're a good man, Henry. A man I know your mom and dad would both be proud of. Maybe whatever's going on between you and Edith right now has nothing to do with something you did. It might just be God's way of making sure both your hearts are in the right place so you can finally move on. *Together.* I don't know what's happened in Edith's past, but I feel like I understand yours pretty well. And I don't see any reason why you should ever give up hope. You're a forgiven man, Henry. Stop punishing yourself over things God already wiped clean. And on that note—" she patted his shoulder and winked— "I'd say our little Hallmark movie is due for a commercial break."

Henry reached out and gave Peg's hand a soft squeeze. "You know something, Peg? You're a heck of a lot better at passing out wisdom than my physical therapist is."

Peg laughed. "I'm a little longer in the tooth than your physical therapist is too." She went back to her desk and grabbed her purse from the bottom drawer. "I better head out. My other half signed us up for ballroom dancing lessons, if you can believe it. I swear I could be married to that man for a hundred years and he'd still find ways to surprise me yet. G'night, Henry. Oh—" She snapped her fingers and paused in the doorway. "One other thing. I went ahead and applied for that Charles Henderson grant I kept telling you about that you kept ignoring me about, so hopefully we hear something back in the next couple of weeks. You're welcome and good night."

"The what grant? Charles who? Peg—"

She slipped out, waving her fingers with a saucy smile, before slamming the door shut behind her. "Peg," he growled. *That woman.*

Henry sank back in his chair. She never was one to pull any punches, was she?

But what if she was right? Not about the grant. He didn't even know what she was talking about. But what if he hadn't completely blown it with Edith? Was he so used to beating himself up he'd automatically assumed he'd done something wrong?

He winced. He *had* done something wrong. He'd lied. To Edith about his real identity. To Steve about his relationship with Edith. And now half the town assumed he was taking liberties with Edith he had no right to take.

Why didn't he set the record straight the other morning at the coffee shop?

Henry palmed his eyes and groaned. Why didn't he set the record straight weeks ago at the coffee shop when Angela told him they needed to decide where their relationship was heading?

Judging by the sparse amount of text messages between them, he didn't imagine there was going to be any great love lost on her end. Even so. He owed her an apology.

If he wanted to be the type of man Peg claimed he was, a man worthy of Edith, it was past time he started acting like that man.

♥

Edith stifled a curse word. Sweat no longer trickled down her back. It poured. And she still didn't have the car seat secured.

"Oh, for the love of Pete," she muttered as she dug her fingers into the back seat, searching for the clip to latch the car seat on to. The small quarters of the car and the sweltering humidity were not making the process as easy as the instruction manual suggested it would be.

At least Edith had learned a valuable lesson. The next time the social worker forgot to bring a car seat to the crisis nursery house, Edith wasn't going to offer to install the spare they kept in the storage room. No sir. Next time she was going to jump in the bushes and hide until the social worker either retired or died.

With the clasp finally latched, Edith shook the car seat side to side. Seemed secure. She straightened out of the car and fanned herself with her shirt. The cocker spaniel next door had flopped onto his back in the grass, panting with all four paws spread wide. "I'm right there with you, buddy," Edith told him.

The heat this week had been relentless. Edith didn't want to run up Kat's power bill, so she'd left the air-conditioning off. But every afternoon she wilted worse than the potted red geraniums on the crisis nursery's front porch.

"Thanks for doing that, Edith." The social worker, a middle-aged woman with wavy brown hair and a tired smile, held the hand of a two-year-old boy who had been dropped off at the house late last night. "It saved me a trip, and I want to get Tyler to his foster home soon as I can."

"Sure." Edith blew her bangs from her forehead. "No problem. Anything else I can do before you go?"

"No. I think we're set." She settled the young boy into his car seat and tightened the straps. When she closed the door, she lowered her voice and stepped closer to Edith. "Just to give you fair warning, it wouldn't surprise me if Tyler's dad shows up at some point looking for him since he knows Tyler has been brought here before. If he does, just call the police."

Edith's eyes widened. "Oh. Okay." Her first experience with an actual child and she was already wishing for the plants.

"Sorry. I'm not trying to scare you. I just know you're new and work the night shift alone, so I wanted you to be prepared if that should happen."

"Right. Thank you. I appreciate that." Edith waved to the little boy already nodding off in the car seat as they pulled away.

After Sharon and the day crew arrived a little while later and were caught up to date on the early morning activities, Edith left for Kat's house. She had given up her morning coffee routine at Julie's shop, too afraid of running into Henry. It was easier to tell herself she'd only imagined the connection between them instead of seeing him and having to face it head-on.

Although the fact he hadn't tried contacting her since the evening at the ballpark made her wonder if perhaps she had imagined it.

Edith unlocked Kat's door and kicked off her shoes, immediately going to the refrigerator for something cold and refreshing. Something to take her mind off the smothering self-doubt suffocating her peace of mind worse than the hot air in Kat's upstairs bedroom.

Was she truly that unlovable? Past experience suggested she was. People didn't seem to have any trouble turning their backs on her, did they?

Edith sat down at the kitchen table and buried her face in her hands. "Stop it," she told herself. "You're just tired." She fanned her shirt away from herself. "And hot. That's no reason to throw yourself a pity party. Not when there's a two-year-old little boy being driven hours away to some stranger's house because his own parents can't get it together. So knock it off. You have nothing to feel sorry about."

Edith gulped down her glass of iced tea. The image of Tyler, asleep in the back seat, his face full of innocence despite the trials his short life had already thrown at him, stayed with her as she tried to catch some sleep in Kat's room with two fans blowing on her.

"That's it." Edith flung herself out of bed. She was never going to get any sleep at this rate. She searched Kat's house until she found what she was looking for. And then before she could question herself, she wrote a letter to Henry and dropped it in the mail.

CHAPTER TWENTY-SIX

A marble fountain, flanked with ferns, bubbled in the center of the hotel lobby. Henry stood with his hands in his pocket, letting his gaze sweep over the sleek contemporary furniture and Asian art. A coffee bar lined the wall. He was just thinking about fixing a cup when the short quick pace of click-clacking heels grabbed his attention.

"Henry," Angela said breathlessly. She brushed a kiss to his cheek. "What are you doing here? Not that I'm not happy to see you. I just wish you had told me sooner that you were coming. I'm afraid I already have plans for tonight. I might be able to reschedule. Probably not though. Chad's expecting me. I hate to disappoint him but let me see if—"

"Angela," Henry said, gently covering her phone with his hand. She looked up from the message she was texting. "It's fine. I figured you'd be busy. I just wanted to talk to you. In person."

"Oh. Okay."

Now that he had her full attention, the speech he had rehearsed during the three-hour drive to Chicago suddenly felt flat. "Um." He cleared his throat and tugged at his ear. "Angela."

"Yes?" She eyed him warily, shifting a small step back.

"I, uh, have been thinking a lot lately. About what you said. Earlier this summer."

"Okay."

"About us. And the future. And well . . ." Henry wet his lips. "I think we should break up."

"I can't marry you."

They both spoke at the same time, so it took each of them a moment to register what the other had said. "Wait," Angela said. "You're not proposing?"

"You don't want to marry me?"

"Did you really drive all the way here just to break up with me?"

He tugged at his ear. "Well, yeah."

Angela's brows dipped. "If I didn't feel so relieved right now, I'd feel a little insulted." She swooped in, wrapping her arms around him in a tight hug.

"Wow," Henry said, patting her on the back. "I would have broken things off a long time ago if I'd known it was going to be this easy."

Angela stepped back with a smile. "You've actually lifted a huge weight off my shoulders. I've sort of been seeing someone else lately."

"Let me guess. Chad."

"I didn't mean for it to happen. We've just been spending so much time together and then one thing sort of led to another and—"

"Angela. It's fine. I came here to break up, remember?"

"Oh yeah." She trilled an awkward laugh, suggesting she still didn't know whether to be insulted or relieved. "What about you? Did you find someone else? Is it someone I know?" A ping sounded on Angela's phone, tugging her gaze down to the screen.

"You might have seen her around, but I don't think you know her. Remember me talking about a woman who was going to be staying at my house for a while?"

"Yeah, the old lady." Angela tapped back a reply. "Ethel, wasn't it?"

"Edith."

"Right. Edith. She have a granddaughter or something?"

"No. Actually—"

"Sorry, Henry. Chad's texting me, saying we're going to be late if we don't leave now. I hate to rush off. It's just that we're meeting up with another potential client. It could be another big assignment for us."

"I actually need to get going too."

"Oh, good." She flashed a quick smile. "Well, it was great seeing you. I'm so glad you came." Angela stepped toward him for another quick hug. "I'm happy for you. For both of us. Maybe sometime we can all get together. That won't be weird, will it?" Another ping. "Gotta go. Bye, Henry."

Angela's heels click-clacked back across the lobby. "Bye." Henry watched Angela leave, her strides quick, her head bent over her phone, and wondered briefly how she'd lived so long without walking in front of moving traffic.

Blowing out a breath, he glanced at his watch. That whole exchange had gone better and quicker than he hoped. If only things could go half as smoothly with Edith.

A little later that evening, down the road at a twenty-four-hour truck stop and diner, Henry ordered a cheeseburger and fries. While he waited for his food, he pulled out Edith's letter. He had read it so many times he could almost recite it from memory.

Dear Henry,

How are you? I've missed your listening ear these past few weeks. I've needed a good friend to talk to. I hope you don't mind if I unload on you a little now. Feel free to throw this straight into the recycling bin if you have no desire to read the ramblings of a troubled soul. (I only say that because I'm fairly confident you would do no such thing.) In the time I've gotten to know you, I've seen the kind of man you are. And you're the kind of man who lets a woman ramble when she needs to.

Henry, I wasn't completely honest with you. I told you in one of my previous letters that my husband and I shared everything in his dying days. I led you to believe that we were in love and all was right in our world once again. That's not true.

You want to know the reality of it? The final week before Brian's death, a woman from his office came to the house to see him. She had brought food. I went to put it away in the kitchen and when I came back, I saw her for a moment before she realized I was back. I saw the look in her eyes as she gazed down on him sleeping on the couch. And that's when I knew.

I didn't know how long it had been going on. I didn't know how much it had meant to Brian. But I could tell it obviously meant a great deal to her.

I did the only thing I could think to do at the time. I thanked the woman for coming over and I never said a word about it to anyone. As far as I was concerned, when Brian died, we loved each other, and we were at peace. I forgave him and moved on. And up until a few weeks ago, I think I even believed it.

Remember Steve? Of course you do. He drove me crazy. But you want to hear something even crazier? Part of me was flattered the whole time he was here. Why? Because I'd convinced myself he really cared for me. That I was such a catch, he was having a hard time letting me go.

But as we both know now, my money was the only thing Steve was having a hard time letting go.

Do you understand now why I will never remarry? Probably not. I'm rambling. Stick with me a few minutes more.

Henry, I didn't even have feelings for Steve, and he still managed to hurt me. I don't think I could survive it if someone I did care for cast me aside like that. Not after what I went through with my parents. Not after what I went through with my husband.

I just can't go through that again. No matter how much I may be tempted to with the right sort of man. Not even a man I love. Not even you.

It's not worth the risk.

Thank you for listening, Henry. You've been a good friend and I hope you know how much it's meant to me.

Love, Edith

"Here's your order, honey." The waitress slid a plate and Coke onto the table. "That looks like a heck of a pen-pal letter you got there." The waitress swiped a ketchup bottle from the table behind her and plopped it next to his plate. "Or is it from your girl?"

"A friend," Henry said, folding the letter back up.

"But you wish she was your girl."

"Excuse me?"

"Honey, I been working this truck stop for years. I've seen every sort of face a man can make when he sits down to eat and has nothing but time to think. And you're thinking about that girl, ain't ya? Wishing she was more."

Henry looked at the name tag. "Phyllis," he began.

"Around here, they call me Dr. Phyllis. I've been known to dish out as good of advice as I do burgers."

"I see." Maybe it was her hound dog eyes. Or the pencil sticking out of her hair that Henry was pretty sure she'd forgotten since she carried another two in her apron pocket. Whatever it was, Henry found himself nudging the chair next to him out with his foot and saying, "What do you know about women, Phyllis?"

She wasted no time settling into the seat. "Considering I've been one for sixty-two years, I'd say I know quite a bit."

"Then tell me this. How do you go about getting a woman to trust again?"

"Trust in what exactly? Relationships in general or you in particular?"

"Both."

A bell dinged on the counter. "Order's up!" a voice shouted from the kitchen.

"Hold your horses, Gary!" Phyllis yelled over her shoulder. "Give me a minute to stew on this . . ."

"Henry."

"Henry. I like that name." She popped out of the chair. "You start on your burger and I'll be back in a few to tell you what I think."

By the time Henry dipped his last fry in ketchup, Phyllis was back, pulling out the chair across from him. "So it's like this, Hank. I married the man of my dreams. He is the kindest, most hard-workingest man I've ever known. It was like a rainbow appeared just for me the day we got married. Guess how long we've known each other."

"Long time," Henry answered.

"You bet. Forty-five years. Now guess how long we've been married. Better yet, let me just tell you. Two years. That's right, Hank. The man of my dreams was under my nose for forty-five years and it wasn't until two years ago that I finally realized it."

"I see."

"Do you?"

"Not really." Henry wiped his mouth off with a napkin as Phyllis leaned forward with her elbows on the table.

"Don't be spreading this around, Hank, but truth is, a lot of us women, why, we're all mixed-up. Things happen in our lives and it gets us thinking things we'd be better off not thinking. And nine times out of ten it's because of daddy issues. Does this woman of yours have daddy issues?"

"Her dad died."

Phyllis leaned back and slapped her knee. "There you go. It's daddy issues."

"Well, I think there's more to it. She and her husband had some marital problems as well."

Phyllis's eyebrows almost reached her hairline. "Your girl was married?"

"Her husband died too."

"Oh, honey, it sounds like she's got a world of hurts bottled up inside her tighter than this here ketchup bottle."

Henry sighed. "And she's afraid to take any more risks on love."

"Well, of course she is. Who wouldn't be? I sure was. I can tell you that much."

"How'd you get past it?"

Phyllis's face softened into a wistful smile. "By letting a man with the patience of Job show me the type of love I'd been running circles around most of my life. See, that's the thing, Hank. This girl of yours, she's gotta figure it out. Just like I had to figure it out. And if you really care about her, you're just gonna have to trust that she'll eventually get there, and then be willing to wait until she does."

"You know something?" Henry stared into Phyllis's droopy eyes. "I'll bet if your husband was here right now, he'd say you were worth waiting for."

Phyllis tipped her head back and laughed. "Let's see if you're right. Gary! You glad you waited all those years for me?"

A bald man poked his head out over the counter that separated the dining area from the kitchen. "Sweetheart, there's not a day goes by where I still don't find myself waiting for you." He plunked two plates filled with sandwiches on the counter. "If I didn't think you were worth it, I'd have fired you by now. Order's up." He threw her a wink and slapped a palm on the bell before disappearing again.

Phyllis beamed like he'd just spouted poetry at her. "I better get back to work. You want any pie?"

"Better not. I need to get going. I appreciate the advice though."

Phyllis waved her hand in the air. "It was my pleasure. Good luck. Just remember this, Hank. No matter what that woman's been through or what she decides to do, you show her plenty of kindness and a whole lot of patience, and she's gonna know one thing for sure. She's gonna know you're the real deal. And I'll tell you what, I ain't ever met a woman who can resist the real deal. Why, when I was—"

"Phyllis!" The bell dinged again. "Just 'cuz you're worth the wait doesn't mean this pork tenderloin needs to be."

Henry left Phyllis a hefty tip and waved goodbye.

CHAPTER TWENTY-SEVEN

What was I thinking? I should know better than to write letters when I'm tired, overheated, and emotional. And I should definitely know better than to mail said letters when I'm tired, overheated, and emotional! Next time I'm feeling lonely and reflective, I'm going to do what every other self-respecting woman does. Instead of spilling my guts, I'm going to fill my guts. With ice cream. Oh, please, let it still be here. This isn't a big town. Maybe they don't even deliver on Saturdays.

"Ma'am, are you all right?"

Edith whipped her head around. A postal worker dressed in blue, wearing a bag slung over his shoulder and more hair in his two bushy eyebrows than on the top of his head, stared at her.

"It's okay, Mr. Walton. Her face just looks that way when–

ever she's gathering wool. Or having an allergic reaction. You're not having another allergic reaction, are you?"

Edith turned around to see Gabby walking toward them. "No. I'm fine. Must have been the wool again."

"Good thing. I'm running low on EpiPens. See ya. Bye, Mr. Walton."

He waved to Gabby, then took a step closer to Edith. "I had a great-uncle who was allergic to wool." He hitched his bag higher and clicked his tongue. "Real shame. He had to sell the entire sheep farm. Never was the same after that. At least that's what I'm told. He died a long time ago." He made a drinking motion with his hand, then shook his head with pity.

"I'm sorry to hear that," Edith said, not sure what else to say. Edith blew her bangs from her eyes, wondering if he ever had to blow his eyebrows out of his.

"Yep." Mr. Walton sighed, then clicked his tongue. "Real shame." He looked Edith over from the toes of her sandals to the bangs on her forehead. "Say, you new here or something? You seem familiar but I don't recall ever meeting you before."

"Oh, well—"

Before she could say anything else, his eyes widened and he snapped his fingers. "I know! You're Henry's girl, aren't you? *Yes sir.* I heard he had himself a real beaut. And that she was volunteering at that baby house." He belted out a laugh. "Well, good for him. It's about time he settled down with the right woman. Welcome!"

He nearly pumped her hand out of her shoulder socket, then laughed again. "Oh, man, his mom and dad would be so happy if they were still alive." He lowered his voice to a stage whisper. "Well, they wouldn't be thrilled about you two living together, but—" he shrugged—"I know Henry will make it right. He's a good man, that boy."

"He is. Yes." Edith tugged her hand from his. "I think there's been a little misunderstanding though."

"Oh?"

"Yes. We were never really living together. I mean, we were. But we're not anymore. Especially since, well, since . . . things have changed between us, you see."

"I think I know what you're saying."

"You do?" Because that would certainly make this exchange a whole lot easier.

"Yep." His bushy eyebrows waved up and down. "And I think it's about time. Julie! Look who I've got here." Mr. Walton waved over Edith's head. "Henry's girl. And guess what! They're tying the knot!"

Edith gasped and would have corrected him if she thought there was any chance to be heard over the sudden screaming behind her. The plump bakery owner was running a crazed fifty-yard dash down the sidewalk. And apparently Edith was the finish line. She lifted her arms as Julie barreled into her for an out-of-breath hug. "I can't believe it! I can't believe it!"

"You shouldn't," Edith said, her voice spinning in circles, along with the rest of her body, as Julie swung her around like a rag doll, all while Mr. Walton shouted to anyone within hearing distance.

"Please say you'll let me make the cake," Julie said, dropping Edith to her feet so she could grab hold of her shoulders. "Oh, please, *please*. I've been dreaming of this day for ages.

It'll be the most gorgeous cake you've ever seen. I promise. Oh, this is wonderful news."

She let go of Edith and fanned her teary eyes. "Just wonderful. I've gotta go tell May. She'll want to do the flowers of course." She blew a kiss to Edith and took off across the street. A car squealed its brakes to avoid hitting her.

"Henry and Edith are getting married!" Julie pumped both fists into the air.

When the car tooted its horn and a voice yelled, "Congratulations!" Edith wanted to crawl down the manhole.

"Well, I better get started on my route," Mr. Walton said. "I imagine I'll be delivering invitations soon." He shot her a wink and began to whistle a jaunty tune as he walked away. Edith half expected him to jump in the air and click his heels.

By the time Mr. Walton disappeared, retrieving the letter was the least of her worries. She grabbed the red bike she'd found in Kat's garage and climbed onto it. Before she made it down the street, two more people shouted their congratulations, and at the corner, a woman she could only assume was May knocked on the window from inside her flower shop to give her a thumbs-up.

Edith gave a half wave back. She didn't know what to think anymore—other than she was going to need a lot more butter pecan ice cream before this day was over.

───── ❤ ─────

Later that night a knock sounded against Kat's back door. Edith pulled the plug from the sink. Sudsy water drained as she rinsed off the last dish. She was still toweling her hands off when she opened the door.

And groaned.

"Wow, that's some greeting," Henry said. "I sort of expected a little more warmth from the woman I'm engaged to marry."

Edith opened the door wider and stepped back, giving Henry space to enter Kat's small kitchen. She raised her shoulders, lifting her palms in surrender. "I don't know what happened. Honest. I just went to the post office to check on something, and next thing I knew, we were engaged."

"I see."

"You do?"

"Not at all." Henry pulled a glass out of the cupboard with a chuckle and filled it with tap water, unable to hide his lingering smile as he leaned back against the sink. "I haven't heard anything from you in over two weeks. I leave town for one day, and now my office manager is congratulating me on my upcoming nuptials. That's going to require some explaining."

"Stop laughing. This is horrible."

"I'm not laughing."

"The sound you're making sounds a lot like laughter." And she didn't realize how much she had missed it until now.

"Sorry. I'll be serious." He took a drink of water. "So it's my job to plan the honeymoon, right?" He blocked the fist she directed at his abdomen. "Hey now. I hope you're not this physical after we're married." He smiled. "Although on second thought—"

Edith tipped the bottom of his glass, dumping water down his shirt. "Whoops."

Henry looked down at his chest for a moment, then

turned around to set his empty glass on the counter. "I see how it is." In a flash, he spun with the spray handle, dousing the front of Edith's shirt.

She gasped at the cold water flooding her chest. "Oh no you didn't."

"Oh, I'm pretty sure I did. Here." Henry handed her a dish towel, then leaned against the counter and folded his arms.

"So where were you?" Edith asked, dabbing her shirt, hoping her voice sounded casual enough.

"Hmm?"

"You said you were out of town. Where'd you go?"

"Oh. Up to Chicago."

"For your job?"

"Not exactly." He rubbed a palm across the five-o'clock shadow on his jaw. "Had some personal things I needed to see to. Things that were long overdue."

Edith continued patting her shirt dry, willing her hands not to shake. Or her voice. "And you just got back a little while ago?"

"Yeah. I had to swing by the office to grab some papers. Peg left me a note congratulating me on our upcoming winter wedding. I thought I better swing by here and see what was going on."

"I see." *Dab. Dab. Dab.* "So you haven't been by your house yet? Haven't, I don't know, watered the plants? Checked the mail?"

His warm palm stilled her arm, then removed the dish towel from her hand. "I got your letter, Edith." His voice was quiet, all teasing gone.

Shoot. She squeezed her eyes and spun in a slow circle, needing a second, maybe two, before she faced him again. "You weren't supposed to get it."

"You didn't mail it?"

"No. I mean, yes. I mailed it. But then I realized I shouldn't have mailed it. It's why I went back to the post office this morning. To get it back. Then things took a really weird turn. How did you get it so quickly?"

"I must have just happened by the post office right after you mailed it. Mr. Walton flagged me down and hand-delivered it. Not even sure if that's protocol."

"Of course. Mr. Walton."

Henry looked at his watch. "I just realized how late it is. Do you have to work tonight?"

"No. I'm done with the overnighters. All the regular staff is back from vacations, so Sharon has me filling in for just a few hours here and there now. Basically, I'm just killing time until my passport arrives. Should be any day now." Edith folded her arms and lowered her gaze.

Henry didn't say anything for several seconds. He refilled his water glass, took another drink, then dumped the rest down the sink. "When's the next time you're going in?" he finally asked.

"Monday evening."

"Can I see you after you get off? I can grab some dinner, swing by, and pick you up." He must have sensed the rebuttal clawing up her throat, because he lifted his hands to her shoulders. "I didn't like how things ended between us the other week."

To be honest, neither did Edith.

"There's some things I think we should talk about."

"Oh, there definitely are now," Edith muttered.

Henry's eyes crinkled in a smile as he lowered his hands back to his sides. "Why don't we hold off until we're both well rested. Or at least until I'm well rested."

She noticed the shadows beneath his eyes. "You do look tired. Downright ragged, really."

"Thank you."

"Wrung out."

"I get it."

"Dragged through the mud."

"I'm going now."

Edith followed him to the door, their familiar banter more welcome than the cool breeze slipping in through the open window above the kitchen sink. "Henry, I am sorry about this whole engagement thing. I did try to straighten it out. Really, I did. But there was so much . . . *screaming*. And happiness. I didn't know what to do."

Henry's lips lifted in a tired smile as he squeezed her hand. "It's just a little misunderstanding. Nothing to worry about."

Edith wasn't so convinced. Whenever she closed her eyes, she still had flashbacks of the maniacal grin on Julie's face as she sprinted toward her with chest heaving, fists pumping. That was one very excited woman. And Edith sure as heck didn't want to be the one to tell her the engagement was *just a little misunderstanding*.

But that wasn't even the most worrisome thing on Edith's mind. "Henry, wait." She opened her mouth but couldn't seem to make any words come out of her mouth.

"The letter?"

She nodded.

He held her gaze for several beats before leaning down and placing a soft kiss against her brow. "Like I said, we'll figure it out later. Good night, Edith."

She closed the door behind him and touched her fingers to where his lips had just been, wondering which part was going to be harder to figure out—the engagement or their feelings for each other.

Oh, why did she have to write that last letter?

CHAPTER TWENTY-EIGHT

Frank Sinatra's voice belted out from the speakers late Monday morning, and for once Henry didn't mind.

"I'm officially handing you your walking papers," Lance said. "No more canes. No more therapy. No more restrictions. Well, within reason, of course. I don't think hiking Mount Kilimanjaro should be on your list of activities this year."

"Thanks, man." Henry held his hand out with his palm facing upward.

Lance looked at it and slapped his palm on top of it.

"What are you doing?" Henry asked.

"Giving you five. Did you want to do a fist bump instead?"

"No. I thought you were giving me my walking papers."

"Dude, man, it's just a figure of speech. I don't have any actual papers for you."

"Oh. So I can leave now?"

"Yeah," Lance said with a laugh. "Get out of here. Don't come back. I don't ever want to see your ugly mug pass through that doorway again, you hear?"

Henry started to leave.

"Oh, wait. Stop. Don't go. I forgot. I do have papers for you." Lance flipped through a folder and pulled out a few sheets. "Here's a list of exercises I printed off for you."

Henry glanced down at the sheets, then looked closer. "These are core exercises."

"Indeed."

"What does strengthening my back and abdomen have to do with my knee?"

"Nothing. It has to do with your love handles."

Henry held his arms out and looked down. "What do you mean, love handles?"

"Hey, no need to get defensive. It's common knowledge that the midsection is a troublesome area for men of a certain age."

"I'm thirty-two."

"Exactly. And what with your wedding approaching, and I assume a honeymoon to follow, I figured you could benefit from a little extra attention to . . . you know." Lance waved his hands along the length of Henry's torso. "You stick to it, you'll notice a difference by wedding time. September is it?"

"Unbelievable." It seemed word of this supposed engagement had infiltrated every nook and cranny of the entire town.

"I know. Gonna be here before you know it. Do you have a DJ lined up for the reception? My cousin's always looking for work. I can give you his number. He also does balloon animals."

"I think we're good."

"All right, but if you change your mind, I'm sure he'd be available. Nobody does a monkey like him."

"I'll keep that in mind. Thanks for everything." Henry looked at the sheets in his hand. "Maybe."

"Sure. One more for the road?" Lance lifted his palm. Henry punched it with his fist on his way past. "Cool. A knuckle-five. I like it. Hey, man, if I don't run into you beforehand, I'll see you at the wedding. I mean, I am invited, right?" Henry heard Lance laugh and mutter behind him, "Of course I'm invited."

Henry shook his head on his way past the front desk. What was with this town?

"Oh, Henry, just the man I was looking for."

Henry drew up short. Nearly twenty-five years might have passed since he'd sat in her Sunday school classroom, but the sound of Ms. Appleblossom's voice never failed to transform him into a stammering eight-year-old boy trying to recite his Bible memory verses.

"Ms. Ample-bottom, I mean, Applebottom—" The front of her walker pressed into his toes. *"Appleblossom.* Hi. How are you? You look wonderful. Have you been working out? Your upper body strength seems particularly remarkable this morning."

She harrumphed. "It is. Ever since they made me start lugging this walker around, I've been able to open my own jar of pickles again. Can't say it does much for my balance though."

"Yes, well, perhaps if you pushed it instead of carrying it—" He stopped at the look of disapproval she wore as faithfully as her black curved spectacles.

"Now you're starting to sound like one of my grandsons."

"Yeah? How are Patrick and Peter these days?"

"Living in California." The way she said *California* made it sound as though she believed it to be interchangeable with the word *sin*.

She lifted the walker from his feet and stomped it back down. "But I don't want to talk about them. I want to talk about you. And a nasty rumor I've been hearing all over town." She pressed down as hard as her hefty frame would allow and leaned forward. "Is it true? Please tell me it isn't. Not with *that* woman."

"Uh, well?" He didn't know if his toes could survive much more pressure without telling the truth. "To be honest, there's been a bit of a mix-up."

She straightened up as much as her stooped spine would allow and gave a satisfied smile. "I knew it."

"I feel obliged to say, though, that she really is a great woman. I don't know why—"

"Great woman? *Please.* She is nothing but a busybody and a gossip. But I suppose if you're not using her for the flowers, then it doesn't really matter what you think of her. Here." She shoved a card into his hand. "You tell that little fiancée of yours to call this number. I know for a fact my granddaughter will not only put together a prettier flower arrangement, she'll do it for a heck of a lot cheaper than anything May Pritchard does."

Henry stared at the business card. *Josie's Posies.* "I don't know what to say."

"Say you'll call her. Now excuse me. Time for my therapy session, though Lord knows why. I'm fit as a fiddle." She lifted her walker, all four tennis balls hovering above the ground, and waddled past Henry to the exercise room.

Heaven help Lance. He looked down at the business card again. *Heaven help me.*

Henry skipped lunch and drove straight to where his crew had been hired to build a garage. The familiar sounds of buzz saws and hammers brought him a brief respite from the constant barrage of backslaps and congratulations that had followed him around town like an eager puppy.

He had obviously underestimated the level of enthusiasm this town carried when it came to weddings. Or the rapid wildfire spread of a rumor once it took off.

———— ♥ ————

Edith's stomach growled. She slapped a palm over it before the noise had a chance to wake the baby. That's right, a baby. Part of her couldn't believe it. Not a fern, not a toddler, but an actual living, breathing baby boy. With a mighty set of lungs she did not want to invoke the power of ever again.

Edith grabbed the baby monitor and tiptoed out of his room, trying not to make a peep as she creaked down the stairs. After all the screaming and wailing and gnashing of gums he'd done the past hour and a half, she imagined the baby could potentially sleep the rest of her shift, if not the rest of the week.

So. Much. Crying.

Edith paused on her way to the kitchen and patted the waxy green leaf of a peace lily. "I never knew how much I appreciated you until now," Edith whispered to the plant.

In the kitchen, Edith set the monitor on the counter and opened the pantry door. At least the past few hours had served to keep her mind off her ravenous appetite.

The clock on the wall tweeted with the sound of a cardinal. Eight o'clock. When she'd told Henry she didn't mind eating a late dinner, it was under the assumption she wouldn't be missing lunch. It was under the assumption she could set foot in the grocery store without hearing people shout, "Here comes the blushing bride!"

Edith had immediately turned tail for Kat's house and locked herself indoors for the rest of the afternoon. She wasn't venturing out into public until she and Henry came up with a solid plan that squelched this rumor for good. Hopefully without causing too much disappointment.

Because that was the thing. It wasn't just that Edith had never seen so many people excited over a wedding. It was the fact, in all her life, she'd never experienced so many people excited over *her*.

Goodness, a man she didn't even know stopped her outside the grocery store and gifted her with a balloon animal. She wasn't sure, but it might have been a monkey.

She closed the pantry door, her stomach growling in protest. "I know you're starving, but we've waited this long." Might as well keep waiting. Both the night worker and Henry should be arriving any minute.

"Stella!" A distressed male voice jarred Edith from her

thoughts. She peeked out the kitchen window. Maybe there was a rehearsal going on in the town square for *A Streetcar Named Desire*. Kind of late in the day but—

A fist pounded on the front door. "Stella, get out here! I know you're in there!"

"Oh, my goodness." One hand over her heart, Edith looked toward the ceiling. God help the man on the other side of the door if his racket woke the baby. She lifted the baby monitor to her ear, hearing the soft white noise from the sound machine next to the crib and one tiny whimper.

"Stella!"

Edith rushed to the front door, grabbing her phone off the entry table on the way past, and jerked the door open. "Knock it off or I'm calling 911."

"Where is she?" A giant man with dark shoulder-length hair and an unruly beard stood in the doorway. Between his bloodshot eyes and the slurring of his words that paired nicely with the subtle swaying of his body, Edith guessed he was intoxicated. "I want to see her." One whiff of his breath and Edith no longer had to guess.

"Who?" Edith gulped, her bravado quickly fading.

"Stella. I know she's here. *Stella!*" He shoved open the door, knocking Edith backwards onto her rear end. Her phone flew out of her hand and skidded across the floor as he staggered inside, heading for the stairs.

Edith clambered to her feet and raced after him. "Stop. *Stop!* There's no Stella." But there was a baby. And Edith wasn't about to let this man anywhere near that little bundle.

He stumbled his way to the top of the stairs and paused, looking each direction. Long enough for Edith to shove past, run to the baby's room, and slam the door behind her. A tall oak dresser sat to the right. She shouldered it in front of the door, knocking a lamp and two succulent plants off the top in the process, before scooping the screeching, red-faced baby out of the crib and clutching him against her chest.

"It's okay, baby. It's okay," Edith murmured as the man stomped from room to room, slamming furniture aside and punching walls like a grizzly bear. *Oh, God, help us.* Edith eyed the dresser. It was pretty solid, but still. She'd prefer a few more barricades between them and the lunatic outside. Especially when she heard his footsteps approaching. Was there any point in hiding in the closet?

She clutched the screaming infant tighter, bracing herself for the oncoming barrage. But instead of pounding, she heard a shout from below. Then the slurred speech of the man outside the nursery door hollering a reply.

The police?

"Edith, are you okay?" Not the police.

Henry.

"Don't come up here. Call the—" That was all she got out before the sound of fists on flesh followed by several grunts and more than a few swear words filled the air. Edith covered the baby's ears, wishing someone would cover hers.

Wood splintered. Glass broke. Something crashed. But scariest of all was the silence that followed a deafening thud. Edith held her breath. Why was there silence?

The baby had discovered his fingers to suck on, leaving Edith with nothing but the sound of her own unsteady breaths. Was Henry okay? Was Henry *alive?*

Flashing red lights reflected off the upstairs windows,

accompanied by the short squawk of a squad car siren. And then the most beautiful sound Edith had ever heard in her life.

"Edith, honey? You okay?" Henry's voice. Alive. *Thank you, God.* Edith's lungs fully expanded and released for the first time in several minutes. Her heart rate might have even dipped below two hundred beats per minute.

Edith placed the baby back in the crib with shaky hands, shoved the dresser out of the way, threw open the door, and—gasped. "Henry, your face."

"Yeah, well, you should see the other guy." Henry tried to wink but failed miserably, considering his eye was already swelling.

Edith didn't know what to say. She picked a noodle off his shoulder and held it up.

"You don't mind eating off the floor, do you?" Henry looked over his shoulder. "Or the wall?"

Before Edith could answer, Sharon's dismayed voice carried upstairs. "Oh, my word." The sound of crunching glass followed. "Oh. My. Word."

"I told you to wait in the car," a male voice scolded.

"Don't take that tone with me, James. I am your mother."

"I need to secure the area."

"What's left to secure? You already handcuffed the perpetrator."

"This is still a crime scene, Mom. I need to—"

"What? Draw a chalk line around the chicken lo mein?"

"Don't take that tone with me. I am an officer of the law."

"Don't remind me. Why you couldn't have gone to seminary school like your father—" Sharon's eyes flew up to Edith as she descended the stairs.

"Oh, honey," Sharon said on an exhale, "are you okay?" Sharon gingerly stepped over scattered noodles and broken glass from picture frames that had fallen from the walls and met Edith halfway up the stairs. "You're not hurt, are you? I should have known it was only a matter of time before Tyler's dad showed up and—"

The stairs creaked behind Edith and Sharon's mouth gaped open. "Oh, my word," she said again. Henry, his face bruised and cut, maneuvered down the stairs with the baby cradled in the crook of his arm.

"James," Sharon snapped. "Tell the paramedic to get in here."

"That's not necessary," Henry said, stopping on the stair behind Edith. "Baby's already snoozing and I'm fine."

Sharon rolled her eyes. "Yeah, you look real fine." She tromped down the stairs and headed out the door, no doubt in search of the paramedic herself.

"What about you? You sure you're okay?" Henry readjusted the baby in his arms and moved down a few steps so that he was standing eye level in front of Edith. "I'm sorry I didn't get here sooner."

"Are you kidding? If it weren't for you, that guy would have tried breaking the door down. Who knows what might have happened then? You came at just the right time as far as I'm concerned." She leaned forward and placed a gentle kiss on the lesser of his bruised cheeks. "Thank you."

Henry slowly angled his head so the warmth of his breath fanned over her lips. "I seem to remember your thank-yous being a little more involved than that."

Heat flooded her cheeks. "You're holding a baby."

"He's secure."

"You're bleeding."

"Not from my mouth."

"There's people around."

He slid his free hand around her waist and inched her closer. "They're professionals. They understand the common courtesy of saying thank you."

Unable to hide her smile any better than she was able to keep her arms from sliding around his neck, she said, "I suppose for the sake of not being rude . . ."

Planning to just brush her lips across his for a quick kiss—because, really, he was holding a baby, bleeding, and there were people around—she closed the tiny space between them.

Short and chaste. That was the plan. No chance for sparks. No opportunity for fireworks. Nothing long and drawn out.

So then why couldn't she stop kissing him?

Because she hadn't planned for this. She hadn't planned for his lips to be as warm and inviting as the first bite of a fresh-out-of-the-oven chocolate chip cookie. Or for the scent of his aftershave to be as familiar and welcoming as a pine tree on Christmas Day. Or for the feel of his shoulders, solid beneath her fingers, to be as comfortable and natural as if they were sharing a bowl of popcorn on the couch together.

She hadn't planned for one quick kiss to so quickly feel like home.

"Uh, I'd say Henry's doing more than okay, ma'am," a voice said from the doorway.

Edith broke the kiss and leaned back, giving her a clear view over Henry's shoulder.

Crowded together in the entryway stood the paramedic, his mustache twitching above a smile; Sharon, her eyebrows raised above amused eyes; and James, his mouth slanted above his walkie-talkie.

A young shaggy-haired man elbowed his way inside a second later, wielding a miniature notebook in one hand and a smartphone in the other.

"We seem to have gathered an audience," Edith whispered.

With his hand still planted around her waist and the baby still secured in his other arm, Henry slowly turned around.

The shaggy-haired guy grinned. "Don't move." *Click.* If possible, his grin grew even wider as he examined the image on his phone. "This is going to make a great picture for the article. Mind if I ask you a few questions?"

———— ♥ ————

The next couple hours passed in a blur. Henry gave a statement to the police, then attempted to help with the cleanup while the shaggy-haired man—whom he learned was named Joel, studying journalism at the community college and currently doing his internship at the local newspaper, covering obituaries and weddings though he longed to someday write a Pulitzer Prize–winning article—hounded Henry with questions.

"Where did you find the inner fortitude to confront a dangerous criminal with no regard to your own safety? It was almost like you were a fireman racing into a burning building. Have you ever trained as a firefighter?"

"I think I saw the movie *Backdraft* once."

After helping Edith sweep up all the bits of glass, plaster, and splintered wood—not to mention Chinese food—from the floor, Sharon demanded they go home. "The baby's taken care of. The police have Tyler's dad in custody. I've got a call in to the insurance company, so I'll be here all night anyway. We're good. Please go. And for goodness' sake, Henry, put some ice on that eye."

Henry, placing a light touch to her back, led Edith down the front porch steps. He ignored the pain in his knuckles, the pressure around his eye, and the mounting soreness in his ribs. He didn't even want to acknowledge his knee. Tomorrow morning was going to be rough getting out of bed, no doubt about that. But tonight Henry didn't care.

Tonight all he could think about was the fear that had slammed against his gut the moment he stepped inside the house and realized Edith was in danger. The fight-or-flight response that had kicked in a second later—thankfully fight. And the one-two punch that had sent the intruder to his knees and down half a dozen stairs. Granted, the man's inebriated state had probably tipped the scales in Henry's favor, but still. What a great punch.

Henry inhaled a deep breath, welcoming the tight grip on his ribs. It reminded him of the feeling he'd get in high school after a Friday night football game, taking pride in his pain. The hits and bruises never mattered when they were earned toward a victory.

And tonight was a big victory. Tonight he played the part of the hero. Tonight Henry didn't fumble the ball.

The sound of cicadas surrounded them as Henry dropped his palm from Edith's back and stepped around the truck to get to the driver's side. In high school, he'd always gone out for pizza after a game. Might not be a bad idea tonight. Unless Edith really had her heart set on Chinese. He opened the door, about to slide in, when he noticed she hadn't followed him to the truck.

She stood on the sidewalk, shuffling her feet. "Well, thanks again." She swept her bangs out of her eyes and hitched her bag higher on her shoulder. "And Sharon's right. You should definitely put some ice on that eye. Maybe take an over-the-counter painkiller or anti-inflammatory or . . ." She shrugged. "Something."

"Uh-huh. Yeah, I'll be sure to do that." Henry leaned his forearms over the side of the truck bed, confused as to why she wasn't getting inside the truck. And why she was saying things that made it sound like she didn't plan on getting inside the truck. "Where are you going?" he said, panic overriding the confusion when she started taking steps away from the truck.

"Kat's house."

"What about dinner? I thought—" *I thought I was a hero. Don't you want to have dinner with a hero?* Henry cleared his throat. "I thought we were going to talk."

"Yeah, but . . ." Edith waved to the house. "Aren't you sore? You've gotta be sore. I mean, your eye's all swollen, your eyebrow's still oozing—you really should have let that paramedic look at it—and you're limping. A lot. You're sore, Henry. Just admit it."

"Fine. I'm sore. But I'm also hungry." He pushed back from the truck and straightened. "C'mon, Edith. Eat some food with me. I've got a frozen pizza we can throw in the oven. Won't take long to cook."

A car turned the corner, its headlights washing over the conflicted expression on Edith's face. "Okay. But only because I'm starving and might very well die if I don't get some sort of sustenance in the next fifteen minutes, and I know for a fact the only sustenance I'll find at Kat's house is an expired bottle of Thousand Island dressing." She aimed her finger at Henry. "But as soon as we're done eating, you're icing that eye, taking some medicine, and going straight to bed. I don't want to hear another word about it."

"Yes, ma'am."

He slid into the driver's seat as she yanked open the door and climbed in on her side. "And just so you know," she said, slamming the door shut and reaching for her seat belt, "I will not be thanking you for tonight's dinner. I believe one thank-you is enough for today."

Henry's mouth curved up as he shifted the truck into reverse. "We'll see about that," he murmured before flashing her an innocent smile.

CHAPTER TWENTY-NINE

Filtered sunlight and the tweeting melody of birds beckoned
Edith awake the following morning. She took in the familiar
sight of her surroundings with a contented sigh, then rolled
onto her side.

Her eyes flew open a second later. This *was* familiar. Too
familiar. What was she doing here? In Henry's room. In
Henry's bed.

She flipped back the covers and bolted upright, forcing
herself to remember what happened last night. They came
back to Henry's house. Tossed in a pizza. Turned on the TV.
Started watching a Fred Astaire and Ginger Rogers movie.
What was it? Oh yeah. *Follow the Fleet.*

Edith swung her feet to the floor, taking in her rumpled
clothes from the day before.

She remembered thinking that they should talk about how to handle the engagement rumor, but decided to wait until after the pizza to bring it up. Then decided they might as well wait until after the movie. Then remembered getting comfy . . .

And that was the last thing she remembered.

Edith used the bathroom and brushed her teeth with her finger. How had she gotten upstairs? It reminded her of when she was a kid and no matter where she fell asleep in the house, come morning she was always tucked away in her own bed, with no recollection of how she got there. But that was when she was a child, all arms and legs, easy enough for her dad to heft around.

She wasn't all arms and legs anymore. Had Henry really carried her up the stairs last night? The thought of it sent a quivering heat to her belly.

Edith heard the back door to the house open and shut. She shuffled down the stairs, the boards creaking beneath her as she made her way to the kitchen. The sight of Henry, both hands braced on the kitchen island and head bowed, drew her up short. "You okay?"

He swung his head up, the bruises on his face causing her to suck in a quick breath. "You're awake." He pointed to a brown sack. "I picked up some scones. There's also coffee if you want it."

"Thanks. You didn't have to do that." Edith moved next to him, grabbing a cup of coffee and peeking in the sack. The scent of warm blueberries wafted out. "But I'm awfully glad you did."

She took a bite, washed it down with a sip of coffee, and

waited for Henry to do likewise. But he remained motion-less, head bowed once more. "Is everything okay?" Edith sat down on one of the stools. "Sorry I fell asleep last night, by the way. You should have woken me up."

He finally raised his head, met her gaze, his eyes trans-forming from serious to droll. "I did wake you up."

"You did? I don't remember you waking me up."

"When the movie was over, I nudged you and said we should call it a night and get some sleep. You said, 'Okay. See you later.' Next thing I know, you're halfway up the stairs and, by the time I reach you, crawling into my bed."

Edith sputtered on her coffee. "I did not do that." She coughed and attempted to clear her throat a few times while working hard not to laugh.

"Oh no? Then maybe you can explain to me how I ended up sleeping on the futon again." He handed her a napkin.

"I thought you carried me," Edith said, taking the napkin and coughing into it.

"You thought I carried you."

"Yeah." She wiped her mouth off and cleared her throat again. "I thought maybe you didn't want to wake me or something." She bit her bottom lip to keep from smiling at his wide-eyed expression. "What?"

"I'm just trying to imagine what that would have looked like, is all. I only started climbing stairs myself a little while back, and it's slow going. Lugging your incapacitated body up each and every step . . . wow. You must think I'm pretty amazing."

"Okay. First of all, I was not incapacitated. I was *sleepy*. Big difference. And secondly, all I meant was that I thought perhaps you didn't wake me up because, I don't know, you were being a gentleman or something."

"Oh, I see. So what you're saying is that when a man has an incapacitated woman—"

"Sleepy."

"—in his home, alone, the *gentlemanly* thing to do is carry her straight to his bed."

Edith wadded up her napkin and aimed for his head. "Well, obviously I can see now that you are neither amazing nor a gentleman."

Henry caught the napkin in one hand, turned, and threw it into the trash. When he turned back, the light had gone out of his eyes, and he was wearing the same expression he had on when she first entered the kitchen. *Defeat.*

"Henry, is everything all right?"

He absently ran his hand back and forth across the back of his neck, slowly shaking his head side to side. "Not really."

She stared, waiting for him to elaborate.

"I went out for coffee and scones this morning."

"Yeah," she said, drawing the word out in question.

"What I mean is, I went to Julie's bakery." He finally met her gaze again. "And it's worse than I realized."

She had a feeling where this was heading. "Does this have anything to do with the engagement?"

He nodded. Then with a sigh, he retrieved a newspaper she hadn't noticed sitting on the counter and slid it toward her. On the front page was the picture of the two of them and the baby, looking like the all-American family, with the headline "ENGAGED COUPLE RESCUES BABY."

Edith knew she could catch flies with the way her mouth

gaped open, but she couldn't help it. "The front page?" She lifted the paper, examining the picture more closely. "Look at us. This is ridiculous."

She couldn't help the bubble of laughter that escaped. "I'm looking at you like you're a returning war hero or something. How did they get this picture? I mean, I *know* how they got this picture. I was there. But is this really what we looked like? All googly-eyed and—" She stopped herself before she said *in love*.

"Oh, well," she said, tossing it back on the island. "It's a small town. I don't imagine that many people still read the newspaper, right?"

"It's not just a town newspaper. It's regional. It covers several counties. And lots of people around here still read it."

"You're kidding."

Henry shook his head.

"Okay. Still. It's just a picture."

"Edith, did you even look at the article? This is more than just a picture. This is a public engagement announcement." He sank onto the stool next to her. "You should have seen everyone at the coffee shop this morning." He dragged his hands through his hair. "I haven't had so many people that proud of me since . . . I may *never* have had so many people that proud of me."

They sat in silence for several minutes. Finally Edith asked, "What do we need to do?"

"I don't know." Henry looked at the picture in the paper again, then ran a hand down his face. "I don't know," he said again as he stood and began to pace.

Edith had time to finish one scone and was halfway

through another before Henry stopped blazing a trail between the refrigerator and the sink and settled into the stool next to her.

"Edith," he said hesitantly. So hesitantly that Edith instinctively slid the remainder of her coffee and scone away from her and turned to face him. She had a feeling whatever he was about to say required some space.

Several beats of silence passed before he said, "Why can't it be true?"

"Henry."

"No, I mean it. Why can't we be engaged?"

"You know why."

"I don't." He reached for her hands. "Seriously, Edith. Why? I know you care for me. I know you *love* me. You said so in your letter."

"No." Edith tried tugging her hands away. "No. That's not . . . the exact verbiage . . . Besides, I'm leaving, remember? I'm leaving."

"Why?"

"I told you. I've already gone down the marriage route. I'm no good at it, remember?"

"It'll be different this time."

"Would it? I'm pretty sure a pretend boyfriend and a fake engagement is going to end up in a sham of a marriage. So I don't really see how it would stand a chance of not turning out like the last time. I'm sorry, Henry." Her shoulders slumped. "I am. But I can't. Please understand. I just . . . I can't. This isn't my story, remember?"

Henry released her hands and turned away from her. "I'm sorry. You're right. You deserve better than this. I don't know what I was thinking." He stood up and moved to the kitchen sink, his back facing her.

"Henry."

"No, it's fine. I'll figure it out. I shouldn't have even . . . I'm sorry." He scrubbed a cloth along the kitchen counter. "This is my town. My problem."

Except it wasn't his problem. Not all of it. If it weren't for her, Henry would never have needed to loan his bedroom out to a complete stranger. Never pretended to be someone's boyfriend. Never been mixed up in this whole engagement misunderstanding. Never gotten a black eye.

The list seemed endless.

The ringtone to her phone began playing somewhere nearby. She must have left her cell phone in the living room last night after she'd fallen asleep. "Excuse me," she mumbled.

She found her phone buried in the couch cushions. "Hello?"

"Great! I'm so glad you answered. I thought I was going to have to leave a message, and this is definitely not something I wanted to tell you in a message."

"Sharon?"

"Yes, sorry. This is Sharon. Ha! I'm so excited, I forgot to even tell you who I was. Are you sitting down?"

Edith lowered herself to the couch. "Yes."

"Good. So get this. Your article in the paper today—I'm assuming you've seen it?"

"Oh, I've seen it."

"Well, guess what. It's gone viral."

"Excuse me?"

Sharon laughed. "I know! I felt the same way when I

heard. Apparently that picture of you and Henry gained a lot of attention through social media and now national papers are adding it to their online websites. But here's the real kicker, Edith. Are you ready for this?"

"Probably not."

"People are sending in donations. Can you believe it? People all over the country were so inspired by how you and Henry rescued that little baby they're pouring in money left and right. At this rate, we're going to have enough funds to cover the next fiscal year and then some. Oh! And I didn't even tell you the best part. One of those early morning shows has offered to cover the expense of your wedding if you and Henry agree to an interview. They want to know all about how you two met and fell in love. Can you believe it?"

"No."

"Oh, Edith, isn't this wonderful? Not only are you going to have an unbelievable wedding, but just think of the extra publicity for our crisis nursery center. We may be able to finally hire all the full-time staff we need. Not to mention what this sort of publicity could do for the entire town. All because of you and Henry. I'm so excited I could burst!"

Edith felt ready to burst too. "That's . . . wow."

"I know. I'll let you go, honey. I just couldn't wait another minute to tell you." Sharon squealed into the phone. "God is good, Edith. God is good." The line disconnected.

Edith dropped the phone back onto the couch. Well, God might be good, but *this* certainly wasn't good.

How was she supposed to walk away from this town when everyone believed she was engaged to one of its citizens? How was she supposed to walk away from this town when the funding for the crisis nursery center was depending on that engagement? How was she supposed to walk away from this town when it was the first place that had ever truly felt like home?

Maybe she wasn't supposed to.

"Who was that?" Henry leaned against the doorframe separating the living room from the kitchen.

"What? Oh. Uh, Sharon. Apparently we're celebrities." Edith fiddled with her bangs, trying to decide if she could really go through with the idea that had seemed so outlandish out of Henry's lips but now, rolling around in her own mind, seemed somehow less outlandish. Appropriate even. Certainly possible. And perhaps—dare she admit—enticing?

She stood up from the couch and faced Henry, her decision made in the span of a breath. "You were right. We should make this engagement real."

Henry straightened. "What? You just said you could never do that."

"I know. But now I've had more time to think."

"Two minutes? That's what you consider more time to think?"

"Look, pal, do you want to go through with this engagement or not?"

"Well, gee, *buddy*, when you put it that way."

"How else am I supposed to put it?"

"Perhaps without the yelling?"

"I'm *not* yelling. I'm just trying to carry on a conversation with you! Okay. Maybe I'm yelling." Edith didn't know how they had gotten so close to each other. But they were close now. She could see lightning bolts of white scattered throughout the irises of Henry's blue eyes as clearly as he must see the doubts circling like sharks beneath the surface of her own.

"What happened, Edith?"

"When? Just now? Or twelve years ago when Brian asked me to marry him and I disappointed the two people I cared about most by saying yes?" Edith reached out, running her hands down Henry's forearms until she was clasping each hand. "I don't want to live with that again, Henry. This town, these people, you. Maybe this is my second shot to do things right. Maybe this time I'm supposed to say yes. Maybe . . . maybe this is my story."

She squeezed his hands. "So Henry I-Don't-Know-Your-Middle-Name-Yet Hobbes, will you please do me the honor of asking me to be your wife?"

Henry glanced down at their joined hands. He slowly removed his from hers and brought them up to cup her face. He leaned forward and kissed her, tenderly, sending butter-flies of anticipation throughout her stomach.

See? Being married to this man wasn't going to be so bad. Even when they argued.

"My middle name is Dominic," he whispered next to her ear. "And no. I will not ask you to marry me."

CHAPTER THIRTY

"No?" Edith's arms and shoulders turned rigid as she pressed away from him. "What do you mean, no?"

"We can't get married. Not like this. It wouldn't be right. This whole thing isn't right. I'll call the newspaper, tell them to issue a retraction of some sort. Or I don't know, call a town hall meeting. Something." He would fix this. Somehow.

"It's too late. Don't you get it? It's too late." Edith placed her palms against her cheeks. With eyes growing wider and wilder by the second, she put Henry in mind of that painting *The Scream*. "Sharon's counting on us, Henry. The whole town—" she let out a hysterical giggle—"maybe even the entire nation. It's too late to go back."

"What are you talking about?"

Henry listened as Edith gave a rambling description of

her phone call with Sharon. "But we cannot do any interviews. That is the one thing I refuse to do. I'll pay for the whole stinking wedding myself. Last time I ever spoke live to a crowd was over the intercom in junior high for morning announcements, and it did not go well, Henry. It did not go well."

Pulling her back into his arms, he cradled her head against his shoulder. His intent worked. She stopped talking, allowing him a moment to think.

So okay. Things had escalated even further than he'd thought. A lot further.

"Henry?" Her muffled voice spoke against his shoulder.

"Shhhh . . ." He patted her head.

What options did they have? Tell the truth obviously. Which would mean disappointment, embarrassment, humiliation—basically all the things he'd worked hard to bounce back from ever since high school.

Or option two. Stay engaged. Get married. Then eventually divorced once Edith realized how much she resented him for standing in the way of her dreams. *Ouch.*

"Edith?" He loosened his hold on her enough to lean back. A crease from his shirt had left an indentation on her cheek. Maybe he'd been holding a little too tight. "What's in it for you if we go through with this? I mean, besides not disappointing anybody. Aren't you supposed to leave for South Africa any day now? That's been your dream all summer. Why would you throw it away now?"

"Who says I'm throwing it away?"

Henry's eyebrows dipped. "So you think we can just keep on pretending we're engaged while you run off for the next couple of years? Am I supposed to tell people it's a really long engagement or . . . ?"

"No. I'm not saying that. I'm saying maybe my dream just gets postponed for a little bit. I still go, I just go later."

"Like after we're married? 'Hey guys, we're back from the honeymoon. Now my wife's leaving the country. Oh no, I'm staying here. Absence makes the heart grow fonder and all that.'"

"No. Not . . . I don't know. I'm sure we'll figure it out."

"The same way we'll figure it out if you get pregnant?"

"Wow." A blush spread up Edith's cheeks. "Jumping a little ahead of ourselves, aren't we?"

"Well, it's possible."

"Is it? I'm not so sure. Brian and I weren't exactly trying to prevent it during our marriage and it sure never happened for us." She shrugged uncomfortably. "Besides, we're not exactly spring chickens, you and me."

"What, thirty and thirty-two?" Henry slid his hands around Edith's waist and tugged her closer. "Pretty sure that falls under the spring chicken category in this town. Even if it doesn't, we're going to be going at it like a couple of spring rabbits once we're married."

Edith smacked Henry against the chest. "Real classy."

He chuckled and let her escape his grip. "I'm just saying it's possible, okay? It's something we need to consider. Something *you* need to consider."

A breeze ruffled the curtains and an outdoor wind chime plunked a hollow tune as Edith moved to the living room window. The morning sun cast a honey glow, making strands of her hair appear even blonder than usual.

It reminded him of the first moment he laid eyes on her. A dizzy feeling of breathless wonder. And that was before he had even started choking.

Now it still felt like he was choking. Only this time on all the words he wanted to say. He wanted her to stay. He wanted to tell her he loved her. But he didn't want her to live the rest of her life with regret either. If this town hadn't been enough for Maggie, why should it be enough for Edith? Why should *he* be enough for Edith?

She wanted to get married out of fear of disappointing the people of this town. He didn't want to get married out of fear of disappointing *her*.

He might not have known Edith long, but he knew her well. She would stand by his side to the bitter end if she thought it would keep the peace. Even if it meant killing her own dreams in the process. She'd done it before, hadn't she? With her first husband.

Henry wasn't about to let her do it again with him.

He pressed his lips together, the unspoken words squeezing his throat tighter than any noose. As Edith stared out the front window, probably searching for answers of her own, he stared at her, already knowing what needed to be done.

He was getting that woman on a plane to South Africa no matter what. He might lose a piece of his heart when she left, but better than losing a piece of his soul. This time he was doing the right thing. Letting Edith move on to live the adventure she'd always dreamed of, that was the right thing.

He knew it. She knew it.

He crossed the room. If this was to be the end of them, he wasn't saying goodbye without making it memorable. He'd sweep her into his arms and dip her back like that black-and-white World War II picture of the soldier and nurse. This kiss would be one for the ages.

Before he made it to her, Edith spun from the window and grabbed him by the shirt. Maybe she had the same idea. "There's people outside. And one of them has a video camera."

Or not. "What?"

"A video camera, Henry. A video camera."

"I heard you."

"What do we do?"

The landline in the kitchen began ringing. "Um . . ." Henry backpedaled out of the living room. Honestly he didn't know what to do. "Let me see who that is. Just . . ." He pointed toward the front of the house. "I don't know. Tell them to hold tight if they come to the door."

Seeing on the caller ID that it was Peg—and not *USA Today*—Henry breathed a sigh of relief. "Hey, Peg."

"Henry, where are you?"

"Sorry. Some things have come up this morning and I'm running late. Is everything okay?"

Peg released a throaty chuckle into the phone. "Yeah, you could say that. Charles Henderson just called. He said he happens to be in the area and would like to meet with you. He didn't mention it, but I've got a feeling he may have been influenced by that front-page article plastered all over the region. Nice shiner by the way."

"Thanks," Henry said, racking his brain for the name Charles Henderson. *Charles Henderson. Charles Henderson.* Was he supposed to know Charles Henderson?

Able to read him over the phone just as easily as she could in person, Peg let out an exasperated sigh. "*Charles Henderson*, Henry. Multimillionaire. Philanthropist. Halfway houses. Does any of this ring a bell?"

It was ringing a bell. So were the people at the front door.

"He wants to start a halfway house here?"

"He's the one behind that giant grant I applied for. Remember? I must've told you a dozen times." She huffed out a frustrated sigh. "Just get down here. He's on his way now."

"O-okay." Henry heard foot traffic in the front entryway along with a cacophony of voices. "I'll get there as soon as I can."

"*Now*, Henry. He's not the type of man you keep waiting. Oh, and, Henry?"

"Yeah?"

"No pressure or anything, but for the love of all that's holy, don't screw this one up."

Peg disconnected the call just as Edith flung herself around the corner, barreling into Henry's chest with eyes full of panic.

"It's a news station from the Quad Cities. They said Sharon promised them an interview. Did you hear me? They want to interview us. Live. Now. What do we do?"

Henry shrugged and rubbed his hand along his neck. "Tell them we can't. Or at least I can't. I have to get down to the office."

"What? Now? Are you kidding me?"

"Sorry to intrude." A young woman with a short blonde bob and a megawatt smile that said she was anything but sorry stepped into the kitchen. "But we should get you onto the couch and ready. I think the lighting will work best there." Raising two perfectly groomed eyebrows when nobody moved, she said, "I'm sorry. Is there a problem? I'm Emily Goodbar, reporter for KWQP TV 8 news."

"I know who you are." Henry cleared his throat. "And yes, there is a problem. Neither of us agreed to an interview. And even if we had, now is not a good time."

"Oh, I see. Perhaps if we added a little makeup, you might feel more comfortable."

"Huh?"

"Your eye. It is rather disconcerting, isn't it? All that swelling and bruising. How about if we—?"

"The problem isn't my eye. The problem is I need to go."

"Emily, we're gonna be on in five minutes," a voice shouted from the living room.

"I'm aware," Emily replied tersely, glancing at her watch. "Look, we'll keep it short and sweet. We'll be done and out of here in no time."

"I already told you we are not doing an interview. Not now, not ever." That might not have been what he said before, but this lady was starting to annoy him.

"Henry." Edith ran a palm up and down his arm, ever the peacemaker. "You might be able to do an interview at some point, right? Maybe in the afternoon?" Edith flashed a placating smile toward Henry followed by an apologetic one to the reporter. "How about if you came back later? Maybe tomorrow. Would that work?"

"I'm not sure you guys really understand the concept of how a *live* story works."

"Edith, I'm sorry." Henry unlocked the iron grip she had clamped on his wrist. "But I really do have to leave."

"You know what?" The reporter waved Henry away. "It's fine." She turned the full force of her smile toward Edith, appearing much like a crocodile facing a live chicken, and grabbed on to her arms. "We'll just do the interview with you."

Edith backed into the refrigerator. "What? No. I can't. I'll start sneezing and—"

"Two minutes!" the cameraman shouted.

"Coming," Emily responded.

"Henry," Edith pleaded.

"I'm sorry." Henry watched Emily drag Edith around the corner into the living room.

He should stay. Edith needed him.

He had to go. Peg was counting on him.

Looking at his watch, knowing he didn't have time to waver any longer, he stepped through the door—hesitating just long enough to hear a voice start to count down—then closed it behind him.

CHAPTER THIRTY-ONE

"Honey, don't you think you ought to slow down? That's your fifth one."

"I said hit me again, so I suggest you do as I say and hit. Me. Again." Edith slapped a bill on the counter.

Shooting her a wary look, Julie reluctantly took the cash and dropped it into the register. "Fine. But don't come crying to me when your pants don't fit tomorrow." Julie grabbed another scone from the display case and slid it across the counter to Edith.

Edith bit into it. "What? You going to judge me too?" Crumbs shot down the front of her shirt and onto the floor as she waved her scone. "Et tu, Chester? Et tu?"

Yawning widely, the feline stood, arched its back, then curled into the basket, facing away from Edith. "Oh, I see.

You'd rather just turn your back on me. Seems to be a common theme in my life."

"It really wasn't that bad, you know." The grimace on Julie's face portrayed a different perspective.

"*Not that bad.* Julie, I was there. I know how bad it was." Edith shoved the rest of the scone into her mouth and wiped her forearm across her lips. "How much is that strawberry tart on the end?"

"Absolutely not. I am cutting you off."

"Julie, I made a fool of myself. I need sugar."

"You were nervous. It happens."

"I'm not just talking about the interview. I'm talking about this entire summer. How did I get here?"

"Well, honey," Julie said, wiping her hands on her apron, "I imagine you came in on Route 6 like most folks do. Oh, c'mon. That was a tiny bit funny. No?" Sighing, Julie came around the counter and flipped the Open sign to Closed.

"Isn't it a bit early to be doing that?"

"Not when you've eaten up my entire inventory. Besides that, I'm pretty sure your bellyaching would scare off any potential customers I get."

"I'm not bellyaching. I'm lamenting."

"Right. Well, how about you do your lamenting while you sweep the floor, considering it was you who left all the crumbs I see standing there."

"Is this how you treat all your paying customers?"

"No." Julie smiled and handed Edith a broom. "But it is how I treat my friends."

Unsure how to respond to that, Edith began sweeping the floor. When she'd cleaned up all the crumbs by the display case, she moved to the seating area and swept. Then she found a wet rag and wiped down the tables and chairs while Julie finished cleaning out the display case and coffeepots.

Everything stored away and ready for the next morning, Julie came around the counter, untied her apron, and nodded toward the door. "Let's go for a walk. Looks nice out and heaven knows you could use the exercise after all the calories you've put down this afternoon."

"I think I'd rather just take a nap."

"Nope. Friends don't let friends nap when they're coming down from a sugar binge. You need to walk it off." Julie locked the door, then linked her arm through Edith's. "Here. I'll even let you choose which direction we go."

"Really generous of you," Edith said, squinting first at Julie, then toward the azure sky. No matter her lack of energy at the moment, she couldn't deny the beauty of the day. Or that a walk might do her some good. "Which direction is it to the park with the botanical garden? I haven't been there yet."

Julie unlinked her arm, leaning back to peer at Edith. "That park's on the other side of town. Do I look like the sort of person who makes a habit of hiking to the other side of town?"

"What did you have in mind then?"

"I don't know. Around the block a time or two?"

"Oh, c'mon now, *friend*. If you're going to drag me out here for a walk, then by golly, we're going for a walk." Edith linked Julie's arm back with her own again. "And just think— the farther we go, the longer you get to hear me lament."

Julie's shoulders sank and her feet began to drag. "I think I liked it better when you were just a paying customer."

Brushes of pink and lavender smeared across the sky hours later as Edith and Julie sat on a park bench, watching a family of ducks make their way across a pond in a single-file line.

"I'm starving."

"You're not starving. We stopped for an early supper on the way over here. Besides, you consumed enough calories at the bakery to last you until next week. I'm the one who should be starving. If I'd known you were going to drag me to the edge of civilization when I suggested a nice leisurely stroll, I would have packed a survival kit." Julie threw a piece of cracker toward a duck.

"What are you doing?" Edith angled toward Julie.

"What do you mean what am I doing?" Julie followed Edith's gaze down to the package of crackers in her hands. "This?" Julie shrugged. "I'm feeding the ducks." She broke off another piece and threw it.

"I just said I'm starving."

"Yeah. But obviously you're not starving, and obviously—" she cocked her arm back and sailed a chunk of cracker into a group of three mallards—"these are for the ducks."

"You always keep a sleeve of saltines in your purse just for ducks?"

"Sometimes I keep stale scones." Julie dispensed the rest of the crackers, then brushed her hands together. "There. That ought to keep them happy for a while." She swung her gaze toward Edith's profile, no doubt taking in the forlorn expression on her face, and sighed. "Fine." Julie dug into her purse, then held out her palm.

Edith blinked. "Gum. That's the sustenance you offer me?"

"It's not just gum. It's Big Red. And frankly I'm going to need the sustenance more than you do if I ever hope to make it back to my car again." She pointed at the cross-trainers on her feet. "Pretty sure I have a blister. These aren't exactly hiking boots, you know."

"Aren't those the shoes you normally wear to work?"

"Yeah, I love 'em. They're super comfortable." She raised them off the ground and flexed her feet back and forth. "But I don't usually run a half marathon in them either."

"Julie, you do realize we walked all of a mile to get here."

"Edith, you do realize you ate supper, plus an entire bakery, before we got here."

"Fair enough." Edith slouched on the bench and crossed her arms. A minute later, she unfolded them and leaned forward. "See, here's the thing though. The last time I was feeling down, I wrote this letter, and it turned out to be a big mistake. I poured out things I should have kept bottled in."

Julie snapped her gum and nodded for Edith to continue.

"I told myself the next time I was ever tempted to do that again, I'd do what I should have done the first time. Eat ice cream. In today's case, pastries. Nothing bad comes out of eating ice cream and pastries, right?"

"Possibly diabetes, but you're the nurse."

"So today, after that interview went so horrible—"

"I wouldn't say horrible."

"I sneezed on the reporter, Julie. My snot landed in her eyeball."

"I doubt anybody noticed."

"She squealed and yelled, 'Ewww, my eye!'"

"There was that."

Edith stood and began to pace, sending a lone duck that had wandered close to their bench scurrying back toward the pond. "You want to know the worst part?"

"It was all captured on live TV?"

"The worst part is knowing, right when I needed him most, Henry left. He just left."

"Well, honey, I'm sure he had a good reason. Have you talked to him yet?"

"No. Because that's just it. I'm sure he did have a good reason. Maybe even a great reason. Who cares? It doesn't matter. Because he has the right to walk away. He is under no obligation to me. Why did I ever think it would be different?"

"I don't think I'm following."

Edith brushed her bangs off her forehead and gazed across the pond toward the low-cast sun. "My parents left me when I made a decision they didn't agree with. My husband left me, in a way, when things didn't go as we planned, then for good when he got sick. His brother—why, he left me as soon as his mother dragged him out by his ear."

"Heard about that," Julie said with an amused snort.

"Point is they were all people I loved. Okay, maybe not Steve. But at the very least, they were all people I trusted. They weren't supposed to leave me. So why did I think for one moment a man I barely knew would be the one to stick by me? Why did I let myself get in this position again?"

Edith sank onto the park bench, her energy suddenly spent as she blew out a big breath. "And for crying out loud, why did I ever think bangs would be a good idea?"

Julie patted Edith's leg. "Oh, honey, we've all been there."

But for a squirrel scampering up a tree next to them,

shaking a few walnuts loose from the branches, and the occasional honks from the snow geese gathered nearby, they sat together in silence for the next several minutes. Mosquitoes buzzed near Edith's ear and she swatted them away. Julie lifted her feet up from the ground and rotated her ankles a few times, occasionally slapping her arms when a bug landed on her.

Finally Julie spoke again. "So you and Henry . . . you're not . . ."

"No," Edith said.

Julie nodded, pulled out a tissue from her purse, and blew her nose several times. "Allergies." She dropped the tissue back into her purse. "I didn't want you to think I was crying over you and Henry."

"Right. I didn't think—"

"Even though I feel very much like crying." Julie's voice quivered and she swiped underneath her nose. "What happened? If you don't mind me asking."

"Nothing really happened." Edith held out a hand for a tissue. A sudden attack of allergies had hit her as well. "It was just a misunderstanding."

"Which part?"

Edith blew her nose. "Every part, I guess." Lifting her legs up and curling them beneath her on the bench to protect them from hungry mosquitoes, Edith started at the beginning. The day she met Brian. Edith told Julie about her marriage, then moved on to include everything that had happened this summer, starting with the Heimlich maneuver in the diner all the way up to the interview conducted this morning. By the time Edith finished, the sky was cloaked in deep purple and the only birdcall was the occasional hoot of an owl.

"Honey, I'm so sorry."

"Why are you sorry? I'm the one who's been lying to everybody this summer. Telling Steve I'm dating Henry. Not telling Henry I knew who he was. Letting people think Henry and I were engaged."

"I know, but I'm still sorry. I'm sorry you thought you had to carry on a misconception out of fear for what people might think of you. Whether you're engaged to Henry or not, the people of this town who have gotten to know you over the past couple months are still going to care about you. Just like we're still going to claim Henry as one of our own, no matter what he does or doesn't do. You'd think he'd have figured that out by now."

"Yeah, but what about the crisis nursery center?"

"What about the crisis nursery center?"

"How am I supposed to explain to Sharon that all those donations were given under false pretenses?"

"Honey, I'm going to let you in on a little something. Sharon—and I say this with all the love in my heart—has a tendency to make a mountain out of a molehill. I'll lay you odds that somebody donated an extra twenty bucks, is all."

"I don't know," Edith said, unconvinced.

"All right, let me ask you this then. Has *Good Morning America* contacted you?"

"No."

"And they're not going to. Anytime that crisis nursery center generates the slightest buzz, Sharon's convinced it's going to make national news. You know how many times

I've heard her celebrating in the coffee shop over how they're finally going to get enough funds to hire full-time staff? About as many times as I've heard Opal threaten to call the sanitation department."

"Oh."

"But you wanna know what I think? I think God knows better than to ever give Sharon the kind of funds she dreams about."

"Why do you say that?"

"Because God wants for Sharon the same thing he wants for all of us—to have the kind of faith that knows he'll provide what we need when we need it, even when we don't see how. Especially when we don't see how. Even Sharon would admit God's always come through on that nursery of hers. You're living proof of that."

Edith released a soft laugh. "How do you figure?"

"You're here, aren't you? Why else would a young single woman without any ties willingly spend a summer in Illinois without payment of any kind unless she were answering God's call?"

"Good point." Edith chewed on her lip. "But I'm supposed to be leaving for South Africa soon."

"Supposed to?"

"Well, with everything that was going on, I started thinking maybe I should just stay and . . ."

"And what?"

Edith cleared her throat. "Get married."

"Oh, good golly grief. You are *not* canceling your plans for South Africa. I already told you. Nobody's going to think any less of you when they find out what really happened. It's going to be fine. There's no reason for you to stay. Unless . . ."

"What?"

"Unless you really do love Henry."

"It doesn't matter whether I do or not. You're right. If God is calling me to South Africa for the next however many years, then that's where I need to be."

"I think it does matter though."

"Not when Henry doesn't love me back."

"Of course Henry loves you back. I heard him declare it in front of the entire bakery."

"Yeah, when we were pretending. That's all it ever was to him. Pretend."

"Honey. About fifteen years ago I spent the longest three hours of my life watching Henry play Curly in the high school's production of *Oklahoma!* How he got the lead role, I'll never know, because the boy could not act and he certainly couldn't sing. So believe me when I say, if Henry had been pretending, I'd have known."

"Well, he's never said it to me." Edith stood up. "Anyway, you're right. I can't throw this opportunity to go to South Africa away. Not when I feel such a deep pull to go. I've ignored God's direction in my life for far too long. I can't keep doing that. I can't stay here. Not like this. I have to go."

Julie rose from the bench. "Are you still talking about South Africa, or do you mean the park? Because technically this place closed at sunset, and we do need to go."

Edith laughed. "Why didn't you say something sooner?"

"I was half hoping James would arrest us since the jail is only a block from my car."

"Oh, good golly grief."

"Are you mocking me with my own expression?"

"I am. Now start moving. We've got a lot of ground to cover."

"Don't remind me."

"And for the record, Charlie Brown owns that expression, not you."

"Not the *golly* part. That's all mine."

"Fine. I'll let you have that if you let me have the Snickers bar I saw you trying to hide in your purse."

"What are you, part cat? How could you have possibly seen that in the dark?"

Edith linked arms with Julie. "I have a keen sense of smell. Especially when I'm starving."

As they made their way back to the bakery, the conversation never stalling, Edith felt lighter than she'd felt in years. Just as she knew it was the right decision to board the plane to South Africa, she knew with equal certainty she'd made a lifelong friend in Illinois.

CHAPTER THIRTY-TWO

"I'll have my assistant write up the contract and give you a call." Charles Henderson rose from his chair. "We can set up another meeting next week, sign the papers, finalize the arrangements. I'd like to get up and running on this as soon as possible. No later than September, preferably."

"Sounds perfect." Henry shook hands with Henderson, his mind scrambling with the implications of what he'd just agreed to. "We'll wait to hear from you."

Henderson nodded. Though not a large man, the strong authority radiating out of his brown eyes was as plain to see as the gray fedora he wore on his head. He put Henry a little in mind of Humphrey Bogart.

"You know, son," Henderson said, taking Henry in with one more keen gaze, "I walked away with a few black eyes myself throughout the years. Some of them I deserved; some of them I didn't. But either way, it was always worth it." Turning and nodding his head at Peg, Henderson let himself out the door. His gray fedora disappeared down the steps and past the window.

Neither Peg nor Henry said a word until the sound of his car starting up and driving away had completely faded. Peg spoke first, her voice a reverent whisper. "Well, can you believe that?"

Still standing behind his desk, Henry slowly shook his head side to side. A grin spread across his face. Then laughter. Deep from the gut laughter.

"Oh, Henry," Peg said, getting up from her desk and joining in. "This is . . . this is . . ." She grabbed her sides and bent forward, tears leaking down her cheeks. She never caught her breath long enough to say what *this* was. She didn't need to. Henry knew.

This was a once-in-a-lifetime opportunity. A chance for something bigger than himself. A future that was anything but boring. "I need to find Edith."

"Definitely." Peg wiped her eyes with a tissue. "She'll want to hear this."

Henry bent down, opened a drawer to fish out his truck keys.

"Maybe it'll help her forget about this morning," Peg added.

Henry's head snapped up.

"Oh, that's right." Peg threw her tissue into the trash and grimaced. "You haven't seen it yet."

The interview. How could he have forgotten? Listening

to Charles Henderson spend an hour telling stories, another hour questioning Henry about his work and life experiences, a forty-minute lunch filled with more stories, followed by an afternoon touring the land in question, topped off with the entire last hour gathering information for the plans Henderson wanted Henry to be a part of. That was how he had forgotten.

"It wasn't that bad, was it?"

Peg's silence spoke volumes.

Henry blew out a breath and tossed his keys back and forth between his hands. "Right. Okay. Well, thanks for the heads-up. Maybe I'll—I don't know—pick up some flowers or something. Try to take the edge off." Henry nodded to himself. "Yeah, that might help."

Because now that he had the next several years figured out, not only with his career but a new purpose for his life, the last thing he needed was for Edith to walk out of it. He couldn't let her go to South Africa. Why did he ever think she should go to South Africa? Nobody should go to South Africa. Not when there were dreams to be made here. Adventures to be had. People to help. Each other to love.

"We're getting married, Peg. I'm doing it. Tonight."

"You're getting married tonight?"

"No. I'm asking her—you know what? We'll straighten everything out later. I need to go."

"Henry," Peg shouted after him as he raced to his truck. "If you're really serious about whatever it is you're asking that young woman, you might need more than flowers." She cupped her hands together over her mouth. "You might need pie!"

♥

Henry was worried. He'd been driving around for hours. The last time anybody had seen Edith was at Julie's bakery. When he'd gone by, the Open sign had already been flipped to Closed. He checked Kat's house—dark and empty. No signs of her at the crisis nursery home. No signs Edith had been back to his house either.

No messages on his phone. No notes on the table. Nothing. She was gone. Where to, Henry hadn't a clue.

"I'm on patrol tonight, so I'll keep my eye out," James promised when Henry called him. "But she's probably just lying low. You know, after the interview and all."

"Right." The interview Henry hadn't been able to work up the courage to watch. The more people talked about it, the less he wanted to.

Henry ended the call. A crescent-shaped moon dangled in the night sky. Only the brightest of stars were visible above the pale glow of streetlights running along Kat's street.

Not knowing where else to go or what else to do, he'd come back to his niece's house. With peach pie.

Setting the pathetic peace offering next to him on the top porch step, Henry stretched his legs out. With time and plenty of rehab, he was back to performing all his usual activities. But the stiffness never went away. Probably never would. Just like, he imagined, the ache in his heart if Edith had already left him for good.

What am I supposed to do here, God? I want to be with Edith, but . . . what if she doesn't want to stay? You can't really expect me to go with her. Not now. Why would you hand me this opportunity if you wanted me to leave?

"Oh, my—" A muffled scream startled Henry from his prayer. He looked up to see Edith clutching one hand to her chest and holding the other out to brace herself. "Jeepers," she said. "What are you doing sneaking around in the dark like that? Don't you know I could have shot you?"

"Sneaking? I'm sitting on the porch. And what exactly would you have shot me with?"

"I don't know. A Winchester '73?"

"*Winchester '73*? I'm thinking more like *The Shakiest Gun in the West* if you're going to be naming movie titles. Pie?"

Despite shadows obscuring most of her features, Henry caught the small smile on her lips as she grabbed the container and sat down on the step next to him. "Or rather *The Fastest Gun Alive* you mean. I'd make an excellent shot, you know."

"Sure you would. I've seen what kind of steady aim you have with popcorn."

She punched him in the shoulder. "Stop that."

"Stop what?"

"Being so likable. Not when I'm trying to be mad at you. It's not fair."

Henry twisted on the step to face her. "Listen, about this morning—"

"No, Henry, you don't have to say anything. It's okay. I mean, it's not okay—I made a complete idiot of myself—but it's okay. I think it's what needed to happen, honestly. I wasn't trying to get you to apologize."

"I do want to apologize."

"You don't need to."

"But I want to."

Edith stood and climbed the porch steps. "Well, I don't want you to, okay? I don't want to hear it. It doesn't matter whether you're sorry or not sorry. Or what kind of pie you brought. Unless it's peach. Is that peach? Nope, doesn't matter. I've decided to leave. So if you want to apologize, fine. But honestly it might be a whole lot easier for the both of us if you didn't."

"Wait—" Henry clambered after her with the pie in one hand, gripping the porch rail with his other.

"No, listen," Edith said, pausing to swipe her hair from her eyes with shaky fingers. "I know I said a lot of things this morning. Things I shouldn't have said. It was crazy to think we could ever make a real marriage out of a pretend relationship. I think we both—"

Henry kissed her, dropping the pie container to the ground. He cupped both sides of her face. He couldn't stand it any longer. He was sorry he wasn't there for her this morning. He was sorry he wasn't up-front about his feelings sooner. He was sorry for how much time he'd wasted this summer—how much time he'd wasted in his life.

Feeling her stiffen beneath his grasp, he loosened his hold, prepared to be pushed away. Prepared to have another reason to apologize.

He was not prepared for her to grab on to him and deepen the kiss. "Henry," she murmured, her entire body molding against him. *Sweet mercy.*

And suddenly it was like their first kiss again. She wrapped her arms around his neck like her life depended on him, and he couldn't help sliding his hands behind her back to press her tighter against him. When they finally came up for air, he had her pressed against the front door, their breaths tangled and heaving.

"Come with me," she said.

"What?"

"Come with me."

"Edith." Henry wanted to come with her, all right. Inside and straight to the bedroom. But he knew that wasn't what she meant. And even if it was, he knew he couldn't say yes. "I can't."

"Why not? What's keeping you here? You've said it yourself: you're bored. So come to South Africa with me and we can do something amazing. Together."

"I am doing something amazing."

"What? Painting walls? You could do so much more than that and you know it."

"I know. I am. I will be. I . . ." Henry realized he still had Edith pinned against the door, her palms resting against his chest, fanning embers that hadn't nearly died out. He opened some space between them. "Invite me inside."

She lifted a brow.

"To talk."

Seated a few minutes later in Kat's kitchen with a glass of iced tea, Henry met Edith's questioning gaze. "I don't suppose you've ever heard of Charles Henderson."

Edith's brow wrinkled. "Isn't he that old actor guy who went to prison, then afterward became some sort of philanthropist, starting up a bunch of halfway houses?

"Exactly." Edith knew more about him than Henry had. "And he was here. Today. In Westshire."

"For real? What did he want?"

Henry swiped his thumb across the condensation on his glass, still trying to process the answer to that question himself. "Me, if you can believe it. He has this idea for one of those refuge ranches—you know the kind of place I'm talking about, where troubled kids learn how to take care of horses—and initially it was going to be funded through some sort of grant, which is how he heard about me. Peg sent in an application. I don't know what she said, but whatever it was caught his attention."

Henry heard himself rambling but couldn't stop his words or excitement racing out even faster. "Instead of using the grant money, he's going to fund the project entirely himself. And he wants me, Edith. *Me.* On the plot of land I've always dreamed about. It's like I've always known in my bones that land and I were meant to do something good, and here it is. The opportunity I've been waiting for. A chance to do something big. From scratch. He wants housing, stables, a recreation center, everything. And he wants me as his contractor. Not his painter. Not his kitchen cabinetmaker. His contractor. This is . . ."

Henry took a deep breath. "This is huge, Edith. And I haven't even told you one of the best parts. A camera crew is going to film the whole thing for his YouTube channel, which has over a million followers or something crazy like that. Talk about great exposure for Westshire."

The ice maker in the freezer churned the next several seconds. He waited for Edith to say something. *Please say something.*

Henry scooted his chair closer to the table, wanting to reach for her hand. Touch her. Somehow keep her connected to him and this life they could both share.

"Wow," Edith finally said. "You're right. That certainly is amazing."

She rose from her chair, turning to face the sink as she emptied the remainder of her tea down the drain. Henry watched her rinse her cup, wash it, rinse it again, then take her time drying it before she turned to face him with a brave smile. "Henry, I'm so happy for you. This is a once-in-a-lifetime opportunity for you."

"Think so?"

Nodding, smile wavering, tears spilling over, Edith whispered, "Yes."

His chair scraped back. He rounded the table and tugged her into his arms. "Hey," he said. Her muffled sobs pressed into his shoulder. "We can figure this out. Maybe . . . maybe . . . I don't know." *Dang it.* Now he was choking back tears. "But we'll figure it out."

Edith stepped out of his arms and grabbed a paper towel to wipe her face. "What's to figure out?" She pointed to the counter, where a thick envelope sat. "My passport arrived. If that's not a sign that it's time for me to go . . ." She inhaled a shaky breath. "We're both going to be helping people. We're both going to be chasing after our dreams. Let's not turn this into something sad."

Henry couldn't have gotten any words out past the thickness of his throat even if he'd had the right words to say. Why didn't he ever have the right words to say?

So he just nodded. Followed her to the front door. Let

her talk, say things like "Thanks for a memorable summer" and "I'll never forget you" and something about being busy packing. Then "Goodbye" as she closed the door on him.

He wasn't sure what he managed to mumble back. In a trance, he climbed into his pickup truck and drove home, his mind placing a roadblock on any messages sent from his heart.

Don't think about it. It's what she wants. Can't make her stay. This is for the best. Let her go. Don't think about it. Don't think about it.

He made it past the front door of his house. Stood in the middle of his empty living room. Then he covered his face and cried.

CHAPTER THIRTY-THREE

In the distance, a dog barked. Outside the window, a chicken clucked. Next to her ear, three tiny voices giggled. *"Molweni, iibhokhwe,"* Edith said without opening her eyes.

More giggles followed. It took her a second to realize it was likely because she'd just called Kaya's three children *goats* instead of *children*.

"Abantwana," Edith quickly amended. "Hello, *abantwana.*"

Edith cracked open one eye to discover the three mischievous grins staring back at her had nothing to do with her butchered attempts to speak Xhosa. And everything to do with the giant hairy spider resting on the oldest sibling's palm.

"Look who's joining us for school today," Theo said.

"Oh, my—" Edith flung herself out of bed, scrambling as far away from the arachnid monster as possible in a bedroom the size of a closet. "Is that a tarantula?"

"A baboon spider," four-year-old Annika said, petting the creature as if it were a baby bunny instead of an eight-legged demon. "Mom says they're poisonous."

"Wonderful," Edith said, clutching her chest. "And I bet your mom would also say to drop it. Not here," she added a beat too late.

Edith watched the spider fall, as if in horrid slow motion, onto her foot. Her bare foot. Her bare foot that obviously had a very strong survival instinct, because it punted the furry beast against the opposite wall with the might of an NFL field-goal kicker on the fifty-yard line.

Which was apparently not the best move. As soon as the fat sucker smacked the tile floor, Sam, the middle sibling, began booting the hostile predator like they'd started a rousing game of kick the can.

"Stop!" The rabid sack of venom flew past Edith's shoulder. "Don't!" The hissing creature whizzed past her ear. "Enough!" The vile alien bounced off her thigh. "I'm telling your mother!"

That did the trick. Everyone, including the concussed spider, fled the room. Edith didn't waste any time slamming her feet into her shoes. Well, she didn't waste any time once she'd shaken her shoes a dozen times to ensure no other spiders lurked inside.

Sweet mercy, those three kids were going to be the death of her—assuming a spider didn't get her first.

Inhaling a couple of deep breaths, Edith waited for her

racing heart to slow. At least drop below a hundred and fifty. Talk about a morning wake-up call. Who needed coffee when you shared housing with the three Reddy children? Their love for nature knew no bounds. And since they were homeschooled by a mom who excelled at turning that passion into a hands-on curriculum, Edith never knew what to expect.

Three days ago, Edith's breakfast of *putu pap* had landed in her lap when an African goshawk flew through the open kitchen window, much to the children's squeals of delight. And Edith's . . . well, squeals of fright. But in her defense, the African goshawk is a *predatory* bird. Nobody would have trusted that pointy beak swooping past their head. Nobody but the Reddy children, at least.

Edith dressed and readied herself for the day. After sharing a bathroom and kitchen in a three-story residence with a revolving door of hospital staff, volunteers, and visitors whose degree of cleanliness varied as much as their consideration in noise level, she had to admit, spiders notwithstanding, living with the Reddy family this past month had been a welcome reprieve.

But enough was enough.

Edith's shoes kicked up puffs of dirt as she hustled along the path that led from the little housing community of healthcare workers to Ithemba's Organizational Headquarters—a rather fancy title for a converted storage shed that more than one mama goat had used as a maternity ward when it was time to deliver her babies.

"Hi, Siyabonga. Sorry, honey. Not today." Edith waved to the petite girl hawking her grandmother's vegetables from the side of the road. "Oh, fine." Edith spun back, digging into her pocket to cover the cost of two tomatoes.

But that was it. No more delays. This five-minute walk could take an hour if Edith didn't avoid all the well-meaning interruptions from local villagers.

Forty-five minutes later, hefting four pumpkins, two tomatoes, a leather key ring, and a woven grass mat into Ithemba headquarters, Edith conceded she hadn't done a great job avoiding all the well-meaning interruptions.

"Kaya—" Edith banged a quick knock on the door with her elbow, then rushed inside to unload her armful onto the chair across from Kaya's desk. "Sorry to barge in like this, but we need to talk." In addition to homeschooling her children, Kaya Reddy had served as Ithemba's operational manager the past five years. More importantly, she was the closest thing Edith had to a friend.

Leaning back from her desk, Kaya dropped her reading glasses onto a folder with a sigh. "I heard about the spider incident. I'll have a talk with the kids."

"It's not that. It's—wait. How did you hear about the spider incident?"

"Edith, everyone in the village has heard about the spider incident. In fact, one of our patients in labor told my husband about the spider incident right before he started her Cesarean a half hour ago."

"Stop it." Kaya was joking. Of course she was joking. But sometimes Edith marveled how similar this village was to Westshire. Namely in the manner of how quickly—and falsely—news tended to spread.

"Listen," Edith said, shoving the pumpkins aside to make

room in the chair. "I hope you know how grateful I am to volunteer for your organization. I don't regret coming here. Not at all. I mean, my goodness, I don't have to tell you how beautiful and amazing this area of South Africa is."

"No, you certainly don't." Kaya nodded to the view past her window, where scattered beige rondavels dotted gentle slopes of green, disappearing into deeper shades of scattered forest. A stunning view. And that didn't even account for the picturesque beach that couldn't be seen from this window.

"But . . . ?" Kaya asked, dragging out the word.

"But . . ." Edith adjusted the grass mat beneath her rear end. "It's been six months. I can't help wondering when I'll get the chance to do something important."

Kaya folded her hands on top of her desk and peered at Edith over her clasped fingers. "What makes you think you aren't already doing something important?"

"I paint toenails."

"That's not true."

"I know, but you get what I'm saying. Isn't it time I do something bigger? Like drive to Mthatha the next time a patient needs an emergent supply of blood or something?"

"You didn't make it past the first curve in the road the one time we sent you for Twizza." Their local version of Coke. "As I recall, it took six people to push you out of the mud."

"That was once. Okay, so maybe it's happened a few times since then. But it hasn't rained for a while now. I bet I could manage. Maybe." If Kaya ever loaned Edith her vehicle again.

Kaya smirked. "I think I know now why God had us start you off with painting toenails in the delivery ward. He wanted you to be familiar with the Xhosa word for *push*, seeing as how often you were going to need it."

Edith's lips twitched despite her best effort not to smile. Kaya thought she was so funny, didn't she? "I just want to do something important."

"You are doing something important."

"Painting toenails? Playing Go Fish?"

"Showing patients they're valuable. Remember our expression? *Njengosisi wam*. It means—"

"'As if she were my sister,'" Edith said, moving the pumpkins onto her lap. "I know. I remember. The head nurse, Mama Peace, told me about it the first week I was here—right after she dressed me down for calling an older patient by her first name instead of Mama. I'm not going to lie. I've been scared of Mama Peace ever since."

"There's always a learning curve. Don't take it personally."

"I'm trying not to. I just thought . . ." Edith slumped back in her chair. "I thought I would have made a bigger difference by now. I'm not even sure half the people here like me."

"Relationships take time. And when you make the effort to give someone your time—even if it's as simple as painting their toenails—you offer them not only a relationship. You offer them hope. Don't ever underestimate the difference that can make. That hope could be the difference a patient needs someday when deciding whether to make the long trek to get their HIV medications or giving up and swallowing a tank pill."

Edith nodded. She'd heard about tank pills. A poisonous insecticide that very few survived after ingesting. "You're right. Of course you're right. I'm not sure what's the matter with me. Being here is important. And it's what I wanted."

So why, after six months, did she still wonder if she'd made the right decision in coming here? "I'll let you get back to whatever you were doing." Edith stood, forgetting about the pumpkins. They rolled off her lap onto the floor.

"Tell you what, Edith." Kaya rounded the desk to help retrieve the runaway squashes. "I understand painting toenails and playing card games after you've worked as a registered nurse for several years might feel a bit . . . unsatisfying. Truth is, we didn't train you for anything more, because . . . well, we didn't think you'd last more than a month here."

"Thanks a lot." Edith pretended to send Kaya a withering glare.

"Since you can't do anything clinically without a nursing registration, what if we try something away from the hospital? What do you think about moving in with one of the families outside of the village? Not that we haven't enjoyed having you."

"I don't mind." Especially if it spared her from waking up to Godzilla hovering two inches from her face. "What will I be doing?"

"Making home visits with Amahle. She's what we refer to as a positive deviant. Despite growing up in the exact same circumstances as her neighbors, her babies have always thrived. We believe it's because of her strong commitment to breastfeeding. Which is why we asked her to partner up with us in making home visits to see if she can encourage more of our mothers to breastfeed and make referrals on babies who don't appear to be thriving."

"Okay. Yeah. I think I might like that."

"I think you might too. Plus, it'll be good for you and Amahle to spend some time together, what with you two about to become family."

"Right." Edith adjusted the pumpkins in her arms. "Wait—what?"

"Amahle. She's Junior's sister."

Edith trapped a pumpkin against her thigh before it fell. "Oh, I see. Yes, very funny. Ha-ha." Junior ran this area's version of Uber. He owned a run-down clunker, offering private transport to the few locals who could afford it. She'd met him her first evening in the village. And once he concluded she was a wealthy American, he'd been proposing to her at least three times a week ever since.

"I heard you accepted a chicken from him."

Edith gave up and let the pumpkins bounce to the floor. "Yeah, his aunt was in the hospital with tuberculosis the other week. She must have been one of the patients whose toenails I painted. I guess he was saying thank you."

Kaya pinched the bridge of her nose. "Edith, I hate to break it to you, but accepting a man's chicken in these parts is the same as accepting a man's engagement ring."

"What? No. He never said anything about—well, I mean he has. Other times. But not this time. He just plopped the chicken into my hands. What about the chicken some guy gave me a month ago?"

"You're engaged to *two* men?"

"No, I didn't know. I didn't—" Edith pressed her lips together the second Kaya's lips started to lift and her shoulders began shaking. She smacked Kaya on the arm. "You are *not* funny."

"I wish I had a picture of your face."

"I'm leaving now."

"Don't you want your pumpkins?"

Edith spun and poked her head around the doorjamb. "Why? So you can tell me in this culture that's a symbol of my eternal agreement to babysit your children? I don't think so. Have fun with the pumpkins."

"Have fun with your sister-in-law," Kaya's amused voice called back.

———— ♥ ————

A week later Edith sat cross-legged on the dirt floor, sharing dinner and bashful smiles with Amahle's brood of children. She didn't know how long it would take for the newness of her presence to wear off. They stared at her with wide-eyed wonder, probably amazed at the limitless ways she managed to mangle their language.

Amahle, whom Edith suspected was with child again, thankfully extended Edith some grace. She always tried speaking to Edith in English, even if it was a bit broken.

"Good?" Amahle asked, pointing her eyes toward Edith's bowl of *chakalaka* and *pap*.

"Yes. Very good. Thank you."

"More?"

"No. Full." Edith rubbed her belly and Amahle quirked her brow. Dropping her hand, Edith tried again. "No hungry." *No hungry?* Amahle wasn't going to make much progress in her English if Edith continued speaking like that. Edith rose from the floor and started gathering the children's bowls. "Let me wash these for you."

"No. No." Amahle waved her back. In rapid Xhosa, she gave the children their washing orders. "You, come." She motioned for Edith to follow her. "Come," she said again.

Edith followed Amahle to a small bench perched outside her grass-thatched rondavel. Amahle sat and patted the space next to her. Amazed the wobbly structure held Amahle, Edith wasn't convinced she should add her weight.

"Sit." Amahle caressed the surface. "My husband make this. He tell me, when gone, sit and think of him. I do." She smiled at Edith, and Edith smiled back. "Sit," she said again.

All right. Here goes nothing. Edith gingerly lowered herself onto the bench. When it didn't splinter or crack, she released the breath she'd been holding.

Like many men in the area, Amahle's husband had to travel to find work and was often gone for long stretches of time, working in one of the mines. Edith would have felt awful if she'd smashed a symbol of their love into the ground as soon as she sat on it.

Edith and Amahle sat in silence for several minutes before the children came outside. As had been the custom every evening since her arrival, they headed straight for the soccer ball Edith had brought with her. The sound of it skimming over the ground was as effective as any trumpet call. Soon other kids joined them, ready for the impromptu game that would last until dark.

"You?" Amahle patted the bench again. "Someone on bench thinking?"

"About me?" Edith gave a small laugh. "I doubt it. I'm pretty sure I burned that bench."

Seeing Amahle's furrowed brow and tilt of the head, Edith expelled a deep sigh and shrugged. "I couldn't stay; he couldn't leave." She swiped her hands in front of her. "No bench."

"You left?"

Edith nodded.

"To come *here*?"

Edith smiled and nodded again. "I left to come here. Yes."

Amahle tucked her chin and blinked several times before—"Why? You have man. You have bench. Why?"

"Oh, you know . . ." Edith turned her hands into fists and pumped them into the air. "Adventure."

Amahle mimicked the same gesture. "Adventure?"

"Adventure."

Amahle shifted her weight on the bench, appearing to contemplate Edith's explanation. Shouts and cheers, spattered with a few arguments, sprang from the children. A few roaming chickens, not happy with the evening activities, clucked their disapproval from the sidelines. Above it all, the sun cast a faded-orange glow. Beneath it, in the distance, Edith recognized the tiny clump of squares and rectangles where the village hospital was located.

"Why here?" Amahle finally asked.

Edith swept her hand out in front of her. "All of this is an adventure for me. I'm happy I came."

"Hmm. Mouth happy, but eyes . . ." She shook her head.

Edith shrugged. "My eyes are tired."

As much as she'd enjoyed trekking up and down the

beautiful hills this past week, visiting members of the community inside their simple rural homes, Edith couldn't deny it was getting harder and harder to climb out of bed each morning—though the aches from sleeping on a dirt floor with nothing more than a thin mattress usually drove her out of it.

Good thing she still had a couple of Tylenol pills left at the bottom of her satchel. Which reminded her, she needed to show Kaya the pills she found during one of their home visits. They didn't look like anything that came from a prescription. But maybe she was snooping into things she shouldn't be. Which was why she hadn't said anything to Amahle.

Edith stretched her back. "I'll admit being here hasn't exactly been a walk in the park. But adventures aren't supposed to be a walk in the park, right? That's why they're adventures." She punched the air again.

Amahle slowly nodded her head, keeping a steady gaze on Edith's face. Eventually she turned her head and jutted her chin toward her posse of children while touching a palm to her abdomen. "My adventure," she said with a soft smile.

"Congratulations."

Amahle dipped her head in acknowledgment. "But—" she pointed to the warped bench—"you are right. Not easy." She raised a knowing eyebrow. "*Very* not easy."

Edith met Amahle's warm cocoa eyes, filled with a gentle understanding, before turning her gaze upon the children. They were racing against each other and time to move the ball from one end to the other before daylight faded.

As dusk turned into twilight, and one by one the children

disbanded to their homes—including Amahle and her youngsters—Edith stayed outside. She found herself questioning why she had never viewed love as an adventure before. It was certainly full of risks. No doubt it carried unexpected twists and turns, sometimes resulting in joy, sometimes resulting in sorrow.

Perhaps she had been living a life of adventure long before she ever set foot in South Africa. And for the first time since her arrival, she wondered if it was time to write another letter.

CHAPTER THIRTY-FOUR

After breaking ground last fall, Henry had hoped to have more to show by now than a single foundation. But considering the record snowfalls and windchill factors they'd faced all winter long, he should probably be grateful his crew had accomplished anything at all.

Henry tilted his head back in the crisp morning air. A far cry from balmy, the sun shining on his face at least offered hope. The fact that baseball pitchers had started reporting in for spring training was another promising sign it was about time to kiss old man winter goodbye.

Henry leaned against his truck and folded his arms, gazing at the evidence of his work so far. Nothing but a slab of cement now, it would one day be the focal point of the campground. A place to gather, a place to fellowship, a place to eat, play, create, entertain, learn . . .

Henry had a lot of work waiting for him this spring. And he wasn't the only one anxious to get started. Henry lost track of how many phone calls he'd received from Charles Henderson over the winter with another idea or adjustment. Good thing Henderson had a hefty budget to make the elaborate plans he envisioned not easy but possible.

While snow had fallen over frozen ground, Henry had spent the winter months designing blueprint after blueprint, ensuring every code would be met, every design plausible, every expectation filled.

"I'm proud of you. Mom and Dad would be proud too." Those words, spoken by his brother a month after Edith left, spurred Henry forward. Kept him from dwelling on what might have been. Kept him planning for the future.

But now he was tired of planning. Now he itched for action.

Ignoring the stiffness in his leg and the ever-present ache in his chest, Henry climbed back inside his truck and gave one more parting glance to the bare-bones structure waiting to be completed. His legacy.

Back at his company's office, he'd no sooner shut off the engine and had one leg out the door when Peg barreled toward him from the office with her red coat draped around her shoulders. "Get back," she whispered, looking around her as if afraid of being overheard.

"Why? What's the—?"

She cut him off with a piercing glare and frantic headshake. Henry raised his palms in surrender, sliding back inside the truck. A moment later, Peg climbed into the passenger seat. "Just act natural," she panted.

"Sure." He'd act as natural as a man could sitting in a truck on a frigid late winter morning with a seventysomething-year-old woman doing pursed-lipped breathing next to him. "You okay?"

She nodded her head. "Just need a minute." Her breathing eventually slowed. "I just got a weird phone call. About Edith."

"Edith?" Henry darted a look toward his office windows as if he might be able to catch a glimpse of her through the narrow slats of the blinds. "What about Edith?"

"I don't know. The person kept cutting in and out. But she mentioned your name. I got the impression Edith must have put you down as an emergency contact or something. How they got our office number, I have no idea. But the lady on the phone sounded frantic. She said she had to talk to you right away. She called you Edith's fiancé."

"Why does everybody keep calling me that? I'm not." He shrugged one shoulder. "What? Don't look at me like that."

"Henry. Please. I don't care whether you were actually engaged or not, you two were in love and the whole town knew it. Why do you think it was so easy for everybody to jump to conclusions like they did? And if you still care for Edith even half as much as I think you do, then the least you can do is try to find out what's going on. What if she's in some kind of trouble? She's in South Africa, for crying out loud. For all we know she's been captured by pirates."

"Pirates."

"Yes. Didn't you ever see *Captain Phillips*?"

"I did actually. Which is why I'm fairly confident that's not the case." Henry ran a hand back and forth across his forehead, trying to sand away the mounting headache. "Pirates," he muttered again.

Still, why would someone be calling him about Edith?

He'd never breathe a word of this to Peg, but he'd been reading up on South Africa ever since Edith had left. And one of the things he'd come across—and wished he hadn't—was that the practice of abducting women and forcing them into marriage still existed in some parts.

But surely that wasn't . . . *Of course it wasn't.* Peg's talk of pirates was making him twitchy. "Did this person leave a number?"

"She tried. I only caught part of it."

Great. He rubbed his forehead. "I'll figure it out. But I'm not pretending to be her fiancé. If they don't want to talk to me knowing that, then—" He blew out a breath, hoping to dispel the growing queasiness in his stomach along with it. "There's nothing I can do about it."

Peg's wrinkled brow and pursed lips told him exactly how she felt about that, but all she said was "Fine." Then she latched on to his wrist. "Wait. I forgot to tell you why I came out here. One of Henderson's men is inside with a video camera. Wants early footage for that YouTube channel. Anyway, I didn't want him to hear about Edith and turn it into national news. So I'm going to cause a diversion while you make the phone call and find out what's going on. Deal?"

Henry climbed out from the truck and started toward the office door as Peg walked the opposite direction. "What are you doing?" he whispered after her. "I thought you were creating a diversion."

She buttoned the top button of her coat and pulled her hood on. "I am. I'm going to Julie's for scones. Tell that guy if he wants one, he should come with me."

"That's your idea of a diversion?"

"Bet you a dollar it works." Looking like an older, slower version of Little Red Riding Hood, Peg ambled down the sidewalk, dodging the patches of ice that still hadn't completely thawed. Henry shook his head, watching her leave.

Then he shook his head a minute later when he watched the cameraman leave. How about that? Looked like he owed Peg a dollar.

———— ♥ ————

By the time Peg returned, Henry wasn't thinking about the dollar.

As Peg walked through door, he was only thinking about how to breathe.

Not taking the time to remove her coat, Peg raced for his chair and wheeled it behind him. "Sit," she ordered. A moment later she handed him a small paper cup filled with water. "Drink." Then she crouched before him, her knees creaking in protest, and said, "Breathe."

Slowly, breath by breath, the pressure within his chest released until all that remained was the familiar ache that had taken up residence ever since Edith's departure.

"Better?" Peg asked.

"A little."

"Good. Now help me up." Henry lifted her by the elbows. "Oh, it's a terrible thing to get old, you know that?" She hobbled side to side back to her desk and, with another wince, sat down in her chair. "Now tell me the truth. It's pirates, isn't it?"

Henry shuffled through the items on his desk, picking up the scrap of paper he'd dropped. "I don't know. All I could make out was that she's in the hospital. We kept getting disconnected. They gave me a different number to try." He dialed the number on the paper, hoping this time for better reception. Better news. Something other than Edith in trouble.

He was put on hold. Forty minutes later he reached a different department, which promptly placed him on hold. A dozen departments and one eternity later, someone who seemed to know more of what was going on picked up the phone.

By the time Henry ended the call with the information he needed, Peg was halfway through the turkey sandwich she'd rushed out to buy for lunch when she decided the cameraman needed another diversion.

She pointed to a brown sack on Henry's desk. "Hope you like roast beef. So? What did they say? Is Edith going to be okay? Is there anything we need to do?"

"There is something we need to do." Henry leaned forward in his chair. When he met Peg's gaze, he could only pray someday she would forgive him. "We need to break out of our contract with Charles Henderson. I'm not going to be able to finish what I started." Henry rose from his chair. "I need to get to Edith."

About to take a bite, Peg lowered the sandwich away from her mouth. "Today?"

"Yes."

"Right now?"

"Yes."

Peg dropped her sandwich with a plop on her desk. "Henderson may be a philanthropist, but he's also a shrewd businessman. You know your name will be mud if you do this, don't you?"

"I know."

"This is a once-in-a-lifetime opportunity."

"I know."

"And you're absolutely positive you want to walk away from a multimillion-dollar contract just because the woman who walked away from you might be sick?"

"Yes."

"Well, then." Peg folded her hands in front of her. "I guess all that's left to say is . . . I've never been prouder of you in all my life. Because you are finishing what you started."

Henry nodded, a burst of gratitude preventing any words from making it past the thickness in his throat.

"But, Henry?" Peg dabbed the corner of her lip. "Just because I'm proud of you doesn't mean I don't think you're an idiot."

"Excuse me?" Henry paused in grabbing his truck keys.

"You heard me. You're an idiot. How can you even think about throwing away an opportunity like this? I'm calling your brother."

"How's he going to help?"

"He's retired, not dead. Do I need to remind you the name

of this company? Is it Henry's Painting and Construction? No. It's Hobbes Painting and Construction. Got that? *Hobbes.* A family name. Your family name. So let your family help you out before you do something stupid. And yes, I absolutely include myself in that definition of family."

Henry's arms fell to his sides as he stared at the woman who'd come to mean as much to him as his own mother. "Peg, I love you."

"I know you do. Now get out of here before that cameraman gets back."

Right. Henry sprang into motion, feeling his back pocket for his wallet as he headed toward the door, his only plan to swing by the house for his passport and catch the first flight out of the Quad City airport to Chicago and go from there.

"Oh, and, Henry?"

Henry paused halfway out the door, ready for one of Peg's "For all that's holy, don't screw this up" comments.

What he got was a soft "I love you too. Now go get our girl."

He smiled and closed the door, aiming to do just that.

CHAPTER THIRTY-FIVE

Sometime after sitting on a warped bench and talking about adventure with Amahle, Edith had entered *The Twilight Zone*. She heard Rod Serling narrating her life. Or was that a doctor?

No, it was her dad. Wait. No. It couldn't be her dad. Could it? Why was her dad here?

He peered down at her, shaking his head side to side as if disappointed she was trying to follow him into the afterlife. She wasn't, was she?

Edith tried to speak but couldn't form any words. Her body shivered and her teeth chattered around a tongue that had shriveled up like a raisin. *I'm sorry,* she wanted to say. After all these years, she wasn't sure what she was even sorry for anymore. She only wished they would be reconciled at last.

But when her dad leaned closer, it was no longer him. It was Dr. Reddy's worried face. Or Mama Peace's stern face, speaking in tongues right before she jabbed a needle into her arm. Once, Edith opened her eyes to see that the hands replacing a cool washrag to her forehead belonged to Kaya. Then the next moment she swore she saw Junior standing next to her bed holding a chicken.

But the one person Edith longed to see more than anyone never appeared.

Edith called for him on the nights she thought she was at his home, tucked under the cool sheets of his bed, and he was only one floor below her. She yelled his name when she thought they were back in the crisis nursery house and he was fending off an intruder. She asked for him when she thought she was at Julie's bakery. "Is Henry here? I'm looking for Henry."

"Shhh. Quiet." Mama Peace again. "We call Henry. But first, you drink." She poured a pungent medicine down Edith's throat. "See? Better."

Edith didn't think it was better. She returned to her restless sleep.

Sometime later she heard more voices. But the heat that raged within her body held her prisoner. She couldn't fight off the weights pressing down her limbs. Or break through the haze fogging up her mind.

Like a radio station filled with fluctuating static, voices volleyed back and forth above her. *A mix-up . . . tank pill . . . expired . . . hopeful . . . fever . . . asking for her fiancé . . . talk to her . . . wait and see . . . pray . . .*

The voices and static dimmed like someone turning down

the dial. But before they disappeared, cool fingers traced her cheek. Warm lips grazed her brow. Then she heard his voice.

"It's me, Edith. I'm right here beside you. No more adventures without me, okay?"

She didn't know if he was real or not, but for the first time since entering *The Twilight Zone*, she fell asleep in peace.

———— ♥ ————

Henry had initially wanted to relocate Edith to a hospital in a bigger city. But after speaking to Dr. Reddy, who assured Henry there was nothing a larger hospital would do for her that they weren't already doing here, and after speaking to an intimidating nurse who assured Henry that Edith was like a sister and she'd receive no greater care anywhere else, Henry agreed the best move was to stay put.

Gritty eyes, unshaven whiskers, rumpled clothes—Henry knew he looked a mess. But he couldn't leave her side. Not yet. Not until she made it out of the woods.

At times he thought she had. Then her cheeks would go all flushed again, and she'd start talking to her deceased father.

Henry never knew what to say to her in those times. "I'm sorry, Dad," she'd say again and again. "I'm sorry."

"It's okay, Edith. Everything's going to be okay."

"I messed up."

"Hey. Don't worry about any of that right now. You just need to get better, okay?"

"I shouldn't have left." Edith's eyes would close, her voice slurring whenever she began drifting away. "I should have stayed . . . with Henry."

Henry squeezed her hand. "No, sweetheart. I should have fought harder to stay with you." Maybe if he'd been here, Edith wouldn't have accidentally swallowed an aluminum phosphide tablet. How that happened, he still didn't understand completely. Somehow a tank pill had gotten into her satchel. She must not have realized what she was swallowing when she took it during the middle of the night.

Henry's stomach growled. Not for the first time either. How could he eat? It felt like a betrayal when Edith could barely take in a cupful of liquids. But willing Edith better through starvation didn't exactly make a whole lot of sense either.

He ought to go find some food. Henry stood from his chair, reaching for his back pocket. But instead of a wallet, he pulled out a crinkled envelope. What? Oh, that's right. He'd left his wallet in his bag, which he'd given to . . . Oh, gosh, who had he given it to?

He scrubbed his face. Kaya. That's right. Kaya. She'd taken his things for him and promised to keep them safe. Then Edith's host—Amahle?—had slipped this letter into his hands outside the hospital. *For you, I think.*

Pushing his hunger off a bit longer, Henry sat back down and opened the letter.

Dear Henry,

So much is in my heart that I want to share with you. I'm not sure where to even begin. I love you. How about I begin with that? I think I fell in love with you the

moment you showed up in the coffee shop
pretending to be my boyfriend. I knew it was
just pretend. I knew it didn't mean anything.
But still. I can't remember the last time
someone came to my rescue like that. (The fact
that I was already half in love with your
blue eyes probably didn't hurt matters.)

Then when I discovered that you were
also the man I'd been exchanging notes and
letters with . . . Well. Suddenly you were more
than just a handsome man helping me out of
a sticky situation. You were Henry. The real
Henry. My Henry. I had shared things with
you. Things I'd never shared with anyone else,
so now you knew me better than anyone else.

And it scared me to death. I saw the
future I thought I wanted so badly slipping
through my fingers and a repeat of the pain
I'd already experienced happening all over
again.

So as much as I loved you, I continued my
plans for leaving, knowing the other shoe would
drop eventually. The day of the interview, when
you left me for work, I thought that was the
shoe dropping. Then that night, when I asked
you to come with me, and you said you couldn't,
I thought that was the other shoe dropping.

Now six months later, living the adventure
I dreamed of, I'm starting to realize

something. I don't think the other shoe ever dropped. I think I took it out of your hand and flung it before it had the chance to drop.

Is this making any sense? Probably not. I'm very tired. And between you and me, my back is killing me. But that's not the point.

The point is I love you, Henry. I know I already said that. But I'm saying it again. I love you. I don't regret coming here. I love the people I've met and the experiences I've had.

What I regret is not asking you to wait for me. Why did it have to be all or nothing when I left?

Will you wait for me, Henry?

Love, Edith

Henry folded the letter. He lifted Edith's hand to his lips, then leaned down to press his forehead against hers. No words were necessary. Of course he'd wait. As long as it took.

CHAPTER THIRTY-SIX

Edith blinked open her eyes to the hum of voices and foot-steps. Where was she? Her gaze swept across the confined space of her bed enclosed by three walls of curtains. An IV pole with a bag of saline hung above her head. Next to her side, an empty chair.

That's right. She was in the hospital. Edith lifted a hand to brush her hair out of her face, noticing the IV tubing secured to the back of her hand. How long had she been here?

"Edith," a voice breathed.

Edith glanced up to find Kaya peering back at her from next to the curtain. She shoved it further open and rushed to her side. "You're awake. And you look so much better."

"I feel so much better. What happened?"

"You swallowed a tank pill."

"*What?* Why would I do that?"

"We were wondering the same thing. It seems there were many mistakes involved, not that I'm pointing the finger at anyone, though if I had to point the finger at someone, I'd point it at you. I mean, really, Edith. You swallowed a tank pill. Thank God it was expired, and you puked the whole way here. Even so, you were incredibly sick. Do you know how worried we've been? You could have died."

"I'm sorry. I swiped them from one of the homes we visited because I had a feeling that's what they were. I only saved them so I could show them to you. I honestly don't know how I made such a stupid mistake."

Kaya's features softened as she sat on the side of the bed. "Well, if it makes you feel any better, the grandmother of the girl who had the pills is convinced you saved her granddaughter's life. And maybe you did."

"Really?"

"I said *maybe*. Don't look so pleased. I'm still mad at you." Kaya squeezed her hand. "And so very glad you're alive."

Tears pricked Edith's eyes. "That makes two of us."

"More than that. Mama Peace has been sneaking to your bedside in her pajamas to say prayers over you during the night." Kaya rose and pointed to the empty chair. "And don't forget about your fiancé. The only reason he's not here right now is because I forced him to bed before he collapsed from exhaustion."

Oh, ha-ha. Kaya the comedian, everybody. Still making jokes about Junior. Edith would applaud if she could muster the energy. Her head sank against the pillow.

"You've been through a lot. Get some rest. I'll check back on you later."

Edith nodded, hardly able to keep her eyes open. Before her thoughts drifted away in a lazy river of slumber, she thanked God that she was better. Then prayed she might dream of Henry again.

———— ♥ ————

Henry hadn't meant to stay away for so long. After filling his belly and changing into clean clothes, he planned on coming straight back to the hospital. But then Kaya and her husband had convinced him a few hours of rest would be okay. Convinced him to use the bedroom Edith had used as a guest. Convinced him to lie down and close his eyes . . .

When they snapped open, the sunlight blazing through the window told him he'd slept more than a few hours. That and the fact he felt somewhat refreshed.

Henry glanced out the window to see a few goats helping themselves to the vegetable garden out back, then reached for his phone to check the time. Shoot. His reflection stared back at him from a blank screen. No wonder his alarm hadn't gone off. Before he could hop out of bed, tiny whispers caught his attention.

"Mom said not to bother him."

"I'm not. I just want to find out what he can build."

"How can he be Edith's husband if Edith is marrying Junior?"

"Where did you hear that?"

"From Junior."

"You think he knows how to build go-karts?"

"Who, Junior?"

"Henry."

Henry poked his head around the door to find the three Reddy children huddled on the floor outside his bedroom. He had met the three rascals yesterday when they visited Edith and left her a surprise. "Who's Junior?" Henry asked.

The little girl giggled. The oldest boy smiled. And the boy whose age was somewhere in the middle returned his gaze with a nonchalant shrug. "Help us build something and maybe we'll tell you."

Henry leaned against the doorframe and folded his arms. "Is this how you treat all your guests?"

The boy shrugged again. "Mom says every person we meet has a chance to teach us something."

"Can't argue with that. What did Edith teach you?"

"Funny stories," the little girl said.

The older boy grinned. "Our favorite was about the lady who swallowed a hot pepper."

Henry dipped his head with a soft laugh. "Yeah, Edith has some pretty great stories, doesn't she?" Slowly his head rose, an idea sparking to life. "What kind of supplies do you have available, saying we do build something?"

CHAPTER THIRTY-SEVEN

Edith figured she must be dreaming again. Henry sat in the chair next to her bed, his arms folded across his chest and a baseball cap pulled low over his face. Instead of looking at her lovingly and whispering words of encouragement next to her ear, he appeared to be sleeping.

Man, her dreams had lost a lot of luster ever since she started feeling better.

She closed her eyes. Opened them. He was still there.

When she reached out to touch him, a folded sheet of paper rustled beneath her hand. She lifted it in front of her face.

Dear Edith,
   I love you.

      Henry

A faint whistle sounded with each of his breaths. She might not trust her eyes, but she believed her ears. This wasn't a dream. Henry was here. Snoring. Next to her. In South Africa. And he loved her.

"Henry," she whispered, despite the urge to shout with joy. "Wake up."

The whistling stopped. Slowly he reached up and tipped the bill of his cap away from his face, allowing her full access to those blue eyes that had captured her from the first moment she saw him.

Except it wasn't his eyes that drew her attention this time.

"What happened to your forehead?" A bruise spread above his left eyebrow.

He shifted forward as a smile lifted his lips. "A little misunderstanding. Nothing to worry about.'"

"We seem to have a lot of those in our lives, don't we?"

He nodded, his gaze never wavering from her eyes. "But hopefully not when it came to what I wrote." He tapped the note in her hand. "Because I meant every word."

Edith reread the note, then folded the paper in half with a contented sigh. "Maybe we should always try to keep things short and simple. Seems to be working better already."

Henry's eyes crinkled in a smile as his calloused palm slid against hers and wrapped around her fingers. "Short and simple, I like the sound of that." He squeezed her hand, staring into her eyes like he'd never get tired of the view. Like he could gaze upon her face the rest of his life and never get bored. Like he could remain rooted to her side and—

"I have to go."

—never have to go. Wait. What?

Henry released her hand and stood. "I have a few messages I'm supposed to relay to you first."

Edith blinked up at him. *He had to go?*

"Let's see." He shifted his weight from one leg to the other. "Amahle said to tell you she likes your man on the bench. Not really sure what that means. Her brother Junior said to tell you he can get you more chickens if that changes your mind. I might have an idea what that means. And last but not least, the Reddy children said to be sure to look under the sheets for the surprise they left you."

Edith jerked her knees up as she flung off the sheets, certain they'd left a horde of spiders or vipers or frogs or—a splash of color caught her attention.

Edith stared. Frozen. Then slowly straightened her legs.

"My toes," she whispered, wiggling her feet back and forth. Bright-pink polish spread across every one of her nails, smearing onto her skin. "They painted my toenails."

"You were pretty out of it, but they thought it might help you feel better."

"It did. It does." With a laugh and a sob, Edith collapsed against her pillow. "I feel very loved, Henry."

"Hey, and that's just a few of the messages from people I've met here." Henry helped situate the sheets back over her. "I don't know if you're ready to hear what everyone back home has to say. Julie's been trying to figure out how to get a delivery of her scones past customs, and Peg wants the US Coast Guard to put a bounty on every pirate's head." He brushed a strand of hair behind her ear. "Oh, you're loved, sweetheart. There's no doubt about that."

Edith let herself get lost in Henry's gorgeous blue eyes,

a part of her still unable to believe they were really together. Here. In South Africa. Had she ever been happier?

Yes, actually. The moment before he said he was leaving. She gripped his hand. "Stay. I'm finally awake. We have so much to talk about. Don't go."

"I'm so sorry." Henry dropped a kiss on her forehead. "But I have to. Now that you're doing better . . ." He shrugged. "There's things I need to take care of." A sense of urgency hummed in his voice.

Sure. Edith nodded. Of course. Just because he loved her didn't mean his responsibilities back home disappeared. He still had a company to run. How much time had he wasted flying all this way just to tell her he loved her? Too much, based on the way his feet shuffled back and forth.

Edith opened her mouth, searching desperately for something to say. *Wait, I'll go with you?* But Mama Peace stepped past the curtain, giving Henry a look that suggested visiting hours were over. Though to be fair, that was the look Mama Peace gave everyone. Either way, it was all the excuse Henry needed to make his escape.

"Take care, Edith. Get some rest," he said over his shoulder.

"Okay, just—" His footsteps faded down the hallway. Edith sank against her pillow. "Don't leave without me," she whispered.

CHAPTER THIRTY-EIGHT

After Henry left, it took Edith less than five minutes to realize she couldn't stick around in this hospital bed a second longer. She needed to go after him.

Swinging her legs to the side, she jumped up from the bed. Then would have promptly face-planted into the chair if Dr. Reddy hadn't entered and caught her under the armpits before the black cloud enclosing her vision knocked her out completely.

"Where do you think you're going?" He guided her back to the bed.

"To stop Henry."

"Yeah, well, that might be hard to do if you're passed out on the floor."

"I feel fine." Well, once she was settled back on the bed

and not quite on the verge of blacking out, she felt fine. "I just got up too fast. I'm better now. See?"

Edith stood, slower this time, while Dr. Reddy wrapped a blood pressure cuff around her arm and started pumping it up. When he released the pressure valve, Edith was just about to wave her arms out to the side and say *ta-da* when that blasted tunnel vision started closing in on her again.

"Yep, that's what I thought," Dr. Reddy said, directing her back to the bed. "You need more fluids. Your blood pressure drops whenever you stand."

"Then get me a wheelchair. I just need to get to Henry. He could already be halfway to the airport by now."

"*Sisi*—" Edith's lips couldn't help quirking into a smile over his use of the Xhosa word for *sister*. "Do you remember where we are? Even if he left two hours ago, he wouldn't be halfway to *anywhere*."

"You and your wife are just full of jokes, aren't you? Fine. One fluid bolus, then I'm out here." She held up her hand with the IV. "Shake a leg on it, Doc."

He rolled his eyes, disappearing behind the curtain as he muttered something about Americans and nurses. Specifically American nurses. But a few minutes later, Mama Peace was at her side, hooking up a bag of saline to Edith's IV.

"Run it as fast as you can," Edith told her. "Which is to say whatever rate you deem appropriate because I trust your judgment completely," Edith added after receiving one of Mama Peace's trademark scowls.

They ended up giving her two boluses, but Edith could tell it had done the trick. No more dark tunnels. "I'm cured," she told Dr. Reddy after she hustled to the bathroom, empty-ing out half the fluids they'd pumped inside her.

"We'll get you out of here soon. We had a power outage, so we're running a little behind. Hang tight."

Hang tight? She was starting to understand why a per-son might tie bedsheets together to escape out the window. Lucky for her, this was a one-story hospital.

"Are you ready to leave?" Mama Peace poked her head past the curtain.

"Yes." Edith tempered her voice. It was Mama Peace after all. "I mean, sure. If that's all right with you. I'm in no rush. I can wait until you're ready."

Mama Peace smiled. The expression transformed her face so much she almost looked friendly. Maybe Kaya hadn't been joking about Mama Peace sneaking in at night in her pajamas to pray over Edith.

But the next moment the smile disappeared, replaced by Mama Peace's typical frown. *"Uyanuka,"* she muttered.

Edith was far from being fluent in Xhosa, but . . . "Did you just tell me I stink?" Not that Edith could argue. She *did* stink.

Mama Peace clucked her tongue. "You can't go out like that."

Before Edith knew what was happening, Mama Peace was stripping her down and scrubbing her clean. Edith's grimy undergarments somehow got exchanged for clean ones. And from somewhere—the woman must be part magician—she retrieved a dress and slid it over Edith's head.

Edith gazed down at the colorful embroidered designs

on the ivory material. "Is this how you discharge all your patients?"

Mama Peace stepped back, looking Edith over from head to toe, then back up again. She shook her head. "That won't do."

"What won't—? *Ouch*."

Mama Peace had grabbed hold of Edith's hair, working with deft fingers to transform the tangled mess of knots into some sort of braid. "There," she said after she finished sometime a quarter of a century later. She stepped in front of Edith to assess her work. "Hmmm . . . no."

"What *hmmm no*? Mama Peace, I have to go."

Mama Peace held up a finger, plucked the flower someone had left in a jar next to the bed, then, using a pin from her own hair, attached the flower to the braid in Edith's hair.

Finally Mama Peace nodded approvingly. "Now you are ready."

Sure. Henry's plane was probably two minutes shy of touching down on American soil at this point, but so long as Edith met Mama Peace's standard for discharge, great. Perfect.

Edith used her last shred of patience listening to her discharge instructions. *Never take medications in the dark. Got it.* Then leapt from the bed and rushed down the hallway, pausing briefly when she realized she'd forgotten her shoes.

Oh, well. Who needed shoes? She took two more steps before deciding she did. In a world full of spiders, Edith needed shoes.

Unfortunately South African hospitals were apparently as adept at losing patient belongings as American hospitals.

It took several staff members and an in-depth investigation worthy of an entire *Law & Order* episode before Edith's missing shoes were located in the exact spot she told them to look in the first place.

If she didn't know any better, she'd think they were stalling her on purpose.

Lacing her shoes tight, Edith refused to let any further delays keep her from getting to Henry. Wherever he was.

She hustled toward the orange-yellow glow of sunset beckoning her down the length of the shadowed hallway. This area must not have gotten its power back from the outage. Good thing she waited for her shoes. Otherwise, this walk might have been creepy.

Who was she kidding? Even with shoes, it was creepy. And dark. And long. Much too long. She'd run if she had the strength.

When Edith burst outside, she sucked in a giant breath, never so glad to step into the light in all her life.

Except the sight in front of her had clutching her stomach as if all her air had been knocked right back out of her again.

What?

An arch, constructed out of broken hospital equipment from the looks of it, stood lopsided and perfect outside the entrance beneath the setting sun.

And beyond the arch, people. Hospital workers. Villagers. Children. All of them together. All of them . . . *singing?*

Their smiling faces began to blur as Edith's eyes filled with tears. "What's going on?"

"It's the closest I could get to a softly singing choir of angels."

Edith hadn't noticed Henry standing off to the side of the

hospital doors. He stepped toward her with that wonderful, beautiful, uneven gait of his.

"Henry." The tears spilled and ran down Edith's cheeks. "You're still here."

"Of course I'm still here."

Edith covered her mouth. So this was why he had rushed off earlier. And why everyone had conspired to keep her from chasing after him. He needed time to give her a story.

The glow of the sun dipped beneath the horizon, gentle shades of orange warming the landscape and lighting up her heart.

"Well, go on." Henry motioned his head toward the arch. "Step through it."

Edith looked through the arch. At the familiar faces gathered beyond it. *For her.*

Amahle and her brood. Dr. Reddy, Kaya, and their three little explorers. Mama Peace. And dozens of others. All of them blending their voices together in a song of hope.

Edith turned back to Henry and grabbed his hand. "Not without you. I don't want any story that doesn't include you." She pressed a kiss to his knuckles. "I want to sit on your bench, Henry."

His blue eyes sparkled with unshed tears. "I'm not really sure what that means."

"It means you better carry me through that arch and never let go."

"Yes, ma'am." Henry swooped her up in his arms and stepped through the arch.

Edith's foot banged against a slanted IV pole missing its wheels. "Ow." The arch teetered.

"Sorry about that." Henry swiveled to make room for her legs and something cracked. "That wasn't your head, was it?"

A bucket bounced off her shoulder. Before Henry made it another step, the structure collapsed into a heap of mop handles, poles, basins, and broken crutches. Edith buried her face against Henry's shoulder as the singing came to an abrupt halt, replaced with shrieks and laughter.

"Well, that wasn't supposed to happen," Henry murmured.

"Who built this flimsy contraption anyway?" Edith said, trying not to laugh or sneeze from the tufts of dirt circling around them.

"Flimsy? Did you hear that?" Henry swung Edith around so they were facing the Reddy kids, who were all jumping and pointing at the rubble. "After all the work we put into it?" Henry lowered his face close to Edith's. "Just for that, I'm feeding you to the crocodiles."

"Oh, please don't." No wonder Henry had a bruise on his forehead if the Reddy kids were involved. "I didn't say flimsy. No, no. You misheard. I said . . . *whimsy*-cal. Finest arch I've ever seen. Wonderful job, kids."

Henry set Edith down on her feet, keeping his arms wrapped around her as the kids began using the mop handles and crutches as pretend swords. "In my defense, the original idea was to do all this at sunrise tomorrow. But then we ran into some logistical issues. Mainly how to keep you in bed five more minutes, let alone an entire night. It turned into a rush job."

"I was afraid you were leaving me."

"Why on earth would you think that?"

"Because you said you were leaving me."

"I said I had to go, not that I was leaving you. I needed time to finish the arch." He waved to the pile of rubble. "A smashing success if I do say so myself."

"What about your job? Charles Henderson? Don't you need to get back? That's a once-in-a-lifetime opportunity for you. I don't want you to mess it up because of me."

"Edith, *you* are my once-in-a-lifetime opportunity. Don't you see that? You're stuck with me, babe."

"Even if I want to stay here? What would you do?"

Henry wagged his head side to side as if giving it some serious consideration. "Seems rather obvious. I'd open an arch business. Word of mouth about this project has probably already spread across the region."

He pressed his forehead against hers, turning serious again. "Truth is, no. I can't stay here forever. At some point I do need to get back to my job in Westshire. But I'll wait for you, Edith. As long as it takes, I will wait for you. I'm not here to pressure you into coming back with me. I'm only here to tell you I love you and I'm willing to wait."

This man. Edith closed her eyes and simply breathed him in.

"You know, one of the reasons I came here was because I thought this was my big shot to do something important with my life. I figured I'd be able to make a huge difference simply because the people here desperately needed my help."

Edith opened her eyes, taking a moment to glance around her. Amahle, Kaya, and Mama Peace stood together, looking back at her with gentle, knowing smiles. Okay, maybe not Mama Peace. But Edith had the feeling it was the sort of smile Mama Peace might give to a sister—a sister who annoyed her but she couldn't help loving anyway.

Edith returned her gaze to Henry's gorgeous blue eyes. "But now I'm thinking maybe the reason God placed this area on my heart was because all along he knew there'd come a time when I needed them. Desperately." She clasped Henry's hands between hers as joy washed over her, filling her with a glow to match the South African sun. "I think I'm ready to go home."

And for the first time in a long time, Edith knew exactly where that was.

EPILOGUE

THREE MONTHS LATER

Brilliant sunlight cascaded through the windows of the Westshire Christian Church's family room. Edith ran her palms down the bodice of the ivory embroidered dress Mama Peace had given her in South Africa and met Julie's gaze reflecting back at her from a floor-length mirror. "I made a mistake, didn't I? And now there's no going back."

"Oh, honey . . ."

"I don't know what came over me. Obviously I got caught up in the moment. And now here I am, once again, having to live with the weight of that decision forever."

"I'd hardly say forever." Julie fixed a loose pin in Edith's hair, then turned Edith to face her. "Your bangs will grow out eventually."

"I never should have set foot in that hair salon. When will I ever learn?" Edith blew out a large breath, fanning the offending strands away from her eyes. "But at least my dress looks nice, right?"

"Your dress looks gorgeous. And so does your hair. Face it, Edith. You're gorgeous, bangs or no bangs." Julie squeezed Edith's hands. "Welts or no welts."

"You told me they weren't visible." Edith spun to the mirror and examined her neck.

"Nooo. What I told you was to avoid the buffalo chicken wraps on the left. Especially since they're for the reception."

"I was starving. And I didn't know if you meant my left or the refrigerator's left."

"That doesn't even make sense."

Edith scratched at her neck. "Just do me a favor, will you? Keep Gabby and her EpiPens away from me."

"I will if you stop scratching." Julie batted Edith's hand away from her neck and smiled. "Have I told you how happy I am you and Henry are back?"

"Only about seventy-six times in the past twenty minutes."

"I am so happy you two are back."

"Make that seventy-seven."

"I love that you're working at the crisis house. I love that Henry has a new logo for his company. A stork with a bottle, is it?"

"A pelican with a hammer."

"I just love everything." Julie handed Edith her bouquet of orchids and lilies. "Thank you for humoring us by having another wedding by the way. I know you guys have been busy getting settled back in and all, but half this town was ready to riot when they heard you'd married in South Africa. The only reason the other half didn't riot was because they were convinced it couldn't possibly be legal, and you'd have to come back at some point to make it real, at which time they'd get their wedding cake. This town lives and breathes for wedding cake, you know."

"Don't we all," Edith responded.

A knock sounded at the door. "They're ready for you, Edith," Kat said, poking her head inside, her eyes lighting up. "Yowza, you look gorgeous."

"See?" Julie smacked Edith on the arm.

"Are you allergic to the flowers?" Kat pointed to Edith's neck.

"See?" Edith smacked Julie on the arm.

In the next minute she stood at the back of the sanctuary, her itchy neck forgotten. Because up front, staring back at her with eyes bluer than the sky, stood her greatest adventure. And she couldn't wait to walk down the aisle to him. Again.

Though Edith had been ready to come back to Illinois right away, Henry convinced her to stay a few months longer. Then Edith convinced Henry to stay. Neither had to work very hard at convincing each other to get married.

"Well? What is she waiting for?" Gladys said from her motorized wheelchair near the front of the sanctuary. "Let's get this show on the road so we can get to the cake."

"Quiet," Peg shushed her. "Let her go at her own pace and take in the moment. Can't you see she's a happy girl?"

"What'd Peg say?" a man in a John Deere hat asked.

"Something about Edith needing to walk slow because

she's having a girl," Mustache Man shouted from two pews over.

"Edith's having a girl?" another voice said. "I didn't even know she was pregnant."

"Edith's pregnant?" several voices responded.

Edith closed her eyes. "Oh, here we go again."

The collective gasp coupled by a chorus of shouts drowned out any possible rebuttal. Several bursts of *woo-hoo,* "I knew it!" and applause exploded around the sanctuary. From behind her, Julie screamed, "I'm baking the cake for the baby shower!"

"We're still getting wedding cake, though, right?" Gladys banged into a floral decoration. "We better still be getting wedding cake. James, do something."

Edith caught a quick glimpse of the preacher shaking his head and closing his Bible behind all the commotion. "I now pronounce you husband and wife," he muttered.

A handful of rice smacked Edith in the face. "Oops. Was I supposed to wait?" a boy asked.

"I call dibs on being the godfather," Lance shouted.

Henry met Edith halfway down the aisle and brushed rice from her shoulders. "Just for the record, you're not . . ."

"No," Edith responded.

"Didn't think so." Henry glanced around the sanctuary. "Want me to try and set everybody straight?"

"Let's just go dance and eat cake. They'll figure it out eventually."

"I like that plan." Henry wrapped her inside his arms as the crowd flowed past them and out the doors.

"Pregnant ladies can still dance, right?" the Mickey Rooney look-alike said.

"Sure they can. Congratulations!" The mailman slapped Henry on the back.

"Yeah, and great wedding," the man in the John Deere hat said on his way past. "Wish all of them could be as straight and to the point."

"You can say that again," his tall friend said.

"Wish all of them could be as straight and to the point."

The tall man groaned. Once everyone had filtered out and left them alone in the sanctuary, Henry released Edith and took a step back. "Can I tell you something? When I saw you at the end of the aisle—you know, for that one minute before everything got weird—I couldn't help thinking about the first time I saw you."

"Because I'm so beautiful and took your breath away?" Edith batted her eyelashes.

"I was thinking more because your face is covered in welts."

Edith smacked him in the stomach. "And here I was about to give you the most romantic gift of your life."

"Hey, I love welts. Welts are beautiful. Give me the gift. Especially if the gift involves making that pregnancy rumor true." He scorched a trail of kisses down her neck. She squealed and ducked out of his arms.

"Follow me."

"Yes, ma'am."

She led him down the hallway to the room where she'd dressed to get ready. Then flung open the door. "Ta-da. I made it myself."

"I . . . bet you did," Henry said, rubbing a palm over his mouth and taking a step closer. "And what is it exactly?"

Edith looked from him to the object in question and back again. "It's a symbol of our love. What did you think it was?"

Henry stared at the pieces of warped wood hammered together with love—maybe not precision—and rubbed his palm over his mouth again. "Honey, if that's a symbol of our love . . . we're doomed."

Edith nudged the bench with her foot, not brave enough to sit on it. "So maybe it turned out about as well as your arch. But benches like this aren't supposed to be pretty."

"You know, I really hope someday to understand what all this bench talk is about."

"Next time we go back to South Africa, we'll visit Amahle and I'll have her explain it to you. It's beautiful. You'll be moved to tears."

"Oh, I think I already am."

Edith gave him a playful punch in the ribs, right before he pulled her in for a long kiss that heated her all the way down to her toes.

"Come on, Mr. Hobbes," Edith said, eventually breaking away from the kiss long enough to slip her arm through his. "There'll be time for that later. Let's get to our reception before all the cake is gone. I don't know what the next chapter of our story will be, but this is one page in our life we don't want to miss."

"How much do you bet people already think we're having twins?"

"Twins? Henry, Henry, Henry. You underestimate this town. We're certainly up to triplets by now."

"And you still want to live here?"

Edith dropped her head on his shoulder as they walked out of the church side by side, Henry limping with his uneven gait, Edith blowing her bangs from her eyes. "What can I say? I love an adventure."

Keep an eye out for the next swoon-worthy romantic comedy by Becca Kinzer

A NOTE FROM THE AUTHOR

Dear Reader,

It's no secret the path to publication is full of challenges, setbacks, and failures. But thankfully it's also full of wonderful surprises and blessings. One of those wonderful surprises and blessings while getting this book to publication was the discovery of the Jabulani Rural Health Foundation at a time God knew I needed them most—not only as a writer, but as a nurse in desperate need of encouragement. Based in Zithulele Village, this foundation is the inspiration behind my fictional Ithemba organization. You can learn more about them at their website, jabulanifoundation.org.

And if you're interested in reading the true stories that inspired a few of Edith's experiences in this remote South

African setting, while also serving as a great source of encouragement to me in my United States critical care setting, then I encourage you to read Ben Gaunt's book *Hope, a Goat, and a Hospital*. Who knows? Maybe God can use some people from South Africa to bring a little hope into your life just when you need it most too.

ACKNOWLEDGMENTS

When I was much younger, before I ever dreamed of pursuing publication, I never understood why an author thanked all those people on the acknowledgments page. Didn't the author write the story? What did all those people do? Well, now I know better, and I am eternally grateful for what all *those people* do. Starting with *those people* I'm blessed to call *my people*.

Dave, Maria, and Charlie—since the moment I started writing, you've listened to me ramble at the dinner table (over many a subpar and mediocre meal) about characters and plotlines and writing insecurities and writing joys and everything in between. And not once did you try to have me committed. I appreciate that. And I love you!

Mom and Dad, thank you for giving me a love for story

by infusing my childhood with tons of great stories, whether real or imaginary. Mom, you introduced me to some of my favorite books and authors. And, Dad, I'm pretty sure nothing I write will ever compare to your Air Force story—or take as long to tell.

To my fabulous in-laws, thank you for all the times you've "borrowed the kids" and given me some peace and quiet to write. Your "Oh, honey, that's wonderful!" with every writing milestone I've hit has been a huge source of encouragement to me.

To my brothers, Matt and Nathan, bless you for reading the first manuscript I ever wrote. Now that I'm a little further down the road with my writing, I realize that must have been a special sort of torture only brothers who truly love their sister would ever endure. And, Kristin, thanks for reading a few of my other early stories that hopefully weren't quite as torturous to endure.

Katie, Alaina, Toni, and Megan—thank you for your over-the-top enthusiasm. And I do mean over-the-top. Please, no more T-shirts with my face on the front. Alicia, thanks for answering my questions about visas and travel (because I clearly never leave Illinois). Cath, thanks for all the great information you provided about Jabulani.

To the crew at My Book Therapy, you taught me how to write a novel. Then you taught me how to get it published. Thank you. I wouldn't have reached this point without all the knowledge I've gleaned from you. And I'm especially grateful for the writing friends I've met through MBT. To my huddle group—Becky, Christina, Denise, Debb, Wendy, and Lynn—thanks for walking this crazy writing journey with me.

To my agent, Rachelle Gardner, I'm still a bit shell-shocked you wanted to take a chance on me. But I'm so very glad that you did. Thank you for your guidance, suggestions, and hard work helping me get this story into readers' hands.

And to the entire team at Tyndale, thank you. I'm so grateful my first-ever book baby had the honor of getting placed in your capable hands. To Elizabeth Jackson and Kathy Olson especially, thank you for your kindness and feedback. You made this story so much better.

And last but not least, I am most thankful to God for giving me a reason to write and a story to write. And thank *you*, dear reader, for taking the time to read it.

DISCUSSION QUESTIONS

1. Both Edith and Henry get the wrong impression about each other before ever meeting. Why did they so easily jump to the wrong conclusion about each other's age? Have you ever had a similar experience with making the wrong assumption about a person or someone making the wrong assumption about you?

2. Even though Edith quickly bonded with Sharon the first time she met her, she practically ran from the house to avoid a potential conversation about her previous marriage. Why then was it so easy for Edith to write a letter to Henry later that night that shared personal information about her marriage?

3. Westshire is a small town with a cast of quirky characters. Did you have a particular favorite character? Why?

4. Once Henry realized the truth about who Edith was,
   what did you think about his decision to pretend to be
   Henry?

5. Part of Edith's motivation to go to South Africa stems
   from wanting to find her story. Is this desire to find
   a story something you can relate to? How would you
   define "finding your story"?

6. We don't meet any friends from Edith's past, but we
   see her develop new friendships with Sharon, Julie, and
   Kaya. (And Mama Peace, though Mama Peace would
   probably never admit it.) We also see Henry become
   friends with his physical therapist due to the amount of
   time they're forced to spend together during his rehab.
   How does this compare to your friendships? Are your
   closest friendships those from your past? Or have you
   ever developed a deep friendship with someone simply
   because you were forced together due to a particular
   situation?

7. Julie tells Edith that God wants us "to have the kind
   of faith that knows he'll provide what we need when
   we need it, even when we don't see how. Especially
   when we don't see how." In what ways does God come
   through for Edith and Henry? Can you think of real-
   life examples of this kind of faith?

8. Edith says, "Adventures aren't supposed to be easy, right? That's why they're adventures." Do you agree? Disagree? How does that idea compare to Jesus' words to his followers, "My yoke is easy to bear, and the burden I give you is light" (Matthew 11:30)?

9. Edith's view of what an adventure should look like shifts by the end of the story. Do you find your definition of adventure changing as you get older? Do you think a person like Henry, who longs to build a life in his hometown, can still live a life of adventure?

10. Is there a place in the world you long to travel to? Who or what inspires you to want to go there?

ABOUT THE AUTHOR

Becca Kinzer lives in Springfield, Illinois, where she works as a critical care nurse. When she's not taking care of sick patients or reminding her husband and two kids that frozen chicken nuggets is a gourmet meal, she enjoys making up lighthearted stories with serious laughs. She is a 2018 ACFW First Impressions Contest winner, a 2019 Genesis Contest winner, a 2021 Cascade Award winner, and an all-around champion coffee drinker. *Dear Henry, Love Edith* is her debut novel. Visit Becca online at beccakinzer.com.

CONNECT WITH BECCA ONLINE AT

beccakinzer.com

OR FOLLOW HER ON

 @beccakinzer

@beccakinzer

@Becca_Kinzer

TYNDALE HOUSE PUBLISHERS IS CRAZY4FICTION!

Fiction that entertains and inspires

Get to know us! Become a member of the Crazy4Fiction community. Whether you read our blog, like us on Facebook, follow us on Twitter, or receive our e-newsletter, you're sure to get the latest news on the best in Christian fiction. You might even win something along the way!

JOIN IN THE FUN TODAY.

 crazy4fiction.com

 Crazy4Fiction

 crazy4fiction

@Crazy4Fiction

By purchasing this book from Tyndale, you have
helped us meet the spiritual and physical needs of
people all around the world.

Tyndale | Trusted. For Life.